Sultry with a Twist

MACY BECKETT

sourcebooks
casablanca

Published by Sourcebooks Casablanca, an imprint of Sourcebooks, Inc.
P.O. Box 4410, Naperville, Illinois 60567-4410
(630) 961-3900
Fax: (630) 961-2168
www.sourcebooks.com

Printed and bound in Canada.
WC 10 9 8 7 6 5 4 3 2 1

For Steve, my hero.
All my love
—M.

Chapter 1

JUNE AUGUSTINE PURSED HER LIPS AND GLANCED AT the cashier's check in her hand. It didn't feel as heavy as it should. Heavenly beams didn't part the clouds and shine upon it. The shimmering watermark didn't sprout lungs and burst into the "Hallelujah" chorus. In short, there was no magical quality to this paper, nothing to reflect all the sacrifices she'd made in earning this money.

For eight years, she'd pulled double shifts, choked down ramen noodles, and haggled over two-dollar yard-sale dresses, while her friends planned destination weddings and delivered blue-eyed newborns that smelled of sweet talcum powder. Instead of a husband and a cuddly baby, June had an incontinent three-legged cat, a ten-year-old purple hatchback she'd nicknamed Bruiser, and this check. She held her whole life right here in her fingers, including every penny of the profits from her condo, which she'd sold earlier that morning.

"*Bonita*," Esteban said, tugging gently at the other end of the check. "Let go."

"Oh, sorry." June bit her lip and released payment to her old friend and new business partner. Now she was officially half owner of Luquos, soon to be the hottest martini bar in Austin. Hopefully. No, definitely. Custom orders for her signature drink recipes poured in so quickly she could barely keep up, and with Esteban's connections and experience, they couldn't fail.

Esteban tipped her chin with his index finger. "You don't have to put in this much. I can get other investors."

"Which means more people telling me how to run my bar." June shook her head and took a deep breath. Who needed money? She might not have a place to sleep that night, but she was officially her own boss, a dream nearly a decade in the making. No more mixing sticky blender drinks for glassy-eyed drunks who didn't tip. No more taking turns cleaning up vomit in the restrooms. Luquos was her baby—her creative vision—and her heart beat faster in anticipation of opening night in six weeks.

Esteban admired the check. "I see closing went well. Where're you staying now?"

"I paid a college kid twenty bucks to deliver his old futon to Luquos. I'll crash in the office until I find a new place." *Which shouldn't take long*.

"And your things?"

"Sold most of them. The rest's in the trunk of my car."

"You can stay with me anytime." He dipped his head and whispered, "*Amigos con derechos*. Business partners with benefits."

"Ah, nice try," she said with a laugh. Sex ruined friendships—she knew firsthand. Esteban was attractive in a successful-older-man kind of way, but she'd never risk losing him as a mentor just for a sweaty good time.

Fierce, early September sunbeams pierced the clouds, and she moved into the shade of a cedar tree before her fair skin baked. After checking her watch again, she straightened her black pencil skirt and picked an errant cat hair from the shoulder of her green silk blouse.

"Stop fidgeting. You look perfect. This is the easy part."

"Tony's late." She took a deep breath of cedar-perfumed

morning air and ran down a mental to-do list. First, the liquor license interview. Esteban was right, easy-peasy. Then bar- and wait-staff interviews, furniture delivery, the marine biology consultation—

"There he is."

Tony bounded up the steps from his car and smoothed the wiry strands of his graying beard. "Hey, boss. Got held up with the contractor. You might have to redesign that back wall."

"Son of a biscuit-eater," June muttered. There wasn't time to redesign it. Three hundred Atlantic jellyfish would arrive next week to take up residency inside that back wall—the largest private aquarium in the city. "Let's hurry and get this finished." She led the way into the—thankfully air-conditioned—Texas Alcoholic Beverage Commission office and waved two fingers at the receptionist. "June Augustine, Esteban Morales, and Anthony Grimes to see Agent Perneras."

She popped a stick of sweet cinnamon gum into her mouth and inspiration for a new recipe struck: the red-hot martini. Which ingredients to use? Top-shelf vodka, of course, like vanilla Grey Goose, then a dash of Goldschlager, perhaps garnished with a candy swizzle. Mmm. She added it to her mental list while making her way to the conference room. A single curly, brown strand of hair escaped her twist, and she tucked it back in place before taking a seat at the head of the long mahogany table.

"Hot enough for ya?" An elderly, balding man with a bushy white handlebar mustache extended his hand and grinned. He reminded June of Yosemite Sam after a few too many decades bushwhacking those pesky varmints. "Barty Perneras."

After a round of introductions, he settled beside her, leaving one empty seat between them, and opened a manila file folder. He thumbed through page after page while humming an indistinct tune. "Here we are…Mae-June Augustine." A soft snicker puffed out the tips of his moustache. "Mae-June?"

"My parents thought they were funny." She elbowed Esteban in the ribs before he had a chance to announce her middle name: July. Actually, her mama and daddy had been the wildest, most lovable, booze-swilling fools in Sultry Springs, Texas. God rest their pickled souls. It was a miracle they hadn't named her Jägermeister. "I go by June."

"Right." Perneras returned his attention to the paperwork. "So you and Mr. Morales are co-owners, and Mr. Grimes is…"

"Our bar manager," June said.

"Mmm-hmm." A trio of deep wrinkles zigzagged across his forehead. "It looks like all the applications are complete except for yours." He raised his gaze to hers. "It's been flagged."

"What does that mean?" Had she forgotten to mail the fee? With everything going on, it could have easily slipped her mind. Wait, no—she remembered paying online with her new business MasterCard. It must not have gone through.

"We can't approve it until you resolve that warrant."

June tipped her head back and laughed into the air. Warrant? In all her twenty-seven years, she'd never even been pulled over for a traffic ticket.

Barty Perneras wasn't smiling. He read from the page. "Bench warrant issued by Judge Arnold Bea of

Sultry County, Texas, for indecent exposure, lewd conduct, and trespassing at Gallagher pond. It's dated nine years ago."

June gasped like a free-diver surfacing for air after five minutes of submersion. The spicy cinnamon gum lodged in her airway, and she clutched her throat while Esteban and Tony took turns pounding her back until she coughed the rubbery pink wad onto the table. Sweet mother of Stevie Ray Vaughan, she hadn't thought about that hellish afternoon at Gallagher pond in ages! Heat rushed into her cheeks, and the musky-sweet scents of algae and coconut tanning lotion seemed to clog her nostrils.

Barty Perneras used a tissue to dispose of her gum. "I take it that jogged your memory?"

"It's not what it sounds like!" She turned to Esteban and Tony, who seemed to appreciate her in a whole new way.

Tony let out a low whistle. "Lewd conduct, Miss June?"

"*And* indecent exposure," Esteban said with a saucy grin. "Sounds like there's someone fun hiding inside the workaholic. Can she come out and play?"

She whipped back around to Barty, who casually scribbled notes in her file as if this sort of thing happened every day. "But I was never arrested! I had no idea about any of this. How could I have a warrant for nine years without knowing?"

Barty shrugged. "If they didn't have your address, the only way you'd find out is if an officer stopped you and ran your license number." He glanced back down at her paperwork. "Looks like we didn't catch it when you got your bartending certification."

She pulled a deep breath through her nose and held it.

How or why Judge Bea issued the warrant didn't matter. A bar without a liquor license was about as useful as a concrete parachute, and every day they delayed opening was another day in the red. She exhaled and glanced at her watch. "It's six hours to Sultry Springs. If I get on the road now, I can be there by four. I'll ask the judge to fax you confirmation when the warrant's rescinded."

Esteban tapped his cell phone screen. "I'll have my attorney meet you there."

"No." She pushed her chair away from the table. "Judge Bea's practically family. I spent my last three summers in Sultry Springs watching his grandbabies. This whole thing's probably a mistake, and it'll tick him off if I bring a lawyer." Worst-case scenario, she'd offer the judge some of her Grammy Pru's pumpkin butter and all would be forgiven. Of course, she'd have to get Grammy to speak to her first…

She gave Esteban and Tony a quick hug and walked to the door, calling over her shoulder, "Be right back."

Waves of pure heat rippled up and distorted the air above the hood on Luke Gallagher's dusty black Ford F-250. He grabbed his paperwork and used his steel-toed boot to push open the door, feeling a nearly solid block of humidity on the other side. Days like this, he could almost wring water straight from the air. Shoving his baseball cap into his back pocket, Luke ran a hand through his damp hair before making his way inside the Sultry County courthouse.

The dim lobby always smelled a little dank, and the scent reminded him of old Mr. Jenkins's drywall after last year's flash flood. Now six months later, he and the ragtag crew from Helping Hands, his nonprofit group, had almost finished repairing the place. All he needed was a permit to add a deck off the back stoop and he could finally wash his hands of this project. He checked the clock and hurried to the county clerk's office before they closed.

Once there, Luke bent down and balanced a chipped brown clipboard against his thigh to complete Mr. Jenkins's permit application, which brought him eye-level to the very round ass in front of him in line. Sweet Jesus, it was clad in one of those tight, black skirts, somehow modest and sexy-as-hell at the same time, gripping a slim waist and clinging to a pair of luscious, wide, wide hips, then stopping just below the knee. It showed very little skin, but drew his attention to everything that mattered. *Nice.* Fair, slender calves narrowed to a delicate set of ankles, and then down to a pair of black leather high heels tap, tap, tapping impatiently against the scuffed marble floor. He glanced down at his pen and scrawled one final signature before standing up to fully appreciate the figure before him.

Little Miss High Maintenance exhaled loudly and placed a hand on her hip, and Luke could see the out-side swell of her breast straining against her silky green blouse—the kind of material that would slide right to the floor and pool around her feet when she unbuttoned it. *Very nice.* And no wedding ring. Maybe he'd ask her out.

Oh, hell, who was he kidding? A woman like that was more trouble than she was worth. Still, he couldn't quit staring at one curly brown strand of hair that fell out of her bun. It hung down, practically advertising that little strawberry birthmark on the side of her neck, practically begging to be tasted—

Suddenly the air was too thick, too humid to breathe. He knew that birthmark. Knew it from a thousand summer afternoons back when she'd worn pigtails and followed him around like a Labrador. And unfortunately, he knew the skin right there on her throat tasted exactly like kettle corn, salty and sweet.

"Ho-o-ly shit," he whispered.

She must've heard, because she turned her head and quirked a perfectly arched brow. It was her. June was back. The freckles that used to sprinkle her nose were gone, as was the roundness of her face, now replaced by high, distinct cheekbones. But her mouth was the same, still soft-looking with that pouty lower lip. And her eyes—the same wide, brown eyes that used to gaze up at him the way a half-starved dieter watches the last piece of chocolate cake. Those eyes regarded him now with curiosity, bordering on amusement. She didn't realize who he was. While he stood there like a slack-jawed mute, she tipped her head and wrinkled up her forehead, as if trying to solve an algebra problem. Then, slowly, recognition dawned across her face, and her cheeks flushed scarlet.

She gaped like a catfish, those red lips opening, closing, opening, while the soft whirr of an air conditioner droned in the background.

They both just stood there for a full minute, too stunned to speak, until she cleared her throat and said, "You broke your nose."

That was it? *You broke your nose?* No apology, no explanation? He hadn't expected her to smile and rush into his arms, but hell. She chewed the inside of her cheek the way she always did as a kid when Pru had caught her doing something naughty.

Luke dipped his chin in a tight nod. "Twice."

The rosy flush in her cheeks drained away, and she glanced down at her black handbag, rubbing the leather like she was trying to summon a genie from its bottle. And probably wishing she were anywhere but with him. She peered up from beneath thick, dark lashes. "I didn't think…" She swallowed and shifted her weight to the other hip. "How've you been?"

"Fine," he said. But that was a lie, and she'd know, if she'd bothered to read his letters all those years ago.

The clerk waved his hand and called, "Next." June backed slowly toward the counter before turning around.

"June Augustine. I spoke with Judge Bea this morning. We have an appointment." She used a low voice, but it carried in the open office.

"Mae-June?" the clerk asked, removing his glasses and inspecting her like she might be an impostor. He squinted and sat back in his chair. "Prudence Foster's girl?"

"Uh, yes. Her granddaughter. Is the judge ready to see me?"

"Yep, come on back." The clerk continued watching her through narrowed eyes.

June spun around and held up one hand in a shaky good-bye. "Nice seeing you." She looked like a suicidal ledge jumper the way she clung to the counter and inched toward the judge's office door. "I'd love to catch up, but I'm heading back to Austin in a few minutes."

Right. She wanted to stay and talk as much as he wanted scorpions stuffed down his Jockeys. A tiny, hot ache writhed inside his gut, but he flashed his best I-don't-give-a-shit grin. "Take care, Junebug." Then he moved to the counter and thrust his paperwork at the clerk. Good thing she was leaving town. Some friendships were better off dead.

Chapter 2

IT TOOK THREE TRIES, BUT JUNE FINALLY TWISTED the doorknob in her sweaty grip and rushed into Judge Bea's office. Immediately, she slammed the door and leaned back against the solid oak. The judge's balding head popped up from where he sat hunched over a stack of files, and he raised a wrinkled, spotted hand to his chest.

"Tryin' to give an old man a heart attack?" Taking a deep breath, he lifted his chin and studied her, his gaze moving across her face, probably noting how she'd changed over the years. Then he rolled his chair away from the cluttered desk and crossed a blue-gray braided rug to where she still stood, plastered to the door. "Come here and gimme a hug."

When Bea's thin, weathered face broke into a smile, June relaxed her shoulders and released the breath she'd been holding. He'd gained some weight in his belly, but otherwise looked exactly the same, and when she bent down to wrap her arms around his neck, she inhaled the familiar scent of sweet pipe tobacco that had always clung to his collar.

"Looks like you've seen the devil. Y'okay?" He gripped the tops of her arms and stepped back, lowering his haywire eyebrows in concern.

The devil. How appropriate. If any mortal could raise hell on earth, it was Luke Gallagher. Holy sugar, seeing him out there was like waking up and finding a pine tree sprouting at the foot of her bed—he simply didn't belong. A hundred questions had flashed through her mind in the lobby: What was he doing back in Sultry Springs? Why wasn't he in Europe? Wasn't he still in the army? And where was his perfect little German wife? But she'd just stood there like an idiot and asked about his nose. God, she needed to get a grip. She shook her head and wrangled Luke to the back of her brain. "I'm fine. Good to see you."

"Mmm-hmm." Bea nodded and ambled back to his desk, pausing to brush the dust off a stuffed trout mounted on the wall before taking his seat. "Been too long, Mae-June. Way too long."

"Just June." She sank into a burgundy leather chair opposite Bea and tucked her fingers beneath her skirt. Though it was nearly a hundred degrees outside, her hands felt like blocks of ice. "I didn't know about the warrant until today, or I'd've come sooner."

Bea didn't make eye contact. Instead, he focused on stuffing his pipe with dried brown shreds. After lighting the tobacco and taking several quick puffs, he sat back and gave her a hard glare. "Shouldn't take legal action to get you back in town, Mae-June. Nine years is an awful long time."

"Yes, sir."

"You look just like your mama."

"I'll take that as a compliment."

He nodded, still unsmiling. "Hope that's where the similarities end."

June stared at the leather clutch in her lap while her cheeks burned. This was one of the many reasons she'd left Sultry Springs—the relentless judgment, the weight of three hundred watchful Baptist eyes just waiting for her to turn out like her heathen mother. None of them understood how much she missed her parents. Sure, her folks might've forgotten to cook dinner most nights, and maybe they laughed a little too loud, but they were always there for her. Every tee-ball game, every soccer tournament. Did they show up singing and dancing, with a box of wine in tow? Yeah, but she remembered feeling loved. And after their car wreck, June couldn't jaywalk without someone tattling to Grammy, as if the smallest morsel of freedom might trigger a genetic predisposition to bat-shit—oops, sugar—crazy and send her to an infamous premature death too.

She checked her watch, even more eager to return to the glorious anonymity of Austin. "I've got a long drive back. Can we take care of this warrant?"

Judge Bea exhaled a cloud of sweet smoke and reached into his desk drawer. He pulled out a thin stack of papers bound with a rubber band and handed it to her. "All right, then. If you wanna get down to it, I'm offerin' you a deal to avoid jail time."

"Jail time?" She snapped off the rubber band and flipped through page after page of legalese. It was like trying to read Latin. "But for what? You and I both know how harmless—"

"Don't you sass me, Mae-June." Bea pointed his ball-point pen at her like a pistol. "You committed a crime and never accounted for it. Don't make me call a grand jury for this."

Her stomach dipped into her lap like an internal

yo-yo. Maybe she shouldn't have been so quick to refuse Esteban's attorney.

"You wanna get a lawyer? Take this to trial?" It was
like he'd read her thoughts. He gave a casual shrug.
"Fine. But I'll have to detain you till we set a date.
Could take weeks."

"No. Please, let's talk about the deal." She didn't
know why the judge was being so harsh, but he had her
over a barrel, and he knew it.

Bea reclined in his chair and kicked his feet up onto the
corner of his desk, puffing leisurely on his pipe. "Here's
the deal: you stay in Sultry County for one month of community service. I'll release you into Pru's custody."

June bolted forward, clutching her chair's armrests
as her handbag toppled to the floor with a thud. "One
month? That's impossible!"

"Don't interrupt. Like I said, you'll live with Pru and
pay off your debt to society. In four weeks you can leave
with a clean record."

"But my bar!"

Bea raised one bushy brow while June lowered both
of hers. He scrutinized her through a thick haze of
smoke, probably judging her for following in Mama and
Daddy's sinful footsteps. Damn it, she wasn't a drunk,
and she sure as hell wasn't in the mood to defend her
career. As the seconds ticked by, she waited for Bea to
condemn her life choices, but he never did. She let out
a breath, thanking him inwardly. If only Gram could've
shown the same restraint instead of forcing June's hand
with an ultimatum—*Quit peddlin' booze or don't bother
comin' home!*

"If you agree to the deal, I'll fax the TABC right now

and tell 'em to put your license through. You open in six weeks, right? I'm sure your partner can hold down the fort for a while."

Living with Grammy for one month versus several weeks in jail and no liquor license. It was a tough call.

"But I haven't talked to Gram in ages. We're not exactly on good terms. What if she doesn't want—"

"She already agreed." Bea's lips curled into a sly smile, and he seemed a bit too pleased with himself, the way he used to look after polishing off the last slice of pecan pie after supper. Then she understood the real purpose behind that bench warrant. What a sneaky, underhanded old coot.

"This has nothing to do with trespassing or lewd conduct, does it? You just want me to fix things with Grammy." Son of a biscuit-eater. She should've known. "Is this even legal?"

"You bet it is. And don't think for one second, Mae-June, that I won't throw you in jail if you get ornery. I love you like my own grandbaby, and I'm not gonna let you ruin things with the only kin you got left."

"It's none of your business." She folded her arms, feeling like a helpless child again.

He tapped his pipe against an armadillo-shaped ashtray and pushed to standing. "As for community service, you have two choices: the Holy Baptism by Hellfire Church—though they won't let criminals work with the children—or Helping Hands. They do home repairs for the less fortunate 'round here. Bring me your time sheet every Monday morning, so I can see you're on track."

"Can't I just take a few days to tie up loose ends in Austin?" There were so many things on her to-do list, it dizzied her mind. Esteban would flip—she'd promised him an effortless silent partnership. To dump the entire workload on him now was unthinkable.

"No, ma'am. Once you sign this deal, you're not to leave Sultry County. Take it or leave it. And be quick makin' up your mind or I'll be late for my supper." He handed a pen across the desk. "Trust me. This is your best option."

She tugged the signature page from the bottom of the stack and took Bea's pen while frantically searching her mind for a way out of this mess. Nothing came. Damn it, he was right. If she didn't agree to his ridiculous deal, he'd bind her in so much red tape it would take months to wriggle free. It wasn't fair, but what choice did she have? The sooner she started serving her sentence, the sooner it would end. She pressed ink to paper and signed away a month of her life.

Very little had changed in the nine years since June graduated high school and left Sultry County. While driving back from the courthouse, she noticed Main Street still boasted more Christian-themed shops than any normal town could possibly support. Of course, Sultry Springs, *population 973 righteous souls*, wasn't a normal town. Wood signs contrasted against faded brick facades, clamoring for the attention of saints and sinners alike, all with one common business principle: in God we trust. All others pay cash.

Kingdom Comb, the old beauty parlor, had changed names to Blessed Bangs, and Bible Thumpers, the Christian bookstore, proclaimed itself *Under New*

Management!, which probably meant Billy Tucker had finally inherited the place from his dad.

After leaving the bustling metropolis of downtown, June noticed the family restaurant where she'd once waited tables was now a McDonald's, and a few Dollar General stores had popped up like mushrooms along the ten-mile stretch of country road leading to Grammy's house.

At home, the majestic pecan tree in Gram's front yard might've grown a foot or two, but it was hard to tell. Confederate gray paint still peeled in curlicues off the ancient, two-story farmhouse, and five whitewashed rockers and a front porch swing still welcomed guests to come and sit a spell. Waist-high, leafy green soybean plants covered twenty acres to the left of the home, and Gram's garden—ripe with tall cornstalks, bean-wrapped poles, tomatoes, squash, and watermelons—spanned half an acre to the right. June didn't have to stroll into the backyard to know a swing set and a huge metallic gas tank rusted together among the tall weeds where Gram's property met the Gallagher land. Just beyond the overgrowth, she'd surely find Luke's childhood home rotting away, neglected since the day his mother left him with Pru and skipped town with his little sister. It had taken several years before June understood why he never wanted to play in the abandoned house.

She carried her luggage to Gram's front porch, grateful she hadn't had time to drop it off at Luquos before leaving Austin, and then paused on the top step with Lucky's kitty-carrier in her lap. A breeze stirred, and the familiar high, metallic tinkle of wind chimes sang out from above.

"Now, don't be scared," she whispered, reaching one finger inside the crate to scratch beneath Lucky's chin. "My gram's harmless, mostly. You'll see."

Lucky purred and tipped his head to the side. He didn't give two figs about Gram, and June wondered who she was trying to convince. Heaving a sigh, she set the carrier down and marched to the door with her shoulders firmly squared. Before she lost her nerve, she punched the doorbell and held her breath.

Almost instantly, the front door swung open and Grammy Pru glowered from inside, wearing a long floral cotton dress and a scowl. Other grandmothers offered soft hugs and gathered little ones onto their plump laps for story time. Other grandmothers smiled gently below rosy cheeks. They spoiled and cuddled, bragged and loved, smelled of cookies and hair spray. Then there was Pru: six solid feet of bony elbows and sharp knees, the edges of her face death-gripped into a bun so tight it made June massage pinpricks of sympathy pain along her own scalp. Armed with a prayer on her lips and a wooden spoon in her hand, Grammy ruled with an iron fist that would make Samson cower in fear.

Luke had once said, "Before Freddy Krueger goes to sleep at night, he checks his closet for your grandma." All the kids in class had laughed, and though June's face had flushed hot with embarrassment, she hadn't tried to deny it. But Luke wasn't laughing a few years later when he came to live with the object of Freddy Krueger's nightmares.

After nine years, Gram looked even stronger, as if she'd told Father Time to quit lollygagging and get the hell out of her kitchen. She stepped onto the porch and grabbed June's suitcase before she could object.

"That's heavy, Gram. Let me get it."

But Grammy just grunted and carried the luggage into the foyer while June followed with Lucky's crate, her laptop bag, and a box of assorted junk from her condo.

Once they were inside, Gram placed a hand on her hip and took a long, silent look at June. Even though it went against every instinct, June raised her chin and locked eyes with her grandmother, issuing a silent statement: *I'm a grown woman now, and you don't intimidate me. Much.* She tried to concentrate on the warm, tangy scent of roasting chicken and vegetables wafting from the kitchen, instead of on Gram's cool, blue eyes.

Gram nodded approvingly and gestured toward the stairs. "Your room's ready. I 'spect you remember the way"—then added a dig—"even after all this time."

"Yes, ma'am."

"I got supper to finish." Gram turned and stalked away, and June relaxed her shoulders. *Whew.* No griping, no rehashing their last argument. And that was fine by June. She'd had all the emotional upheaval she could handle today.

It didn't take long for June to haul all her worldly possessions upstairs, since she didn't possess much. Hard to believe she'd owned a condo—a private space all to herself—just twelve hours earlier. It felt like a lifetime ago. She tossed her suitcase onto the lumpy single bed and turned to the nicked pine dresser, scanning rows of cross-country trophies that had tarnished to a lackluster gray. Gram hadn't touched a thing—the room felt like a time capsule. A single photograph remained taped to the dresser's mirror, the last picture of June and her parents taken just shy of her seventh birthday. Her mama and daddy had laughed and sandwiched her into a hug. It was her favorite. Odd, she didn't remember leaving it behind.

She walked to the window and opened the mini-blinds to let in some light. The bare, dingy-white walls of her old bedroom seemed to close in like one of those carnival funhouses, though there was nothing fun about *this* house. Not now, anyway.

Back when Luke still lived here, back before everything fell apart, things had been different. The sounds of laughter and clomping sneakers used to echo in the now silent home. She bit her lip and glanced into the hall. Would his room look the same—a black-draped double bed, wood floor littered with engine parts and CDs, and Army posters covering the walls? Or had Gram burned everything Luke owned after he'd stormed out? If she were a betting woman, which Grammy never would have allowed, she'd put her money on the latter. She slipped off her leather pumps and tiptoed down the hall to the last door, then opened it slowly and peeked inside.

The air smelled like leather and something she couldn't place, maybe aftershave or cologne, which seemed odd, since Luke hadn't occupied this room in almost a decade. The same black comforter concealed his mattress, and aside from the pine desk in the corner, the room was empty. Every single recruiting poster had been removed; every trace of the old Luke was gone.

She padded to the desk, wincing when she stepped on a creaky floorboard, and quietly slid open the largest file drawer. Luke smiled at her from inside a simple black lacquer frame. He had his arm around a stunning young woman with tanned skin and cropped blonde hair. Was this his wife? She didn't look German. The photo seemed recent based on what she'd seen of Luke earlier that afternoon. The tips of his hair brushed his shirt collar, and they were reddish brown at the ends, the way his hair always looked at the end of summer. His slightly crooked nose gave his face a masculine ruggedness and saved him from being too beautiful, as he'd been in high school. Not that it had stopped every girl in the county from falling head-over-Keds in love with him—herself included. But he was somehow even more attractive now. All grown up. And up. He must've sprouted three inches since graduation.

She closed her eyes and remembered the way his sweaty T-shirt had clung to the hard contours of his chest and flat belly at the clerk's office. And good God, those dusty jeans, worn paper thin, practically plastered against his long, muscular legs. She'd enjoyed ogling him so much she didn't notice his eyes right away. But that's when she knew. His eyes were the same—a warm green, the exact shade of lichen in the sunlight. She'd never seen another pair like his. But she wouldn't give him a second chance to kick a hole in her chest, not after what happened last time. Gorgeous or not, Luke Gallagher was off limits.

She set the frame on Luke's desk and pulled out the only other item in the drawer, a Converse All-Stars shoebox. When June pulled off the lid, she couldn't help smiling at what she found inside.

"Look at you," she whispered, lifting a GI Joe action figure from the box. It was Snake Eyes, Luke's favorite character, and he'd only let her play with it twice:

once when he'd accidentally nudged her out of a tree and sprained her wrist, and again when she'd taken the blame for something-or-other he'd done.

She pushed her fingers through the box, identifying all Luke's favorite action heroes and Matchbox cars. Every single one had been a gift from her. He'd saved them all. An unexpected warmth blossomed within her chest, and she shoved the shoebox back into the drawer before the warmth had a chance to grow. *Off limits*. She stood and took a quick peek in the closet, which was empty, except for a few oversized cardboard boxes stacked neatly at one end and marked "Gallagher" in black marker. Of course Gram hadn't burned anything—she was hard, but not heartless.

It was time for June to put Luke out of her mind and do something she'd been avoiding for hours—call Esteban. Returning to her bedroom, she took a deep breath and flipped open her archaic, pay-as-you-go cell phone. One feeble bar flickered to life and then faded out.

"You've got to be kidding me."

She jogged down the stairs and into the kitchen, where Grammy was leaning into the oven to remove a sheet of fresh biscuits. June couldn't remember the last time she'd eaten a home-cooked meal, and her mouth watered. Gram shook the biscuits into a wicker basket and covered them with a clean dish towel.

She cleared her throat to get Gram's attention. "I don't get cell coverage here. May I use your phone?"

"Long distance?" Pru's mouth pressed into a hard line.

"To Austin."

"Make it quick."

June was about to ask if Gram had Internet access,

but stopped herself. She already knew the answer. She dialed Esteban's mobile line, but it went to voice mail. "Hey, it's me," she said. "I'm still in Sultry Springs, long story. I need you to call me at this number right away. It's important."

After hanging up, June washed her hands in the kitchen sink. "Can I help?"

"You can set the table. Four places."

Judge Bea was probably coming over, maybe with one of his fishing buddies. June opened the maple cabinet and pulled out four sets of dishes and salad bowls and began placing them atop the red and white checkered tablecloth. She tried to think of a tactful way to ask about Luke that wouldn't reveal she'd been snooping in his bedroom.

"I, uh…I saw Luke today," she said softly. "At the courthouse."

"Mmm-hmm." Gram stirred a pot of butter beans and added a pinch of black pepper. "Probably for a building permit."

"How long's he been back?"

"Goin' on five years."

June dropped a fork, and it clanked against the beige linoleum floor. Her voice rose an octave. "Five years?"

"Mmm-hmm."

"Does he, um"—June folded a napkin in half and creased it with her thumb—"live here again? With you?"

Gram didn't say a word for a full minute. The sounds of bubbling beans and sizzling chicken filled the small kitchen. Then she turned around and pulled off her apron. "Not anymore, 'cept for a night or two, if I need help. But he stayed here awhile to get back on his feet."

"Back on his feet?" June asked, frozen in place with a drinking glass in one hand and a butter knife in the other. "What happened?" Luke had probably swallowed a truckload of crow when he'd asked to come back here. It must've been bad.

Gram lifted her wooden spoon from the pot and pointed it at June, and her thigh muscles clenched in response. She'd been on the wrong end of that spoon a time or two. Or twenty. "That's his story to tell. Ask him yourself. He'll be here in ten minutes."

The glass slipped from June's hand, and she performed a feat of acrobatics to catch it before it hit the floor. "Are you serious?"

"Fetch the butter and honey, and put out a pitcher of sweet tea." Gram pointed to the refrigerator. "Lucas's friend Trey is comin' too. I have 'em over three nights a week."

June's stomach did a double flip and she caught herself chewing the inside of her cheek. Sweet mercy, she had to get her shit—oops, sugar—together. It was just Luke, just an old friend she'd lost touch with over the years. No reason to get worked up. Still, she heard the echo of her inner voice calling *off limits, off limits*.

Chapter 3

"YOU OKAY?" TREY ASKED, PULLING OFF HIS SEAT BELT as Luke turned the truck onto Pru's gravel driveway. "Something go wrong at the Hallover place?"

"Nah, it's fine." Luke parked behind the butt-ugliest car he'd ever seen, a purple spray-painted hatchback, and cut the engine. "Just thinking."

Thinking too much about June. After seeing her in line, his brain had relentlessly flashed images of her all afternoon—nine-year-old June in denim overall cutoffs, her face streaked with mud; sixteen-year-old June fishing at the pond in her bikini; eighteen-year-old June sprawled beneath him on a patchwork quilt *without* her bikini. He'd damn near cut off his thumb with the circular saw. Distraction on the job was more dangerous than dry rot, and somehow, he had to get her out of his head. He'd done it once; he could do it again.

Luke yanked the rearview mirror to the side and ran a comb through his hair, still wet from the shower. Pru was bound to say he needed a trim, which was probably true, but lately he didn't have twenty minutes to spare at the QuickClips. He leaned back to tuck in his shirt and then joined Trey at the front door. With a smile already in place, he knocked twice and let himself in, but he stopped short on the other side, smile frozen on his face.

"Hi." June sashayed in from the kitchen, cradling a small black and white cat in the crook of one arm. "You

must be Trey. Grammy told me about you. I'm June."
She shook Trey's hand, then nodded a half-hearted
greeting in Luke's direction. She'd let her hair down,
and it curled around her face in soft, light brown ringlets
that brushed her shoulders. He glanced at her feet—
smooth and fair with pink-polished toenails—somehow
even sexier bare than they'd been in black high heels.
What was she still doing here, and more importantly,
why was God punishing him?

Luke backed up a pace while Trey moved forward to
scratch behind the cat's ears.

"I heard Miss Pru had a long-lost granddaughter. I
was beginning to wonder if you were real." Trey grinned
playfully, but June didn't look pleased. His words probably hit too close to home. Trey leaned down and talked
to the fur ball. "What's your name, little kitty?"

"This is Lucky," June said. She bent over and set the
thing on the floor, and it pattered away, stepping forward
with two front legs and then hopping along with a single
hind leg.

"Lucky?" Luke said with a snort. "Ironic name for a
three-legged cat."

June furrowed her brow and scooped Lucky off the
floor like he'd hurt the cat's feelings or something. She
cuddled it against her chest and smoothed her cheek
over its head. "A dog attacked him at the shelter, and
they wanted to put him down. I paid for his amputation
and adopted him. I think that makes him lucky." She
glared at Luke over a tuft of salt and pepper fur. "Be
sweet. He pees when he's scared."

Luke watched the puny animal rest its chin between
June's high, full breasts while she stroked his fur and

lightly massaged his neck. Yeah, the friggin' fleabag *was* pretty damned lucky.

"Come on for supper," Pru called. June set the cat down and they all headed to the kitchen. The air was hot and thick with steam and the walloping scents of fine, fine country cooking. Luke's stomach rumbled in response.

While June washed her hands, Pru gathered Trey into one of those motherly smother-hugs, then turned on Luke. She shook her head and tugged a lock of his hair.

"Get a cut, Lucas." Pru patted his cheek. "You could be such a handsome boy."

"There'll be plenty of time for that when I get the Hallover property on the market."

Something clattered from inside the white porcelain sink, and Luke turned to see June staring at them, her mouth forming a perfect red oval. It must've been a shock to see him and Pru on such good terms, but what did she expect? He wasn't a rebellious teenager anymore. Now the roles were reversed. June was the outsider, and Pru favored *him*. Half a grin curved his lips before he could stop it.

While Luke stood there gloating like an asshole, Trey held June's chair out for her, and she smiled up at him like he'd just pulled her from a burning building. Luke hurried and did the same for Pru, and they all held hands for grace. After "amen," Luke noticed Trey was half a second too slow in releasing June's fingers, and she bit her lip and blushed before laying the napkin in her lap. What the hell was up with that?

An invisible fist tightened around Luke's windpipe as he slid a glance at his best friend, appraising him for the first time as a man instead of a buddy. Trey was probably an okay-looking guy, if you were into blonde hair, blue eyes, and tanned skin. Was that June's type? He didn't know anymore.

"So," Trey said to June with his mouth half full. "What brings you back to Sultry Springs?"

June froze, holding a forkful of mashed potatoes in midair. "Uh, a little legal misunderstanding." She started to say something else, but shoved a bite into her mouth instead and closed her eyes, chewing slowly like she'd just tasted nectar from heaven. "Mmm." Then she leaned back in her seat and placed a hand over her heart. "Oh, God, that's so good."

"Hey," Pru snapped. "No blasphemin' in my house!"

"Sorry." June scooped a forkful of butter beans. "It's just I can't remember the last time I ate something that wasn't off the Dollar Menu."

While chewing, June kept making these low throaty moans, and Luke had to adjust himself. He needed to get her to stop, or he'd never be able to stand from the table. "What do you do for a living in Austin?" he asked.

June hesitated and her eyes darted to Pru. Then she set down her fork, took a slow drink of iced tea, and sat ramrod straight. She looked at Pru, not him, when she finally answered. "I own a bar downtown. On Sixth Street." June said *bar* with emphasis, as if challenging Pru to denounce her sinful occupation. Lifting a buttered biscuit to her lips, June continued staring down her grandma, waiting for a reaction like a game of emotional chicken.

Pru's mouth tightened in obvious disapproval, but she held her tongue. Which didn't happen very damn often, especially when it came to the subject of fire water. A lifelong teetotaler, Pru still wrote her congressman each year, clamoring for the repeal of the twenty-first amendment.

"Sweet." Trey wiped a sleeve across his mouth, oblivious to the tension between the two women. "Which bar? I've probably been there."

"No, you haven't." June rested her chin in her palm and smiled with a faraway look in her eyes. "We don't open for another six weeks. But it's called Luquos, and it'll be like nothing you've ever seen. Totally upscale, romantic, sexy." She glanced again at Pru. "I've been selling drink recipes and tending bar for years. It took a long time to save enough money for my own place."

Pru patted her bun and grumbled to herself. It was as close as June would get if she wanted approval.

"Sounds great," Trey said. "Do I get a personal invitation to the opening?" He leaned toward June and flashed his dimples—the ones that made panties drop like lead.

Luke knew his buddy would rather roll naked in a bed of pine cones than spend an hour in a stuffy bar like that. For no reason at all, he kicked Trey's chair.

"What?" Trey lowered his brows.

Luke shrugged, pretending like nothing had happened, and lifted his glass to June. "Congrats, Junebug. Makes me wish Sultry wasn't a dry county."

"Ugh," she groaned. "Still dry, huh?" She bit that pouty lower lip and glanced at him through her lashes. "And thanks."

The phone's shrill ring carried through the hallway into the kitchen, and June pushed away from the table like it was on fire. "I'll get it!" she cried, scrambling out of the room.

Luke glanced at Pru for some kind of explanation, but she sat silently and leaned her ear toward the hall. He quirked an eyebrow at Trey, and then all three of them shamelessly eavesdropped on June's end of the conversation.

"Listen, the good news is I talked to Barty Perneras, and our license is going through right on time. But the bad news is pretty bad."

Luke heard the boards creak beneath June's bare feet as she paced the hardwood floor. "I'm stuck here for a month."

Luke coughed and sputtered a mouthful of tea into his hand. Sweet Jesus, a month? She'd half-scrambled his brain after being in town less than a day—how would he survive a month of this? June's voice pleaded in the hall, but he couldn't understand her words over the ringing in his ears. It took a solid minute before he could concentrate again. He thought he heard a man shouting—in Spanish?—from the receiver.

"...and I'm telling you it wouldn't've made any difference! He had it all planned out!"

June spoke with a firm voice now, no longer pleading. Luke didn't know who was on the other end of that line, but she didn't take any shit from him.

"We can waste our time arguing, or figure out how to make this work." She heaved a sigh. "Come on, Este. Do you have any idea how long I've waited for this? How many design journals I've read or how long I've prepared? It kills me not to be there."

June's mystery man must have apologized, because she took a softer tone.

"No, it's okay. *I'm* sorry. Look, I don't get cell service here, and it's long distance to Austin, so if you call me at this number every morning…say, at eight?…we'll go over every detail together. And I'll make this up to you. I promise."

Luke could just imagine all the things Mystery Man had in mind.

"You're so bad," she said with a smile in her low voice.

Yep, exactly.

"So I'll talk to you tomorrow morning. Bye."

Trey crammed half a biscuit into his mouth, Pru speared a bite of chicken, Luke refilled his glass with tea, and they all scrambled to look innocent when June walked in. She smoothed her tight black skirt, adjusted her silky blouse, and sat down, flashing an apologetic grin.

"I wouldn't take a call at dinner, but it was important," she said.

God love her, Pru asked what they were probably all thinking. "Your boyfriend?"

"No." June drizzled honey over her biscuit. "Business partner. He's got a dozen clubs and restaurants in Austin, but he's more a financial backer than a planner. Not used to day-to-day stuff, so this'll be hard on him. But enough about my problems." She gestured at Trey with her biscuit. "I can tell by your accent you're from up North. How'd you and Luke meet?"

"I grew up in Chicago." Trey rested his forearms on the table and shot a nervous glance at Luke. "We met in the army."

"Were you in Germany together?"

"Yeah, and basic training before that."

June took a long drink and studied Luke over the top of her glass. Then she glanced down and used her fork to make swirls in her mashed potatoes. "The army was your dream, Luke. It's all you ever talked about since we were kids. So what're you doing back here?"

"Turns out I didn't like taking orders." It wasn't a complete lie. Luke noticed Trey's jaw clench, and he got that guilty look on his face, just like every time someone asked that question. Trey had nothing to feel guilty about. Hell, if anything, Luke was to blame for what happened.

"Well, that's easy to believe." June turned to Trey. "Did he tell you how he bossed me around as a kid? Always made me play GI Joe, and never—not even once—played house with me."

Trey shook his head. "He's never mentioned you before."

"What?" she asked.

"I heard about you from some local folks," Trey explained. "I work on their homes with Luke, but they didn't say much. Just that Miss Pru had a granddaughter."

June's shoulders rounded forward and she seemed to sink two inches into her chair. Then she gave him that look, wrinkling up her forehead and widening those big, brown eyes. Aw, shit. Somehow that'd hurt her feelings. Why did women try so hard to take offense to every little thing?

"He never told you we grew up together here, in this house?"

"Wait," Trey said, pointing his fork at Luke. "So she's like your sister?"

"Jesus Christ, no!" He'd never, ever thought of June as a sister. A best-friend-by-default, and in later years, an object of lust, but never a sister. The incestuous implication made him shiver.

"Lucas Gallagher, I won't have the Lord's name

taken in vain!" Pru shot to her feet and shook her bony index finger at his nose. "You're not too old for the wooden spoon."

"Yes, ma'am. Sorry."

Trey sat back and rubbed his stomach like he'd filled it too full. "I'm confused."

"Well," June said in a voice sour as a year-old lemon, "I'll be happy to explain, since Luke never did." She focused on the striped wallpaper behind his head. "My parents died when I was seven, and I came to live here."

"I'm sorry."

"Thanks." She smiled at Trey and softened a little. "Luke lived on the next farm, and there weren't any other kids around, so we played together a lot. Then he came to live with Grammy and me when he was twelve. I assume he told you why."

Luke pushed back his chair and began clearing the table. "I told him my white trash mama went Christmas shopping and never came back. Is that close enough to the truth for you, Junebug?"

June's cheeks flushed, and she pressed her red lips together.

But Luke never told Trey about his little sister. Abandonment was one thing, but a mother choosing to take one child and discard the other—like a goddamn game of rummy!—was different. Like he was inferior, not worth keeping. Luke had been a spitfire pistol of a twelve-year-old, all skinned elbows and dirty finger-nails, snatching cookies, burning through his mama's patience, and leaving nothing but muddy sneaker prints behind. Mama'd left a note claiming she couldn't han-dle being a single parent to both kids, so she took his four-year-old sister and hitchhiked to California to find her deadbeat boyfriend. She'd kept the easy child, and left him without another word.

"Let me get this." Pru pulled the butter dish from Luke's hand. "June and I can clean up later. There's a melon in the fridge. You three take it on the porch while I make a call."

June made a move for the refrigerator, but Trey darted in front of her and insisted on carrying the watermelon outside. Luke wasn't hungry anymore—thinking about his mama always killed his appetite—but he followed along and pulled a rocker to the porch rail so he could sit back, kick up his feet, and watch the stars. A cool night breeze rustled his hair and tickled the back of his neck. The air was sweet with honeysuckle, which brought back memories of other summer nights when he and June used to eat watermelon out here and spit seeds onto the front lawn. His always went farther, and one year a melon plant took root beneath the big pecan tree.

"So," Trey said, plunging a heavy butcher knife into the melon and steering the topic away from family. "Why do you have to stay here for a month? Not that I'm complaining or anything." And then he flashed those damned dimples again.

June curled up on the porch swing and tucked her feet underneath her. The moonlight glowed from behind, illuminating the curls of her hair, but leaving her face concealed in shadows. She looked like a dark angel, all soft curves and sensuality.

"It's completely bogus," she said. "But I have to stay for a month of community service. I can work at the church or with some charity that fixes old homes."

Luke nearly fell backward in his chair, and he lurched forward to catch himself. "You mean Helping Hands?"

"Yeah, that sounds right."

"That's great—" Trey began.

"Church," Luke interrupted. "You'll want to work at church. It's air-conditioned."

June leaned forward into the porch light and gave him a glare that said she'd rather burn in hell for ten eternities.

"No, trust me." Luke used his eyes to send Trey an unspoken message: *Back me up, man*. "You're better off working with those nice little church ladies."

"Oh?" June sat up and gripped the edge of the swing. "The ones who think I'm running a den of iniquity? No thanks."

Shit. What had he done to deserve this? "Tell her, Trey."

"Uh, okay." He shrugged, twisting his lips in confusion. "Building and repair is hot, dirty, dangerous work, but you can—"

"Exactly!" Luke nodded and pointed at June. "Not to mention bugs and critters. No scorpions or rabid raccoons in church." If that argument didn't sway her, nothing would. Brave as she always was, June shrieked like a teakettle every time she saw a creepy-crawly. "Or snakes," he added for good measure.

June bit the inside of her cheek and stared into the darkness. "Well...we'll see."

"Here you go." Trey handed June a thick, dripping triangle of melon. Then he grabbed one for himself and joined her on the swing without offering Luke a slice. "One of my friends back home used to cut a hole in the top of the watermelon and stick a bottle of vodka in it, upside down."

"Oh, right. I've heard of that," June said. Was she batting her lashes at Trey, or did she have something in her eye? "You leave it in the fridge overnight, and all the vodka soaks in."

"Yeah. It was pretty good." Trey rested one arm on the swing behind June's neck in a covert wraparound move that every guy learned in high school. "You know, there's a little bar in the next county. Nothing fancy, just a few pool tables, but the beer's wet. I was thinking we could…"

Uh-oh. Luke knew where this was heading, and he didn't like it one damned bit, though he refused to examine why he felt that way.

"…have a drink while you're in town." Trey sucked melon juice off his bottom lip, and not so innocently either. "Maybe the bartender can mix one of your special recipes."

"Time to go." Luke stood and shouted to Pru through the screen door. "Thanks for supper."

Trey tilted his head and stared at Luke like he'd grown a third arm. Luke fished his keys out of his pocket and skipped down the front porch steps toward the truck. "See you around, Junebug."

Luke didn't see June's expression, but she told Trey thanks, but no thanks. She wasn't allowed to cross the county line. For no reason at all, Luke's chest felt ten pounds lighter.

Once he and Trey were on the road headed back to town, his buddy switched off the radio.

"What's with you?" Trey asked. "I had a shot with her back there. And why don't you want her help with the Jenkins place?"

Luke tried to sound casual, but his voice came out ten decibels louder than he'd expected. "Can you imagine her working with Creepy Karl? Just forget about June. She'll be gone again before you know it."

"What's the harm in having a little fun while she's here?"

"A little *fun*?" He glared at Trey, and the truck swerved wildly into the left lane before Luke jerked it back again.

"Whoa, chill the hell out! What's your problem? If she's not like your sister, then why can't—" Trey sucked in a quick breath and turned to face him. "You're into her, aren't you?"

"No."

"Bullshit. You two have a history. What happened? Did you already…y'know?"

Luke's fist tightened against the wheel. Some things a man just kept private. "I want Jenkins's roof finished before the next storm comes in. They deliver the shingles?"

Trey hesitated a few seconds before he said, "Yeah." His best friend wasn't an idiot, so he let the subject drop, and they drove on in silence.

Chapter 4

RANDY TRAVIS CROONED THROUGH ONE HALF-BUSTED speaker in June's car, promising to love her forever and ever, amen. The air-conditioning only worked on special occasions, and today wasn't one of them, so she rolled the window down a little farther and let the warm breeze stir her ponytail. June squinted at the digital clock on the cracked gray dashboard. The faded display read nine-fifteen. If the temperature now was any indication, fall hadn't decided to make an appearance yet. Another scorcher. But not even the lure of air-conditioning could convince her to spend one minute inside the Holy Baptism by Hellfire Church. She'd had her fill of all that as a child, thank you very much.

June glanced out her window at a parched irrigation ditch running alongside an even more parched, withered cornfield. The filmy brown ditch water couldn't compare to Luquos's clear, clean aquariums. She sighed, imagining herself relaxed against a velvet-cushioned booth while watching three hundred graceful jellyfish float delicately inside a pink backlit wall. Her jellies would arrive next week, and she wouldn't be there to greet them. Esteban had phoned that morning, and aside from an argument with the building inspector, things were going more smoothly than either of them expected. She'd tried to sound pleased on the phone, but truthfully, she missed feeling needed.

A dull thunk sounded from the engine, and June eased up on the accelerator. Time to keep it below fifty.

"Come on, Bruiser," she whispered. "You can make it."

With only three hundred fifty dollars in the bank and no means of earning cash during the next month, June couldn't afford another repair. And she'd ride a rusted unicycle before she'd ask Gram for money.

She read the directions Gram had written for her. Only one more mile until the Jenkins house. June held her breath and tried to calm the nervous flutter inside her belly. What did she know about fixing things? Hopefully she'd find a useful way to contribute without making an idiot of herself in the process. She also hoped Luke had exaggerated about the critters.

An old, white colonial came into view, its roof half stripped of shingles and baring the faded plywood underneath. A shirtless man straddled the roof peak, pulling off tar sheets and tossing them behind the house. As June drove closer, she realized it was Trey. He must've recognized her too, because he paused to wave before returning to his work.

Five other vehicles were parked in front of the house, including Luke's big black *Gallagher Contracting* truck. Her heart gave a little quiver—what was he doing there? Taking a deep breath, June pulled Bruiser onto a shaded dirt path around the side. Her engine was more likely to start up again if it didn't sit too long in direct sunlight.

June smoothed her T-shirt, donned a wide-brimmed straw hat, and grabbed a bottle of water from her minicooler. Folding her community service time sheet, she pressed it between her lips while stepping out of the car.

"Hey, I recognize that." A chubby, dark-haired man

with a few days' growth on his face pointed to the paper in June's mouth. "You servin' hours?" He was a dead ringer for John Belushi, and she half expected him to don a toga and start a food fight. Flashing a wide, brilliant smile, he strolled forward and pulled her into a crushing hug, the sour, smoky tang of marijuana practically emanating from his pores.

June stiffened and gave him a quick pat-pat-pat on the back before wriggling free. "Yeah."

"Me too!" he said with way, way too much excitement. "Give your sheet to the boss-man. What's your name, *mamacita*?"

"June." She took a step back and leaned against her car, but the stoner didn't seem to understand the concept of personal space. He eyed her up and down like she was a warm slice of cherry pie, or in his case, like she was an oversized bong with boobs. Then he placed one meaty hand on the car's purple roof and leaned in close.

"*Giiiirl*." He shook his head. "You're finer than a frog's hair split three ways."

"Huh?"

"Karl!" Luke's voice boomed out, and June flinched in shock, clocking the stoner in the nose with the top of her head. She tugged off her hat and rubbed her throbbing scalp.

The stoner—Karl, she guessed—cupped both hands over his nose and hopped in place. He hollered at Luke, pulling his red-stained hands away. "I think it's broken!" Almost instantly, his nose had swollen to the size of a plum, a current of blood streaming over his lips and chin.

"I'm sorry!" June cringed and shielded her eyes. She could handle the sight of all bodily fluids, with the exception of blood. And mucus, she didn't like that either. Or vomit. Heck, to be honest, she wasn't a fan of most bodily fluids.

"Jimmy," Luke's voice called from nearby, but June kept her eyes covered and couldn't see him. "Take Karl to Sultry Memorial. He busted his nose again."

June heard the slap of boots running on the dirt path and Karl's retreating cries. Then a vehicle started and drove away, flinging gravel in its wake. From somewhere behind the house, the shrill buzz of a saw pierced the air, and she realized the drama was over. Everyone had already gone back to work.

Slowly, she peered out from between her fingers at Luke's moss-green eyes, which gleamed with amusement despite the firm set of his lips. From there, her gaze lowered to the hard curves of his bare chest and those broad shoulders. Sweet mother of Stevie Ray. June chewed the inside of her cheek and let her eyes wander to the trail of russet hair that encircled his navel and dipped below the waist of his jeans, which hung low—really low—on his lean hips. *Off limits!*

"Hey," he said, pointing to his face. "I'm up here." He folded his muscled arms across his chest and smirked. "Nice job, Calamity June. In your first five minutes, you managed to send one of my men to the hospital."

"Wanna make it two? I'd be happy to push you off a ladder or something." June smiled sweetly and held up her time sheet. "Who's in charge?"

"That'd be me." He moved closer, bending near enough for June to feel the heat from his bare skin through her thin T-shirt. He smelled like warm leather and sawdust, and June's heart thumped against her ribs. She closed her eyes and held her breath when Luke's lips found her ear-lobe. "And if you're not nice," he whispered slowly, "I'll send you to work for the Baptists." His mouth caressed the helix of her ear as he breathed, "Junebug."

June stumbled back against her car and tried to forget the tingle of his hot breath in her ear. "You run Helping Hands?"

"No. Trey runs it for me. I founded it." Luke pulled off his faded blue baseball cap and raked a hand through his hair. "I come around twice a week to check on everyone and do paperwork."

"You?" June felt her eyebrows rise. "The same Luke Gallagher who used to climb out his bedroom window and pee off the roof started a charity?"

"Technically, it's a nonprofit, not a charity. We need fund-raising and donations to pay for supplies, licenses, and Trey's salary." His gaze shifted beyond her to focus on Bruiser. "Jesus, that thing's older than sin. And twice as ugly."

"Well, it's paid for and cheap to insure, which I think is beautiful."

"Your cooling fan's been running too long. God only knows what's going on under the hood. I'll come by Pru's tomorrow morning and check it out."

"You don't have to do that."

As if on cue, the fan sputtered, rattled, and clunked to a stop. Luke shook his head and pulled his cap back on. "This isn't Austin. You break down, it might take half a day before someone else drives along and finds you. I'll be there at seven." He turned and walked toward the backyard. "Come on, I'll get you started. You already met Karl. He's a criminal like you."

"I'm not a criminal."

"That's what they all say."

"Hey." June grabbed his rounded bicep and the corded muscle bunched beneath her fingers. *Off limits!* "That reminds me."

Luke stopped and his eyes darted from hers down to her hand, which still gripped his warm, damp skin. "Of what?" An emotion she couldn't quite place crossed his face, and she pulled her hand back.

"Did the prosecutor charge you for what happened that day? At the pond?"

"Nope." He picked up a hammer from the dusty ground and continued walking.

"Why not?"

"Your conduct must've been lewder and more indecent than mine."

Not the way she remembered it. Not at all. Luke had done things to her that afternoon she'd never known existed. Things she couldn't think about without feeling heat rise from her chest into her face. The heat spread to other places too.

"Trey's on the roof," Luke said. "I'm *sure* you remember him." June thought she heard a faint sneer of jealousy in his voice. Probably just her imagination. He pointed the hammer to a middle-aged balding man wearing protective goggles and cutting two-by-fours with a motorized saw, then to a group of five men standing nearby who sanded and applied wood stain to the freshly cut boards. "That's Pauly. He's okay, but stay away from the rest of the halfway house guys. They're fresh out of prison, and not because they got busted skinny-dipping. You hear me?"

June nodded.

"Just watch out for yourself. Trey keeps a close eye on the workers, but he can't see everything."

"You don't get paid for this?" June regarded the man she'd known nearly all her life, yet didn't know at all. "Why do you do it?"

The bill of Luke's baseball cap cast a shadow over his eyes, but intensity still simmered there, like he had something unpleasant to say, but didn't know how much to reveal. "Everyone deserves a second chance. Most of these guys need the experience. They're not fit for anything else." He watched the men in silence for a moment, then admitted, "Five years ago someone gave me a second chance. I'm just giving it back."

Did he mean Grammy? June wanted to ask Luke to spill everything—explain what ended his military career and his marriage—but after the way she'd avoided him the last nine years, she didn't have the right to ask what he ate for breakfast.

The Holy Baptism by Hellfire Church was looking better with each passing minute. June had never been a violent woman, but she couldn't stop fantasizing about breaking Karl's nose again, this time on purpose. There were so many ways to do it. Her favorite option involved the use of a discarded toilet seat protruding from the temporary Dumpster out back.

"Hoo!" Karl said in a nasally voice. "It's hotter'n the devil's bunghole out here."

He'd been treated and released from the hospital and had returned two hours ago with his nose packed with gauze. Either he'd toked up again, or he was just a freakishly upbeat man, because he'd been following June around to "help" while singing bad reggae, telling lame jokes, and offering compliments like, "*Giiiiirl*, your body's like an hourglass that went *Bam!*" then smacking his hands together to mimic an atomic blast. June knew her hips were too wide, and she didn't appreciate Karl-the-Kook pointing it out. She'd finally stopped trying to squeeze into ill-fitting jeans a couple years ago and started buying a size too big and having the waist taken in.

June picked up another cracked shingle and tossed it in her black trash bag. Before Luke had left to work on a house he was flipping in the next county, he'd assigned her to cleanup detail. Shingles tossed off the roof, tar paper, old nails, paper cups—the brown lawn was littered with junk, and cleaning it up was boring as a sermon. And painful. She winced and massaged her lower back, stiff from hours of bending. She'd volunteered to clean the gutters—at least she'd get away from Karl that way—but Luke had expressly forbidden her from using the forty-foot ladder.

"Hey, *mamacita*." Karl had turned on the garden hose and stuck it down the front of his pants. "Best way to cool off. Wanna try?"

Oh, sweet mercy. "No thanks, I'm going to clean the gutters. Give me a hand with the ladder, will you?"

Karl pulled the hose out and waddled over with his jeans soaked and clinging to his chunky thighs. He looked like a stoned, bowlegged cowboy taking ten paces before a showdown at high noon. Between the two of them, they extended the heavy aluminum ladder and pushed it into position against the chipped siding near the roof.

The metal rungs burned her palms as she climbed, and she stopped halfway up to give a little bounce and make sure they'd secured the adjustable lock. When June reached the roof, she peeked at the ground, her hands automatically tightening against the top rung. Holy sugar, it was a lot higher than she'd thought. Best not to look down. She focused on watching Trey nail a sheet of new, jet black shingles in place. A battered cowboy hat shaded his face, but his bare back glistened with sweat and had started to turn pink near the shoulders.

"Hey," she called, continuing to grip the ladder instead of waving.

Trey glanced up and smiled, then hammered one last nail in place before joining her. "Fancy meeting you here." He knelt on the exposed wood and grinned, revealing a pair of deep dimples. "How's it goin'?"

June kept one hand on the sturdy aluminum and used the other to scoop dried leaves from the gutter. "Karl's driving me to drink, but there's no alcohol in Sultry County."

"Sounds like a regular day, then." The tan skin around his bright blue eyes crinkled when he smiled, and June felt relaxed. Calm. Not all knotted up and squirmy like when she met Luke's intense gaze. It was kind of nice for a change.

"You can help, you know," she said.

Trey glanced at the gutter and reached out to curl his fingers around it.

"No, not with that." June tipped back her straw hat. "You can help preserve my sanity. I can't leave the county to visit that bar, but if you bring back supplies, I can mix up my favorite drink recipes for you. Maybe at your place?"

A flicker of excitement sparked behind those cerulean eyes, but it was gone in an instant. He chewed his bottom lip and concentrated on pulling clumps of dark debris from the gutter. "Uh, that's a mighty tempting offer, but I'm gonna have to pass. I'm seeing someone."

What? He wasn't seeing someone last night when he'd asked her out for drinks. There was no way she'd misinterpreted his signals—all those flirty looks and the way he'd practically tripped over himself to act like a gentleman. She must've done something since then to change his opinion. Did she have tar on her face? Food between her teeth?

"Oh, sure." She reached in to scoop another handful of leaves. "No problem."

A heavy, awkward silence hung between them like a force field. Trey leaned down to dislodge an old mud dauber nest inside the gutter, and then a loud metallic noise clanked from below and shook the ladder. Stomach dropping, June gasped and grabbed on to the gutter near Trey's hand. It separated from the siding with a dry crack.

Trey toppled forward, panic flashing in his eyes as he lurched sideways, trying to steady himself. She reached out to grab his arm, but the sweaty flesh slipped from her fingers, and he went down, feet first. People always said tragedies seemed to happen in slow motion, but that wasn't true. June didn't even have time to blink before Trey was on the dusty ground, curled up and groaning in pain.

June didn't know how she got down the ladder so fast, and she didn't remember tearing inside the Jenkins house to call an ambulance. But she recalled running outside and identifying the only person she knew besides Karl.

"Pauly!" she shouted. "Call Luke!" Then she knelt down and ran her fingers through Trey's short blond hair, trying to soothe the terror so thick in his voice. "Don't move," she told him. "Help's on the way. You're gonna be fine." He squinted his eyes shut and kept clenching his jaw so tightly, she worried he might break a tooth.

When the ambulance finally arrived, the paramedics let her ride in the back with Trey, and she held his hand the whole ride, apologizing over and over.

Nearly an hour later, Luke came barreling into the hospital lobby, leather tool belt still fastened around his waist like he'd jumped in his truck as soon as Pauly'd made the call. She waved from her seat in the waiting area to get his attention.

"What happened?" he asked. The front of his shirt was slick with sweat, the hollow of his throat pulsing visibly beneath tanned skin.

June handed him her Coke. While he took a long gulp, she told him, "Trey fell off the roof."

"Well, no shit, Junebug. But what happened? Pauly said he didn't see."

June wanted to tell him it was all her fault, that she'd pulled the gutter off the wall and made Trey lose his balance, but the response died on her tongue. She chewed the inside of her cheek and stared at the immaculate black and white floor tiles, because she couldn't bear to look him in the eyes.

"Miss?" the emergency room cleric said from her desk. "They said you can go back now. Room one-eleven."

Luke charged ahead, his strides so long June had to jog to catch up. He pushed open the door to room one-eleven and stopped short for a moment before walking inside. June soon understood why.

"Hey," Trey said weakly, his eyes trying to smile from below a stark white bandage taped across his brow. His bare chest was mummified in tight binding, and one plaster-casted leg hung from a line secured to the ceiling. He looked like death warmed over, cooled back down, and then steamrollered. "Not as bad as it looks. Just a couple cracked ribs and a broken femur."

"Just cracked ribs," Luke muttered to himself. "What the hell happened?"

"That idiot, Karl, accidentally knocked June's ladder with a five-foot lead pipe. We were both holding on to the gutter when it broke, and I lost my balance."

June closed her eyes and felt that sick, sinking feeling in her tummy that always told her she was in big trouble.

"Ladder?" Luke said through gritted teeth.

She opened one eye, then wished she hadn't. She'd seen Luke angry before. When they were sixteen, he'd used his wages from three summers of picking crops to buy a used red Camaro. She'd borrowed it without permission and dented the bumper on a fence post when she'd swerved to avoid a deer. But Luke's reaction then was nothing compared to the hot menace in his expression now.

"Damn it, I told you to stay on the ground for a reason!" As he moved closer, she shrank away from his booming voice. "You both could've been killed! You always *were* a magnet for troub—" Then he froze mid-yell, like he'd just realized something, and his face turned white as a dove's wing. "Oh, Jesus." Luke turned back to Trey. "You know what this means? You'll be laid up for weeks, and I'll have to take over the Jenkins project. How am I supposed to get my house on the market in time?"

"Shit," Trey whispered. His semi-cheerful expression wilted. "We'll figure something out. I can still supervise the crew from a chair."

"A chair?" Luke said, shaking his head. "You won't be supervising anyone but your own busted ass for at least two weeks." He sank down onto a padded seat and held his head in his hands. "Shit. I'm not gonna miss my chance again. I'll just have to work nights at the house."

"Buddy, you're already working nights."

"Then I'll work later nights."

"I'm real sorry," June whispered softly. She didn't dare speak out loud after what she'd done. "I can help you at—"

"I need your help," Luke spat, "like I need a hole in my head." He stood so fast, he knocked his chair over. "I gotta finish Jenkins's roof before it rains. Come on. I'll drive you back to your car."

June started to say she'd take a taxi, but caught herself just in time. Like Luke had said earlier, this wasn't Austin. Suddenly, she ached for home so badly she almost doubled over, but not wanting to upset Luke any further, she nodded and followed him to his truck.

She didn't peer around the cab for clues to Luke's life, didn't hear the music vibrating her seat. Instead, June rested her forehead against the window and stared outside, seeing nothing but a green and brown blur of landscape.

When they reached the Jenkins house, Luke waited to be sure her car started. He didn't look at her when he said, "Call here and let the phone ring once when you get home. I've got enough on my mind without worrying about you breaking down."

"Luke, I'm awful sorry."

"And don't come back tomorrow." He shot one icy glare in her direction—so full of venom it made her breath catch. Then he stalked away into the backyard. A minute later, she saw him on the roof hammering shingles.

June bit her lip and rested her forehead on the steering wheel. Somehow, she'd gone from a responsible business owner to a complete screw-up, sending two men to the hospital and alienating her oldest friend. Hot tears pressed against her eyelids, but she forced them back.

One day down, twenty-nine to go.

Chapter 5

LUKE AWOKE WITH A START, THE WAY HE ALWAYS DID when he spent the night in his old bedroom at Pru's. From the soft light streaming through the blinds and the occasional call of a whippoorwill, he guessed it was about six-thirty. He heard the toilet flush in the hallway bathroom and figured June was up too.

He'd been dreaming about her, specifically about the time she took an ass-whooping for something he'd done. It was just a few months after his mama'd left, and he'd smashed one of Pru's figurines in a fit of rage. June had swept up the glass and told her grandma she'd broken it. When Pru had taken the wooden spoon to June's backside, June hadn't cried. Her chin had wobbled, eyes all red and glassy, but she'd pressed her lips together and held those tears inside. He'd felt so terrible he'd let her play with his favorite action figure the rest of the day.

The reason behind the dream was obvious. She'd looked up at him with that same quivering chin yesterday when he'd told her not to come back. A heavy fog had settled inside his chest ever since. He'd finished the roof around midnight, and then—too tired to drive an hour back to his air mattress at the Hallover house—had come here to shower and sleep. Though he still didn't want June's "help," he needed to smooth things over.

He pulled on his jeans and followed the scent of

coffee into the kitchen. Pru was already working on breakfast, dressed in one of those flowery grandma ensembles. She pressed a steaming mug into his hand.

"Thanks." He sucked down a scalding sip, letting the bitter coffee scorch his throat. "Where's June?"

"Pickin' peppers for the eggs." She added a pat of shortening to her bowl and began cutting biscuit dough. "She looked upset when she came home last night. Eyes all puffy. Didn't say two words at supper. Y'know anything 'bout that?"

"Yes, ma'am."

"Lucas." Pru stopped and gave him a look he'd never seen before. Hard, but soft at the same time. Maybe even sad. "You know I love you like my own kin, but that's my baby girl out there. She's always been so tenderhearted, 'specially with you. I can't have you hurtin' her again. Y'understand me?"

He nodded, setting his mug on the counter. If it was possible to feel any lower, he didn't see how.

In his bare feet, Luke strolled through the cool, damp grass to the garden on the side of the house. Clouds drifted across the sun, and the crisp morning air puckered the skin on his chest into gooseflesh.

Then he saw her, and all the oxygen in his lungs vanished. In her long, white nightgown, June looked mystical, like one of those faeries his mama had told him about. Her curly, brown hair glowed amber as she moved among the tangled vines and leaves with fluid grace—her fair fingers skimming each pepper before twisting it gently from the stem. A breeze swirled the flowing, gauzy gown around her ankles, and she gathered the material in front to hold the vegetables she'd picked. When he approached and cleared his throat, she sucked in a startled breath and dropped everything.

"Sorry," Luke whispered, moving forward slowly, as if entranced.

She frowned at the scattered peppers. "It's okay."

"Not for that." He reached down and took her left hand. "For yesterday."

"You're apologizing?" Her pink lips curved into a cautious smile. "The same Luke Gallagher who—"

"Yeah, yeah. Who stole the county's prize watermelon and terrorized the chickens and never said he was sorry for anything. That same Luke is sorry."

"Me too."

The low morning sun broke free of the clouds, illuminating June's thin, white nightgown and rendering it completely transparent. Suddenly, a pair of creamy, pink-tipped breasts came into view, rising and falling in a steady rhythm with each of her deep, slow breaths. He knew he should look away, but hell, he was only a man, and she was even more spectacular than he remembered. His fingertips twitched—actually twitched—aching to skim across her nipples, to see if they'd still tighten beneath his touch, like they'd done years before. He gazed lower, drinking in the curve of June's tiny waist and the smooth flare leading down to her thighs. Sweet Jesus. She still had those indents at the front of her hips—visible now as shadows beneath her gown. Those small divots were the *exact* size of his thumbs, as if she were custom-made for his hands. He'd once pressed his thumbs there and curled his fingers around her hips before slipping so gently inside her for the very first time. "Ho-o-ly shit," he murmured, gazing even lower to her bare—

"Hey," she said, tipping his chin with her fingers. "I'm up here."

Luke told his left hand to release hers and his feet to return to the house, but his mind and body weren't on speaking terms. He grabbed the front of June's night-gown and pulled her hard against him. She gasped, digging her fingernails into the skin on his shoulders. Christ, she smelled delicious, like oranges and cloves, and he could feel her heartbeat through her gown. The soft curves of her breasts, her hot breath panting against his chest, her silky hair tickling his jaw, all the dizzying sensations scrambled his brain into oatmeal.

He lowered his lips to her ear and tried to form a coherent sentence. "You shouldn't wear this thing outside the bedroom, Junebug."

"I didn't mean to give you a show."

"Oh, I got one, all right." After breathing in her sweet scent one last time, Luke pulled back and gazed into her wide, brown eyes. "You sleep without skivvies."

When June's mouth dropped into a pretty, pink oval, it took every fraction of his self-control not to kiss her silly and lay her down on the soft soil next to Pru's squash plants. He cleared his throat and gently pushed her away. God help him, he was hard enough to crack granite. He sure as hell couldn't go back in the house like this. "I'm gonna get started on your car."

June hung up the phone and slouched against the wall, letting her body sink slowly to the floor. Esteban had hired the entire staff in one hasty round of interviews—bartenders, cocktail waitresses, even a cleaning crew. He didn't seem too discriminating, but how could she criticize his methods when she sat here without contributing a thing? Darn it, she'd wanted to hand-select the most competent applicants, not grab whoever was easy. After nearly a decade of sacrificing and saving to open this bar, she couldn't even help choose the stemware. Esteban had done that too.

She slipped on a pair of flip-flops and shuffled outside to bring Luke a glass of water and a ham biscuit. He'd been tinkering with her car for the last hour and hadn't even come inside for breakfast, which wasn't like him. Nothing got between Luke Gallagher and a hearty meal.

Two jean-clad legs, one bent at the knee and the other extended straight, peeked out from beneath her car. Luke lifted his hips and scooted forward, and June felt a rush of heat pool between her thighs, remembering how those hips had pressed against her in the garden. He'd wanted her—there was no mistaking the very large, very rigid evidence that had strained against her belly. She'd repeated her *off limits* mantra over and over inside her head, but it was useless. Clinging to those powerful shoulders, she'd have let him lift her gown in an instant. Maybe working at church away from him was a good idea after all.

Luke appeared, holding something black and greasy. "This thing's a death trap."

"Hey, you took it apart? How am I supposed to get around?" She handed him the water and kept the biscuit, since his hands were so filthy.

He drained the whole glass and wiped his mouth on the back of his arm. "You're working for the Baptists today, right?"

"Yeah, cutting the lawn. I'll do my best to stay out of the sanctuary, so I don't burst into flames."

"Catch a ride with Pru. She's over there all the time. I need to get a few parts before you can drive that heap again." Luke wiped his hands against his thighs, leaving his jeans streaked with black goop. He reached for the biscuit and his fingertips brushed the inside of her wrist, sending a thrill up the length of her arm. "I'll put it back together tomorrow night."

"Thanks." June sat on the lowest front porch step. "Since when do you know so much about engines?"

In three mammoth bites, he crammed the whole thing in his mouth and spoke with one cheek stuffed with food. "Since the army trained me. But I wound up working on helicopters when they sent me overseas." He refilled his glass with the hose and drained it again.

"Can I ask you something?"

"Sure. Doesn't mean I'll answer."

"That house you're flipping? What's the rush to get it done?" She leaned back on her elbows and tried to read his eyes. It was easy: panic with a dash of stress.

"All my money's tied up in that place. Everything."

June laughed without humor. "Believe me, I know the feeling."

"And I need that money in four weeks."

"Loan shark?" She smiled, trying to lighten his mood. It didn't work.

"Auction." He took a deep breath and released it, puffing out his lips. "Silent, cash auction."

"What is it you want so badly?"

"My land." He nodded toward the back of Grammy's property. "It's in foreclosure again. This might be my last chance to get it back."

"Sure you want it?" There must've been so many

painful memories there. June didn't remember much about Luke's mother, but according to rumors, she'd had an addiction to OxyContin and abusive men, and that was before she'd skipped town and broken Luke's heart.

Luke nodded and joined her on the porch step, sitting so close his white T-shirt sleeve brushed her arm. If she tipped her head a teeny bit, she could rest against his shoulder. Then she could link their arms together and stare into the front yard the way she'd done on a few cool summer nights once upon a time. Instead, she leaned forward and wrapped her arms around her knees.

"I never told you about my granddaddy," Luke said. He fidgeted with his own hands, pressing a thumb inside the opposite palm. "He took me fishing at our pond every Sunday since I was three. And each time he'd tell me that pond would be mine someday, and I'd take my own grandbabies fishing there. When I was eleven, and everyone knew my mama wasn't...well...right in the head, my granddaddy said he was having the land subdivided and leaving ten acres around the pond to me. But he died before the paperwork went through, and everything passed to Mama."

He reached over and took June's hand. His skin was warm and rough—the large, powerful hands of a working man—and she fought the urge to lace their fingers together and hold on tight.

"She didn't pay the taxes when she left town," Luke continued, "so the county foreclosed. It's been bought and sold twice since then, and the last owner lost it to back taxes."

"But the house?"

"I'll bulldoze it and build new. Something closer to

the pond, so I can sit on the front porch with my coffee and look at the water."

June hated to say it, but she knew from personal experience how long real estate could sit on the market. It had taken nine months and three price reductions before her condo sold. "Even if you finish the investment house in time, it might not sell."

"Oh, it'll sell. And fast." He smoothed his thumb over each of her pink nails. "It's right down the street from a brand-spanking-new elementary school, and I've already got four families interested—one of them even tried to buy the place before it's repaired, but the bank wouldn't go for it. So anyway, all I gotta do is finish it up, list it, and let the bidding begin."

"I still want to help."

He laughed in a long, rolling chortle that basically said *forget about it*. "Duly noted. Now, can I ask *you* something?"

"Sure," she parroted. "Doesn't mean I'll answer."

"How come you never came back after college?" He bumped her shoulder, smiling despite the heavy subject he'd dumped at her feet. "All those years, and nothing but a few Christmas cards? I know things were rough between you and your grandma, but I didn't think they were *that* bad."

"They weren't," she admitted. "Not at first." He probably remembered that Gram had tried strong-arming her into living at home and attending the Bible College in the next county. Gram had gone so far as to cut her off financially when she'd applied to Texas State, but that hadn't strained their relationship to the breaking point. June had never felt entitled to a free education.

"But when I left and she couldn't use money to control me anymore, she found other ways." Like relentless, nagging phone calls, guilt-laden letters sprinkled with scary Bible verses, and worst of all, arranging for some Hellfire Baptists in June's town to "check on" her periodically, which had felt a heck of a lot like stalking. "When I started bartending, she completely lost her shit—oops, I mean sugar—and gave me an ultimatum."

"Which backfired."

"Yeah." She shrugged. "I was tired of being controlled."

But her feeling of vindication hadn't lasted beyond a few weeks. Several times, she'd picked up the phone to extend the olive branch, but fear had stopped her. Not fear of Grammy, but of the disappointment and loathing in her voice. She couldn't bear to hear it again.

"Did you miss her?" Luke pressed their palms together, comparing the lengths of their fingers.

"Yes." There was no reason to deny it. "But she made me feel shunned. And each year that went by, it got harder to call. I kept imagining she'd hang up on me, or worse…" *Tell me I'm "trash" like she said in our last fight.* "Anyway, I'm here now."

"Well, Junebug, I'm glad you're back." He released her hand, then patted her knee and rose to his feet.

"Me too." Because it wasn't only Grammy she'd missed. "And I want to help while I'm in town," she reminded him.

Luke didn't answer, just sniggered as he skipped down the steps. He grabbed his wallet off the car's roof and slipped it into the worn back pocket of his jeans, drawing her attention to his magnificent backside. *Off limits!* She glanced away and swallowed hard.

"Tell Pru good-bye for me." Then he hopped in his truck and drove off to supervise the Helping Hands crew.

After one day, not even a *full* day, of working at the Jenkins house, June's back and arms had ached so badly she'd needed two ibuprofen pills to sleep last night. Luke intended to spend his days laboring there, before driving an hour and working all night on his investment property? Impossible. June needed to figure out how to make Luke see she wasn't a walking catastrophe and accept her help before he worked himself into an early grave.

Chapter 6

ABOUT FIFTEEN YEARS AGO, AN ARGUMENT OVER whether or not Jazzercise counted as sinful dancing broke out among the Sultry Springs churchgoers, and a few disgruntled members marched their leg warmers over to a new house of worship: Holy Baptism by Water. The rift had rocked the county, pitting brother against brother, much like the Civil War, but far more serious. These pious soldiers fought for everlasting glory, as opposed to something as trivial as states' rights. The Sultry Springs Holy War raged on for six months, until the Jazzercise instructor ran off to Vegas with her boyfriend. Then, with their heads hung in defeat, the defectors returned home and rejoined the flock. Nowadays, if a person wanted his soul saved, there was only one option: Holy Baptism by Hellfire.

June brushed her fingertips against the shiny oak pew, polished to a high gloss by hundreds of bottoms and decades of use. Years ago, she and Luke had squirmed in these pews and found ways to amuse themselves during the long sermons: passing notes, playing tic-tac-toe or rock-paper-scissors, and her favorite distraction—replacing the nouns and adjectives in the church bulletin with dirty ones. *Mr. Peterson's white corn for sale, you shuck it!* became *Mr. Peterson's sweet ass for sale, you...*well, something obscene that rhymes with "shuck it." Sometimes her ribs had ached from holding in the laughter.

The church had added a new fellowship hall off the

sanctuary—a boxy, red brick structure that looked out of place next to the weathered, white wood of the main building. Otherwise, nothing had changed. The air inside the church still smelled like dusty silk flowers and arthritis ointment.

"Well, look at you, Mae-June." Pastor McMahon ambled out of his office. June recognized his voice—a drawl thicker than molasses that stretched "Jesus" into four syllables, *Jay-ee-us-sus*—but he'd lost all his hair and found a hundred pounds instead. "Sister Pru told me you were back."

Grammy gave June's arm a zealous pat. It was the first time Gram had touched her since she'd come to town two days ago, and June's muscles stiffened at the contact. Her grandmother had never been an affectionate woman to begin with, and after so many years apart, June wasn't used to Gram's touch.

"I go by June now." She folded her arms over her breasts. It seemed wrong wearing an immodest tank top and khaki shorts in the Lord's house, but lawn mowing was hot work, and the temperature was supposed to top ninety again.

"Did I hear Mae-June's voice?" A gaggle of ladies in the lobby shuffled into the sanctuary. Apparently, June was a celebrity now.

Ms. Bicknocker straightened her spine and peered down her long nose. She'd once been the pariah of Sultry County, until she found God after working the pole for twelve years in a Houston gentleman's club. Now she looked just as constipated as everyone else. "I see you're not married," she said, glimpsing June's left hand in clear condemnation. "What're you up to these days?"

June glanced at Grammy, not sure what to say. These ladies were hard-core advocates for the prohibition of sinful vices like booze, and she didn't want to start any trouble.

"Well, now," Gram said, wrapping one arm around June's shoulder. "June's got her own business. A...bar. Sounds real special with an aquarium an' everything." Holy buttered biscuits, she almost sounded proud!

"I see." Ms. Bicknocker shook her head disapprovingly. "And where do you go to church?"

June grinned and slipped her hands in her back pockets. "I belong to Our Lady of Infinite Lazy Sunday Mornings on the Sofa."

That joke usually elicited laughs, at least a snicker or two, but no smiles broke out this time. Tough crowd.

"Mmm," came the disappointed response.

Pastor McMahon wrinkled his mouth and tipped his head forward like he was praying for June's soul. "May I ask why you don't attend service?"

Was there a tactful, mature way to say, *'Cause I don't wanna*? "I've just been so busy."

The pastor nodded in understanding. He'd probably heard that one before.

June decided this was the perfect moment to excuse herself. "I should start on the lawn before it gets too hot."

"I'll walk you out."

Leaving the cool lobby behind, she followed Pastor McMahon outside to the storage shed. "There's a gas can in there," he said. "But don't forget to let the mower cool off before you refill it. And come inside if you get too hot. There's iced tea in the fellowship hall."

She thanked him and tugged open the heavy wood

door. The hot, musty air inside the shed parched June's skin, making her face itchy and tight, and by the time she'd tugged the mower out and found the gas can, her tank top was damp with sweat. That glass of iced tea sounded awfully good, but she had too much pride to take a break before actually doing anything.

After filling the gas tank, June primed the motor and yanked the start cord a few times until the engine turned over and rumbled to life. She started near the building and worked her way out, mowing in meticulous, straight lines. No way she'd mess up like yesterday—this would be the neatest, trimmest lawn anyone had ever seen. An hour later, she stood back and admired her work and then rewarded herself with two tall glasses of tea.

The grass was taller and thick with weeds at the back of the property where the church grounds met a fallow field, so June slowed her pace, lifting the front of the mower every few feet so it didn't choke and shut off. It was dull, monotonous work, so she let her mind wander, imagining opening night at Luquos. But while June tried to decide which outfit to wear, her thoughts drifted to Luke. What was he doing right now? Maybe demolishing Jenkins's rotted back deck. Did he think about her? Doubtful. In every relationship—or in their case, friendship—there was always one person who gave more. That person had always been her. Besides, he was so busy now he couldn't spare a second to think about anything but work.

She probably wouldn't see Luke at supper anymore, at least not until he finished his house, and by then, she'd return to Austin. But perhaps that was a blessing. If June was honest with herself, and she tried to be, she could easily fall for him again in the next twenty-eight days if they spent too much time together. Best to—ouch! Something scraped against June's calf, maybe a patch of thistle. She rubbed the side of her sneaker against her leg, but the prickle intensified, until it felt like her skin was on fire.

Releasing the mower, she glanced down at her legs—and shrieked like a banshee. A stinging, swarming cloud of yellow and black covered her calves and ankles. She must've run over a bees' nest! They crawled in frantic zigzag patterns higher up the length of her body, while some took flight and prepared to attack her face. June's heart nearly seized, and she bolted for the fellowship hall, screaming the whole way. She was still yelling when she threw open the door and dashed inside.

"Grammy! Grammy! Grammy!" June scurried in circles, swatting at her legs, her arms, her face, anywhere she could reach.

Dozens of shoes squeaked and clopped against the tile floor, but June couldn't see anything except a blur of arms as she slapped herself silly.

"Oh, my Lord!"

"Put her in the baptismal font!"

"No! Get the hose."

"Where's the wasp spray?" It was Gram's voice, the only one June could identify in her panicked state.

Within seconds, the air was practically impossible to breathe as Gram fogged the fellowship hall with thick, acrid insecticide. Coughing hard enough to hack up a lung, June bent over and braced her hands against her knees. The scene playing out before her was comical, and she would've laughed had she not been paralyzed in agony and choking on fumes.

Pastor McMahon's stomach bobbed up and down as he jumped to swat a rolled-up newspaper against the low ceiling. Prim church ladies armed with fly swatters whacked and smacked, crouching low and then springing on their prey like kung-fu fighters. Even Ms. Bicknocker joined in, flicking a dish towel with the skill of a seasoned locker room jock. When the last of the bees were crushed, everyone huddled around June's swollen, blotchy legs.

"My daddy used to chew tobacco and spit on the stings."

"Got any tobacco?"

"Nope."

"How 'bout ammonia?"

"We should call Doc Benton."

"He's wet behind the ears. Call Doc Noble."

"Everyone get your credit cards," Grammy said. "And tweezers, if you can find 'em."

Ten minutes later, Pastor McMahon brought June some aspirin and iced tea, and she tried her best to sit still while five gray-haired ladies scraped and plucked the stingers from her skin.

"Quit squirming," Ms. Bicknocker said over the top of her bifocals. "I can barely see as it is."

"Sorry. It really hurts." The throbbing ache didn't subside. If anything, it mounted with each passing second. June grasped the cool edge of her plastic chair and held her breath. Nope, that didn't help.

"Nora," Gram said to June's old Sunday school teacher. "See if you can find a spray bottle. Baking soda and water'll cool the burn."

And God bless them all, it really did. June's temples still ached, but Gram claimed that was to be expected with all the venom in her bloodstream. When the last stinger had been plucked, June thanked everyone for their time and help, and Pastor McMahon suggested she show her appreciation by attending next Sunday's service. She agreed, unable to think of a single excuse not to, and asked for indoor community service hours until her legs healed.

Back home, Grammy made June lie in bed with three pillows under her knees. Then she wrapped June's legs in cool, damp towels soaked in baking soda and ice water.

"Same thing happened to your mama." Gram sat at the end of the bed, and it shook with her weight. "I ever tell you that story?"

June shook her head. She could count the number of times Gram had spoken Mama's name on one hand and still have a couple fingers left over. Like a child at bedtime, she grinned in anticipation of the rare morsel to come.

"Mowin' right back there in the tall weeds. She was eat up with welts." Gram laughed quietly to herself. "While I was in here tendin' to the stings, your grand-daddy took a can of gasoline and set half the lawn on fire tryin' to kill the nest. Nobody messed with his little girl, not even Mother Nature." Shaking her head, she whispered, "Lord, he did love that child somethin' fierce." Gradually, her smile fell, eyes glistening with tears that never quite spilled over. "Probably a blessin' that he went first. He wouldn'a survived losin' her."

Gram pulled a familiar, frayed hair ribbon from her pocket and rubbed it between her fingers. June knew it was Mama's. She'd watched Grammy stroke that green velvet a thousand times over the years, proof that she thought of Mama often, even if she didn't talk about her. Grammy gazed at the worn strip of fabric with so much grief and longing it broke June's heart.

"I miss her too." Every day.

Ever the stoic, Grammy made a noncommittal grunt and tucked the ribbon back into her pocket. She smoothed an imaginary stray hair back into her bun and changed the subject. "You hungry?"

"Not really." June pulled herself to a sitting position, dragging all the pillows and wraps along for the ride. "Listen, don't tell Luke about this, okay? He already thinks I'm snakebit." And maybe she was—misfortune seemed to follow her like a lemming.

Gram smiled once again, sending creases and deep folds in motion over the tops of her cheekbones. "You don't have your granddaddy's luck o' the Irish, that's for sure."

"Can I ask you something about Luke?" When Gram didn't object, June continued. "He said someone gave him a second chance. Was that you?"

"No, ma'am. He never needed one from me." Grammy nodded toward his room. "I shouldn't've thrown him outta the house like that, and I told him so in a letter a few days later. Told him to come back home anytime he pleased. I think it took a long time for him to forgive me, 'cause the first letter I got was invitin' me to his wedding."

June's lungs compressed like someone had dropped a sack of concrete on her chest. She'd received that same letter her freshman year in college, and she'd cried so hard she'd missed two days of class. Even now, all these years later, she couldn't deny the heavy ache that came with knowing Luke had loved some other woman enough to marry her.

June cleared her throat. "Did you go?"

"Yep. He didn't have anyone else. What could I do?"

Gram seemed to understand how June felt. She probably knew June had fantasized for years about marrying Luke and raising their children together on this farm. For Gram to attend his wedding to someone else seemed like an act of betrayal.

"But I didn't like her." Grammy leaned toward June and lowered her voice to a whisper. "I was glad they split up. She wasn't a nice girl like you."

June couldn't help but smile. "So who gave him a second chance?"

"That'd be Morris Howard." Gram pushed herself off the bed with a groan and massaged her lower back. "An old widower who used to court me."

"Grammy! You had a boyfriend?"

"He was a builder," Gram said, smiling and ignoring the question. "Took Lucas on as an apprentice—taught him everything—then left all his equipment and money to Lucas when he passed."

"And he used the money to start Helping Hands?"

Gram nodded and shuffled to the door. "I'm mighty proud of that boy, but there's still room for improvement. His mama didn't set much of an example, June." Gram paused in the doorway for a minute, hesitating to say more. Finally, she lowered her head just a fraction and gave June a solemn look. "He needs someone to teach him to love. Think on that." Then she left that bombshell suspended in midair and walked downstairs to make supper.

June stared into the empty hall. Teach him to love? Apparently, he had a firm grip on the concept—wasn't his ex-wife living proof? Luke knew how to love other women, just not her. And no matter how badly June wanted to, she couldn't teach him how to do that.

Chapter 7

LUKE WASN'T SURE HOW IT STARTED, BUT WHEN HE and June were kids, they used to hold their breath when they'd pass a graveyard. This didn't present much of a challenge while cruising by in Pru's old, brown station wagon, but bicycle rides—and especially walks—had stretched their lungs to the limit, and they'd always made it a contest to see who could reach the rusted, iron gates that bordered the cemetery without exhaling. Funny, he hadn't thought of that in years. But now, as he crossed the threshold into Sultry County Memorial Hospital, he held his breath once again. After all, there were dead people under his feet—several floors below, resting in the morgue.

Luke hated hospitals. In fact, until Trey's accident the other day, he'd managed to avoid setting foot in one for nearly a decade. When he'd broken his nose—once playing a friendly game of football with his squadron, and again during a not-so-friendly bar brawl with some drunken Bavarians—he'd insisted on receiving treatment in the doctor's office. Why would he want to expose himself to the diseases and plagues of a thousand people, all crammed into one foul-smelling building? Nothing good happened within these walls. Hell, at that very moment, a dozen people were probably dying all around him. Morbid? Maybe. But true, all the same.

As he approached the elevators, he slowed his pace,

allowing a group of visitors to file inside and head off to their destinations. He didn't want to share a ride, partly because those strangers were trailing germs from someone's bedside, and also because he'd just left the Jenkins house after eight hours of demolition work, and he smelled riper than a month-old carcass.

"Going up?" A teenage boy with blue hair and a pierced lip held the elevator door.

"Nah," Luke said with a wave. "I'll catch the next one."

Rolling his eyes, the kid let the doors slide shut, and Luke pulled off his baseball cap and used it to press the *up* button. Hundreds of people pushed that switch every hour, and he knew it was crawling with flu viruses, or worse. Normally he didn't fret about that stuff, but he couldn't afford to get sick—not now.

When Luke stepped onto the fourth floor, he immediately flinched back. The odor of bleach and vomit slammed his nostrils with the force of a freight train. "God damn," he whispered. Holding his breath again, and not out of respect for the dead this time, he rushed to Trey's room. After one quick knock that sounded more like a body slam, he tugged open the door and bolted inside.

"Hell, buddy," Trey said with one lifted brow and a sardonic grin, "come on in."

Luke immediately shut the door to block out the smell. Stepping forward, he collapsed into the chair farthest from Trey's bed, but he stiffened and grasped the armrests when a woman's form rose from her chair on the opposite side of the room.

He recognized the perfectly styled, silver hair that curled in a bob and rested atop the lady's rigid shoulders. She glanced down and picked a bit of lint off her designer blouse, then smoothed a set of nonexistent wrinkles from her tan slacks.

Luke stood from his seat. "Sorry, Mrs. Lewis. Didn't know you were here."

"Hello, Private Gallagher." Trey's mom tipped her head in a greeting, polite, but still colder than Hitler's grave. Her eyes, bright blue, just like Trey's, turned to slits, somehow managing to look down at him, despite the fact that he towered two feet over her. He'd only met her once before, after the discharge, and she didn't seem to like him any more now than she did back then.

"It's just Luke these days, ma'am." He wished he'd stopped at Pru's for a quick shower before coming here. Normally, Luke didn't give a damn what anyone thought, but this woman had a way of making him feel like trash, and he hated looking the part.

"Oh, yes. I'm well aware." Translation: *I know your name, asshole, but I love reminding you of the disgrace you and my son brought upon our family.* Her eyes raked over him, no doubt taking in the sweaty hair plastered to his face, his dirt-streaked T-shirt, faded, torn jeans, and steel-toed work boots. "Thank you for calling me after the accident."

"No problem. I knew you'd want to be here." He glanced around the room for Trey's old man. "Is, uh, Mr. Lewis…" Trailing off, he noticed his buddy's fist clench around a handful of white blankets.

"*Colonel* Lewis," she corrected smoothly, "is at home." She didn't offer further explanation.

"Oh." Seemed the old bastard still hadn't forgiven Trey for all the shit that went down in Heidelberg. For the love of God, it had been five years. How much longer was the sanctimonious fucker going to punish his only son? "How long are you in town?"

"My flight leaves first thing in the morning." She lifted her shiny black handbag from the bedside table and sashayed to the door, wrinkling her nose in disgust when she skirted around him. "I'll get something to eat from the cafeteria while you boys visit." And then she left without saying good-bye.

Trey exhaled, puffing out his cheeks. "That went better than I expected."

"Sorry, man. Why didn't you tell me she was here?" Had he known, he would've skipped this visit and driven straight to Pru's to fix June's clunker, then swung by the hardware store before it closed.

"She didn't call—just showed up a few hours ago."

With a groan, Luke lowered into his chair. "I hate this place, you know that?"

"Cry me a river, you douche." Trey used both hands to fire "pistols" at his leg, trapped from hip-to-toe in thick plaster and hanging from a line in the ceiling. Though his left eye was barely visible beneath its swollen lid, the expression behind it seemed clearer than yesterday. Alert and teasing, just like the old Trey. "I'm feeling better, thanks for askin'."

Scooting his chair closer to the air conditioner, Luke let the frigid breeze stir the damp hair at the back of his neck. He nodded at the traction line keeping his buddy's lower half immobile. "How do you go to the bathroom in that thing?"

"Trust me," Trey's mouth drooped into a frown, tugging one dimple to the surface of his cheek, "you don't wanna know."

"Forget I asked." Poor bugger. Broken bones were painful, but nothing made a man feel lower than losing the ability to take care of his own personal needs. "But at least you're getting sponge baths, right? Bet your nurse loves to get you *reeeal* clean." That's how it had worked in a *Naughty Nightshift Nurse* movie he'd watched once or twice…or a dozen times…as a teenager.

"Yeah," Trey mumbled, glancing away. "He's very thorough."

"*He?*"

"You heard me."

Luke didn't want to laugh—really, he didn't—but the mental image of his buddy gritting his teeth, clenching his eyes, and suffering through a dude-on-dude sponge bath was just too much. "Jesus, man," he chortled, "and I thought I had it bad."

"Shut up. It's not funny." But Trey joined in the laughter before sucking in a sharp breath and bringing one hand against his ribs. "Stop," he urged, trying to suppress a snicker. "It hurts."

"Okay, okay." Luke turned the subject away from awkward bathing situations. "I checked your mail before I came. Nothing but junk."

"You water the fern?"

"You mean that brown, crunchy thing by the TV? Yeah." Hooking one thumb toward the leafy, green potted plants and assorted flowers on the window ledge, he added, "But I think these will complement your classy *dé-coor* a little better."

"Totally. Those carnations over there match the wine stains on my sofa."

"Need anything?"

"Yeah," Trey nodded emphatically. "To get the hell outta here."

"Right, but anything I can do?"

Trey considered a moment, sliding his gaze toward the empty space by the bathroom door. "I can think of one thing."

"What? It better not involve bedpans." Their friendship wasn't *that* strong.

"Take it easy on *Joooonbug*. You practically tore her a new one the other day. This wasn't her fault."

Luke's spine stiffened against the back of his chair. The last thing he wanted to remember was the way he'd lit into June or how she'd struggled to hold back from crying before driving away. "Don't worry about June. I already made things right—it's done."

"No shit?"

"In fact, I'm heading over there in a few minutes. Had to pick up some parts to repair that heap she's driving."

"Mmm-hmm." A sly, crooked grin curved his friend's lips. "You know, she wanted to take me up on my offer. Said she'd mix up a few drinks at my place, if I provided the booze."

Luke's gut clenched like he'd just taken a sucker punch to the crotch. "What?"

"Yep." Trey nodded and beamed. He was enjoying this, the deep-dimpled son of a bitch. "But I shot her down. She might want to ply some guy with liquor and have her way with him, but I can tell it's not me. I don't wanna be her second choice, even if she does have the sweetest backside I've ever seen." Then he made a wide circle with his palms to mimic June's ass, causing Luke's face to blaze.

"That's enough." Luke leaned forward, pointing an index finger at Trey. "Don't talk about her like that."

"What's the matter, buddy? Did I strike a nerve?"

"I'll strike *your* nerve if you don't cut that shit out." Best friend or not, Trey was wandering into dangerous territory, now pretending to smack June's imaginary bottom. Luke wouldn't hurt a cripple, but he could sure as hell wait until Trey was strong again to knock some respect into that blond head.

"Quit stonewalling and tell me what's up between you two. I can tell something happened."

"Don't you have enough to worry about without digging into my private life?"

"No." Sweeping a hand to indicate his battered body, he said, "I'm bored as hell, and I'm stuck here at least another week, or however long it takes these sadists to make sure my effing, swollen spleen doesn't explode. Come on. You never tell me anything."

"I never tell you anything? Jesus, you sound like my nagging ex-wife." Luke stood and tugged at the stiff, white comforter draped over Trey's good leg. "You sure the doctors didn't put a few girly parts in there when you weren't looking? I think you grew a vadge, my friend."

"Yeah? Then eat me."

"Should I pick up a box of Midol the next time I visit? Tampax? Or you want some of that shit with wings?"

"Ha-ha-ha. Very funny. Why can't you just answer the question?"

Three quick knocks sounded from the door, saving Luke from a topic he didn't want to examine. A pretty, young redhead balanced a plastic tray in one hand, gripped a cup of juice in the other, and pushed the door aside with her hip. Luke scrambled to help her, taking the frosty cup and clearing assorted paperwork and crossword puzzles from Trey's bedside table.

"Thanks, hon," she said with an inviting smile. Too bad this wasn't the woman giving Trey his sponge baths. She lifted the domed lid from Trey's dinner plate, filling the air with the mouthwatering scents of marinara sauce, spaghetti, and garlic bread. Waving a quick good-bye, the redhead left and pulled the door shut behind her.

Luke's stomach rumbled loudly, reminding him he hadn't eaten since breakfast. "That doesn't look half bad."

"This right here," Trey said, pointing a fork at the parmesan cheese sprinkled generously on his pasta, "is the only thing that keeps me from hanging myself on the traction line. So back off, man. I'm not sharing."

"That's okay." Luke checked the clock above the television, figuring it was about time to go. "I'll have a chicken leg in my mouth in twenty minutes. Pru's famous biscuits too. Maybe even a slice of pecan pie."

"Hey," Trey said with his mouth crammed full, "why don't you stay the night at Miss Pru's? Take a rest. You look like shit, no offense."

"None taken." Luke knew he'd pushed his body nearly to the limit these past couple days, living on four hours of sleep and chugging enough coffee to power a small town. But it was only temporary, and besides, if he'd survived basic training, then he could manage a couple weeks busting his ass until Trey was back on the job. "There'll be plenty of time to rest when I'm dead."

"Keep it up and you will be." Trey pulled a napkin across his saucy mouth, then held it in the air. "What's one night? Get some sleep."

Pushing up from his chair, Luke leaned in and grabbed the edge of Trey's blanket. Lifting it to peek underneath, he said, "Yep, just as I thought. You've grown lady bits."

A chunk of garlic bread pelted Luke's ear, and he dodged just in time to avoid a salt packet.

With a chuckle, he made his exit, leaving a smile on his buddy's face. Mrs. Lewis would surely erase it when she returned from the cafeteria, but she'd be gone the next day, and then Trey's family-away-from-home—the people of Sultry Springs who'd made this Yankee one of their own—would be here to lift his spirits again.

"Oh, praise be!" Pru jumped back and hit the refrigerator, knocking all June's old cross-county ribbons askew. "Get a shower, Lucas!"

Luke snatched a bite of salty ham from the pot of green beans simmering on the stove, then tossed it into his mouth and sucked in a few breaths to cool his scorched tongue. "I'll just get dirty again when I go outside to fix June's car after supper." When he tried sneaking a biscuit from the counter, Pru advanced and smacked his hand—hard.

"Ouch!" Sometimes he forgot how strong she was. "Aw, come on, Pru. I'll make a plate and eat on the porch."

"You'll do no such thing." Moving to stand between him and the stove, Pru extended one long, bony finger and poked his chest. "What's the rule in this house, Lucas Gallagher?"

With sagging shoulders, he sighed and droned the words, feeling twelve years old again. "A clean mouth in want of bread, with a prayer shall be fed."

"That's right. Cleanliness is nexta godliness. You get a shower, and we'll eat at the table together, the way it oughta be."

"Yes, ma'am."

He trudged upstairs to the hall bathroom and noticed June's bedroom door open. With one hand on the door-jamb, he leaned his head and shoulders inside and found her resting in bed, reading a *Better Homes and Gardens* magazine. She'd propped herself up with pillows and stretched out, and she wore a long, black sundress that covered everything but the tips of her pretty little toes. The outfit seemed out of character for her, considering the casual shorts and skimpy tank tops she'd worn since returning to town.

"Feeling Amish today, Sister Augustine?"

She flinched and brought a hand to her heart, dropping the magazine to the floor.

"Nice dress." He stepped inside, grabbed her magazine, and tossed it onto the bed without getting too close. Judging by Pru's reaction downstairs, he really needed that shower. "Only two days with the Baptists and you're already going modest on me?"

"You look filthy," she said, changing the subject. "And tired."

"Yeah, yeah. I've already heard it from your grandma. She won't feed me till I get cleaned up, so I'm gonna hop in the shower." He started to turn away, but she held her palm forward to halt him.

"Wait." She went silent a minute, and then those brown eyes swept his body from head to toe with such intensity he almost felt her warm, gentle touch all over. He recognized that glazed look. He'd seen it before, her first day—hell, her only day—working at the Jenkins place. He had a pretty good feeling she wasn't criticizing the mud on his jeans when her eyes fell there, and when her tongue darted out to wet her lips, he had to grasp the doorway to keep from closing the distance between them and finishing what they'd started the other morning. He scraped together enough willpower to tease, "Like what you see, Junebug? I can take a picture—make one of those wall calendars for you, even tape it to the ceiling above your bed."

She wrinkled her ivory forehead and pushed up straighter. "I *was* going to offer to wash your clothes while you're in the shower, but since you're being such an—"

"I accept. Thanks." When she started to object, he cut her off. "Especially since I'm here to fix your car. For free."

"Fine. Leave them in a pile outside the bathroom."

"That means I'll be naked when I open the door. You gonna try to sneak a look?"

"You wish."

With a smirk, he left her to grab some clean clothes from his room and then get washed for supper.

While in the shower, his mind conjured naughty images of June. Cranking up the cold water didn't help, and neither did shampooing his hair extra rough, scrubbing with his fingernails hard enough to make his scalp burn. He couldn't stop picturing himself hooking one finger beneath the hem of that long, black dress and sliding it up the length of her smooth legs, then slipping her panties down, down, all the way down past her ankles… Damn it. If he didn't quit this madness right now, his soldier would come to attention, and he couldn't very well relieve it of duty knowing he'd have to hold Pru's hand for grace in ten minutes. Turning off the hot water completely, Luke doused himself in the icy spray, closed his eyes, and recited the Texas Rangers' starting lineup.

———

"What's this thing?" Wedging herself between Luke and the car, June braced on her elbows and bent over the hood, poking at engine parts and bringing her firm, round behind to the front of his hips, where it brushed his fly. Sweet Jesus. He needed to finish this repair and get the hell out of here before he died of chronic blue balls.

"Hmm?" she pressed.

"That's where your windshield wiper fluid goes, Junebug. You couldn't figure that one out yourself?"

The cool evening breeze picked up, swirling June's chestnut curls around the back of her neck, while the setting sun cast pinks and reds over her skin. "Well, what do I know about cars?"

"At the very least, you need to know how to check your oil, especially when you drive something this old." Girls. How did they manage to survive? "Come out of there. I'm gonna teach you real quick."

She stood and turned to face him. "What does age have to do with it?"

"The older a car gets, the more oil it loses. Nobody ever told you this?"

"No." When she shook her head and stirred those curls, he inhaled the familiar, spicy-sweet scent of her orange shampoo. Did other women smell this good? Had he simply failed to notice all these years?

"Okay." Focusing on the task at hand, Luke pulled

a clean rag from his back pocket. "The first thing you gotta do is clean your dipstick."

"Oh, is that what you're calling it now?" she said with a giggle. "I bet you're an expert at that."

"Concentrate, Junebug. This could save your engine." Actually, he'd be surprised if the thing made it another thousand miles. "See this loop?" He slipped one finger into the dipstick pull. "You take it out, like this…" When he turned to make sure June was paying attention—which she wasn't—the wind kicked up again and swirled her black dress up around her calves, drawing his attention to patches of raised welts on her skin. He shoved the dipstick back into place and wiped his greasy fingers on the rag.

"What happened to your legs?" he asked, kneeling at her feet.

"Nothing!" She scurried backward, right over an empty drip pan, and her arms flailed wildly in the air for a few seconds as she tried to right herself. Luke launched forward to steady her, but he wasn't quick enough, and she went down hard on her backside onto the lawn.

He crawled forward with a grin tugging his lips. "You okay?"

Rolling to the side, June rubbed her palm against her fleshy bottom, while her lips formed the word *Ouch*. "Yeah."

"Good thing you had—" Luke bit short his reply. Probably not a good idea to say *plenty of cushion on that big, gorgeous ass*. Instead, he finished, "the thick grass to break your fall."

He rested on one elbow and used his opposite thumb to pull June's dress to her knees. Scenes from the shower flashed in his mind, tying his stomach in knots, but those sexy mental pictures died awfully quick as her imaginary, silken skin was replaced by oozing, scarlet blotches. Bee stings, by the look of them—he'd had enough experience to know. "What on earth did you get into, Junebug?"

She brought her knees to her chest and heaved a sigh, pulling the dress back into place. "It's not a big deal. Happens to people all the time."

"Then stop acting like it's a big deal and spill it." He remembered how Trey had tried to pry information earlier, and he laughed to himself, resolving not to push too hard and lose his man card.

"I ran over a bees' nest mowing the church lawn the other day."

Luke sucked a sharp, sympathetic breath through his teeth. He'd accidentally stumbled over a nest of hornets as a kid and unleashed such a fury he'd had to leap into the pond to escape them. A few of the spiteful little bastards had hung around for half an hour to zap him when he'd waded out of the water. Of course, he'd expect something like that to happen at a wooded pond. Only June could find trouble in a churchyard.

"Who else but you would raise hell in God's house?" he asked.

She snatched a fallen pecan from the ground and hurtled it at his boot. "I knew you'd give me a hard time."

"Ah. This explains the Amish dress." He flipped it to her knees again, scanning her marred flesh. "Trying to conceal the evidence, huh?" Her lack of response said it all. Gently gripping June's ankle, he stretched her left leg to rest on the grass so he could investigate the damage. "You need some Benadryl."

"It's on the list. Grammy's going to the grocery tomorrow." June lay back, resting on her elbows in the tall grass.

"Have her pick up some antihistamine cream too." Using his index finger, he trailed it gently from one sting to the next, like playing connect the dots. "These welts will go down a lot faster that way." Those damn bees hadn't messed around. He followed their stinging pattern, smoothing his palm higher along June's calf, up past her kneecap, and beneath the cotton fabric of her dress to her thigh, where he felt a couple scattered lumps on the surface of her skin. He halted his hand. "Did they go any higher?" he asked softly, half hoping she'd say yes.

June's eyelids fluttered shut, and she swallowed hard. After a while, she said, "No. I ran inside before they—"

"Luke!" When Pru's voice echoed from the porch, he snatched his hand away like a kid caught stealing from the cookie jar. But he wasn't after June's cookies this time. Not really.

"Ma'am?" He rose to his knees and tried to appear innocent, like he hadn't just had his hand under June's dress.

"You stayin' tonight? I stripped your bed, but I'll make it again for ya."

"No. I'm gonna wrap up here and head over to the house. Gotta finish tearing out the old cabinets before they deliver the new ones." Remembering all the work hanging over his head pushed away thoughts of June's thighs. His shoulders tensed, and a heavy weight settled around his ribs. The new doors would arrive soon, right along with the cabinets, which meant pulling off the old doors, unscrewing all the hinges, filling the holes, and prepping them for new hardware.

"You sure?" Pru asked, gripping her hips and probably gearing up for a lecture.

"One hundred percent." Before she had a chance to object, he stood and began clearing his tools from the lawn. "I'm on my way in a minute."

With a loud grunt of disapproval, she said, "Suit yourself," and returned inside.

June helped him clean up, tossing a screwdriver into his toolbox. "Hey." She curled her fingers around his wrist, forcing him to slow down. "Thanks. I'm broke right now, but I'll find a way to pay you back for these parts. And your time."

"Don't worry about it, Junebug. That's what friends are for, right?" He didn't mention that worrying about her car breaking down, stranding her helplessly in the middle of nowhere, had kept him awake a few nights. Replacing the fan and all those belts had lifted an invisible burden from his back.

"Hey, why don't you stay tonight? Come lie down. I can tell you're beat."

"No can do."

"Just a quick nap? I promise I'll wake you in an hour." Her eyes darted to the pecan tree, and she chewed the inside of her cheek. June was a terrible liar. She'd wake him after he'd wasted twelve hours sleeping.

"You're trying awfully hard to get me into bed, hon." He added a wink. "As much as I appreciate the effort, I really have to go. And quit fretting. I'm fine."

He left her with a quick pat on the head before climbing into his truck. When a yawn threatened to stretch his lungs, he stifled it, knowing June was still watching him.

Pulling out onto the main road, he switched on the radio, smiling when the perfect song filled the cab. He sang along with Cage the Elephant, feeling the lyrics deep in his soul—there really was no rest for the wicked.

Chapter 8

"How was your first week?" Judge Bea leaned back in his oversized leather chair and slurped coffee from a Styrofoam cup. The early morning light streamed in from the side office window and lit up what remained of his bushy, mad scientist hair.

"Fine. Well, the first couple days were a little rough, but I'm doing better now." Which was true. June had started to appreciate little things she'd taken for granted before. Like waking up to a soft, lazy whip-poor-will's song accompanied by pattering squirrel paws on the roof, instead of to a shrieking car alarm or a barking dog. And the feel of the cool, dewy grass beneath her bare feet first thing in the morning when she gathered fresh tomatoes.

The judge leaned over his desk and glanced at her time sheet. "Been workin' at church? Didn't expect that."

"It's not so bad. I've been cleaning, mostly, and helping Gram with the newsletter."

"Mmm-hmm." Reclining, Bea kicked up his boot heels and rested them on the corner of his desk. He gave a slow, cautious nod. "How're things 'tween you and your grandma?"

June folded her arms and summoned her best poker face. Things with Grammy were better than they'd been in years. They spent their evenings rocking on the front porch, sometimes shelling beans or pecans, and sometimes just eating melon and listening to the wind chimes.

Grammy had seen June play an electronic, handheld Sudoku game one afternoon, and she'd asked to learn. Since then, they'd worked the puzzles together at the kitchen table each morning while drinking their coffee. Even Lucky had warmed up to Gram. He'd started sneaking into her room at night to sleep curled in the bend of her knees. But Judge Bea didn't need to know that. June didn't want to reward him for forcing her into this situation.

"Fine," she said. When he raised his eyebrows and waited for her to elaborate, she didn't.

"Hmm." Bea tilted his head and narrowed one eye like he was trying to see through her, but she gave nothing away.

"Judge," she said, changing the subject, "I need permission to leave the county." He held up a palm and shook his head, but she cut him off before he could get a word out. "Just listen before you say no. It's not Austin."

"Where, then?"

"Two places. First, I hear there's a little bar right outside county lines. I'm broke, and I need a job. You mind if I apply?"

"That'd be Shooters. Burl Bisbee's hole in the wall." Bea pursed his lips and considered her request. "I'll give you one night a week. That oughta bring enough tips to tide you over."

"Thanks. And then there's Luke's place. He's working on a house a couple counties over, and he needs my help." He just didn't know it yet. But June had a plan. She'd started thinking like a businesswoman instead of a lovesick teenager and put together a proposal much like the one she'd pitched to Esteban the year before.

Sample paint chips, landscape design, staging details, current market trends—everything she had to offer was bound in a clear plastic sleeve. She intended to storm the Jenkins place, deliver her presentation, and if necessary, refuse to leave until Luke agreed.

She wasn't above showing a little cleavage, either. Not exactly professional, but she didn't care. When Luke had returned to fix her car, he'd looked like hell. The dark circles and bags under his lifeless, green eyes had told her what she'd already suspected: he'd been choosing work over sleep. You couldn't get blood from a turnip, just like you couldn't work two full-time jobs and stay healthy. June knew she could lighten the load on his shoulders. She just needed to make the stubborn fool see it.

"Mae-June and Lucas together again," the judge said with laughter in his voice. "I dunno if Sultry Springs is ready for that." He shook his head and heaved a sigh. "I never could get that smell outta my barn after you two—"

"Sorry," June said, wincing at the memory. "You *do* know that fire was an accident, right?" Who knew three gallons of pig lard could be so flammable?

"Yep. Unlike the time y'all killed every trout in my pond."

"Oh, god. I forgot about that." June hung her head and tried not to giggle. The judge had built an Olympic-sized swimming pool in his backyard, but she and Luke had preferred his pond, so they'd decided to do Bea a "favor" and chlorinate it with the chemicals in his shed. "All those poor fish."

"Mother of pearl," the judge murmured. "It's a wonder either of you survived to adulthood." He shook his

head again, probably remembering another June-n-Luke
calamity, and then said, "Okay. You can help him. Y'all
just stay away from my place, y'hear?"

———◦◦◦———

Luke tipped back another Mountain Dew and prayed
the caffeine would last until lunchtime. Maybe then he
could catch a few winks in the shade when his crew left
for the local diner. He tossed the empty soda can into the
recycling bin and winced in pain. Damn it, his shoulder
hurt like the devil. He'd strained it last night lifting a
door off its hinges, and no amount of aspirin helped.

He wedged a crowbar between two wood planks and
levered it back with a grunt, which sent invisible flames
lapping at his muscles. "Sonofabitch!" Grasping his
shoulder, he tossed the crowbar aside and hollered at
Pauly. "Bring two guys and finish up here."

Pauly nodded and got right on it. The crew seemed
to sense Luke's foul mood, and they worked twice as
hard because of it. Even that jackass Karl stayed on task
and kept his head down. Maybe he should hurt himself
more often.

Luke used his good arm to lift his shirt and wipe the
sweat from his eyes. The sun beat down like a sledge-
hammer against the back of his neck, and he wondered
when this damn heat would let up. Then all of a sudden
the crack and creak of boards being pried off the deck
was replaced by cat calls and wolf whistles.

From somewhere to Luke's right, Karl yelled,
"*Mamacita!*"

"Stop screwing around and get back to—" Whoa.
When Luke turned, he saw what had brought his workers

to a dead halt. It was June, and she looked better than a chocolate ice cream cone in hell. A double scoop.

She wore a long, flowing tan skirt with some flowers or paisleys or whatever all over it—he couldn't tell because he was too focused on the ivory swell of breasts heaving out of the top of her low-cut, sleeveless shirt. Her curly hair blew softly behind her shoulders as she drifted forward, just like an actress in some slow-motion television commercial.

"Hey, Luke," she drawled, bending down to adjust the strap on her high-heeled sandal. If she leaned just a little further, those gorgeous breasts would fall right out, and by the look of his slack-jawed crew, every one of those bastards was wishing for it to happen. "Can we talk?"

"Um, yeah." But not around all these salivating jackals. He told the men to get back to work and led June through the side door into the house. "There're a few chairs in the kitchen."

Luke watched her sway those voluptuous hips across the room to a wooden chair, which she dragged over next to his. Then she sank extra slow into the seat and gave him a look that oozed sex. She was up to something.

"Out with it, Junebug." He rotated his stiff, aching shoulder. "What do you want?"

She reached into her purse and pulled out one of those plastic book report covers, the kind he only used for really important assignments back in school, then handed it to him. It was full of paint colors, pictures of model homes and flower beds, and information on girly stuff like furniture and interior design.

"What's this?"

"It's everything I can offer, if you let me help. Despite what you might think, I'm not a dolt. I know a lot about the real estate market from selling my condo and buying Luqu—"

"Stop right there." Luke held out a hand, the wrong one, and sucked in a sharp breath. "I told you—"

"I can't do heavy things, but what about cleaning and painting? And lawn care and landscaping? All that takes time, which you don't have."

He couldn't deny she had a point. She must've taken his silence as encouragement because she smiled and kept talking.

"And I can help you with staging."

"Staging?" Luke leaned forward and rolled his head to the side. Now his neck was feeling stiff.

"Yeah, using the right paint, furniture, and accessories to get the most money out of…" She paused and wrinkled her forehead. "What's wrong with your shoulder?"

"Nothing. Just pulled it last night."

"Take off your shirt." She slipped off her sandals and stood up.

Luke laughed dryly and gave her a teasing grin before she disappeared behind him. "So you can violate me with your eyes again?"

"Look who's talking." June reached down and grabbed the bottom of his shirt and peeled it gently over his head. She moved a little too slowly, sweeping her fingertips over his ribs, and his pulse quickened a beat or two. Or fifty.

Her palm skimmed lightly across the skin on his shoulder. "Doesn't feel swollen," she mumbled to herself. "I think this'll help." And she began kneading his stiff muscles like a pro.

"Oh, god," Luke groaned, closing his eyes and tipping his head back to rest against her belly. He couldn't remember the last time something felt so good. Actually, he could. When he'd held her soft little body in Pru's garden. But this was a close second. Though still tender, the pain in his shoulder nearly evaporated.

"One of my exes was a massage therapist. First guy I ever lived with. He taught me all his tricks."

"My little Junebug shacking up? Tsk, tsk." He tried not to think about another man's hands sliding all over her body. Or warming her bed at night. It was none of his business, and he shouldn't care anyway.

She laughed and leaned down to use her elbow for more pressure. "I'd rather live in sin with a dozen men than suffer through one divor—" Then she froze for a moment.

"Say it. Divorce. You won't hurt my delicate sensibilities. You're right. Nothing's worse than being stuck in a bad marriage."

June straightened again and guided his head back to rest on her stomach. Then she used her thumbs on his neck and Luke thought he'd melt with pleasure. "Was it *really* bad?" Her voice was thick with pity, which would've pissed him off, if he hadn't been so relaxed.

Yes, it was really bad. He'd met Ada when he was barely nineteen, lonely, and stupid—a dangerous trifecta. She'd picked him up in a bar outside Dusseldorf and taken him into the parking lot to have drunken sex in the backseat of her Volkswagen. It was the first and last time he'd ever neglected to wrap his johnson. Big mistake.

Two months later, she'd tracked him down and announced she was pregnant. He did the right thing, of course, but a month after the honeymoon he'd noticed a package of tampons in the cabinet beneath the bathroom sink. That's when she'd confessed there was no baby. There never had been. Like an idiot, he'd let himself get wrangled into a green card wedding. He'd considered getting an annulment, but in the end, shame and embarrassment had won over. How would Pru have reacted to learn his marriage was over in four weeks? So he'd stayed and tried to make it work. Bigger mistake.

Almost overnight, Ada had changed. She'd awoken each morning with poison in her gaze. When he'd asked what her problem was, she'd screamed, "I know about June, your whore!" Apparently, he'd been calling June's name in his sleep, and Ada had assumed he'd cheated. Highly ironic, since she'd *already* been sleeping with an officer on post. And not just any officer—Luke's boss.

"Sorry. It's none of my business," June said softly. Those magical fingers curled over his shoulders to massage the top of his chest in small circles. He wanted her to keep going lower, to feel her firm touch all over. And when she did go lower, ghosting her palms over his nipples, he sucked in a sharp breath.

"Don't be sorry. It's over, and I'm glad." He inhaled deeply and leaned back harder against her belly. "If you're trying to butter me up, it's working."

"Oh, I don't need to." June ran her fingernails from his neck up through his hair, and chills danced across his whole body. Then she leaned down until he felt the soft cushion of her breasts against his shoulders, and she pressed her lips to his ear. His blood turned hot and rushed right between his legs. "I'm coming out there," she whispered, "whether you like it or not."

Luke forced his eyes shut and tried to will away his

erection, but it throbbed in time with his quickened pulse. "God damn, Junebug," he hissed.

As she stepped slowly around to face him, she let her fingernails trail along the side of his neck and down the front of his chest. When Luke opened his eyes, she was bent over, gazing right into his face. He glanced down at her soft, red mouth as she added, "If you want to get rid of me, you'll have to call the sheriff to take me away." She licked her lips and came closer, like she might kiss him, and he gripped his thighs to stop from reaching out and pulling her into his lap. Would the guys outside see if he laid her on the table and pushed up her skirt? Would she let him? "You don't want to see me in handcuffs, do you?"

The mental image made him twitch. "I'll pick you up tonight at Pru's."

"Excellent," she chirped, all traces of seduction gone. June sprang away and grabbed her sandals and handbag, calling over her shoulder, "You won't regret this." Then she practically skipped out of the kitchen.

Damn, that just wasn't right.

Chapter 9

JUNE NEVER UNDERSTOOD WHY SO MANY PEOPLE HATED hospitals. She adored the gleaming black and white floor tiles that squeaked beneath her sneakers. And the biting, yet oddly pleasant scent of lemon ammonia and disinfectant. She pulled in a long breath through her nose and savored it. Once in a while, a woman's soft voice would punctuate the silence to page Dr. Benton. The distant voice was strangely comforting, and June caught herself imagining the details of that woman's life while she navigated the maze of hallways to Trey's room.

More than anything, though, June equated hospitals with tender, loving care. Someplace you could arrive broken and return home whole. Of course, she knew that wasn't always the case, but in her limited experience, this wasn't a place to fear. When June was nine and Luke had accidentally knocked her out of the tall pecan tree, Grammy had rushed her to this very emergency room. Though June's memory was spotty, she recalled gentle touches, heated blankets, and a bitter tasting liquid that made her feel all warm and floaty inside. When the nurse had announced June's wrist wasn't broken, she'd wrapped it in a stretchy tan bandage and given her a bubblegum-flavored lollipop and two Care Bear stickers. What's not to love about that?

When she reached Trey's new room on the fourth floor, she rapped her knuckles firmly against the door and waited before peeking inside. "You decent?" she asked, not wanting to barge in mid-sponge bath or toilet break.

"Only on Sundays, but come on in." He clicked off the television and used the control panel beside his bed to rise into a semi-sitting position. They must've served lunch right before she arrived, because the smoky scent of hamburger still hung in the air.

June returned Trey's infectious smile and noted how much he'd changed since her last visit several days earlier. A sturdy white brace had replaced all the bandages that bound his chest, and the swelling above his left eye had smoothed out and turned the color of a ripe eggplant. Trey's blue eyes were bright and clear again, smiling right along with his dimpled cheeks.

"Going crazy yet?" she asked, placing a foil-wrapped paper plate on his bedside table. Guys like Trey and Luke couldn't stand sitting still too long. "Gram sent snickerdoodles. She said they're your favorite."

"Oh, snap." He tore off the foil and dug right in, littering his starched, white linen sheet with cinnamon and sugar crumbs. "I'm bored outta my mind," he muttered with a mouth full of cookie. "You have any idea how bad daytime TV is?"

June giggled and moved around the room to admire the scattering of potted plants and flowers on the ledge below a thick, beveled window. "Oh, Gerbera daisies!" She lifted one day-glow pink flower to her face, but it didn't smell very good, and she wrinkled her nose. Still, the bright pinks, yellows, and oranges brightened Trey's room and brought a grin to her lips. "Who sent these?"

"My family."

"In Chicago?"

"Mmm-hmm." It sounded like he'd stuffed another cookie in his mouth.

"How'd you wind up here, in Sultry Springs?" June pulled a chair beside Trey's bed and sat down. "You're a long way from home."

"Luke offered me a job." He set the empty paper plate on the table, then balled up the foil and tossed it across the room, where it plunked right into the trash can. "I had a hard time finding work after we got—" Trey paused and wiped the back of his hand against his mouth. "Did Luke tell you what happened?"

June bit her bottom lip. She'd never felt so tempted to lie. If she said yes, Trey might let enough information slip to help her piece together the puzzle of why Luke came home five years ago to "get back on his feet," as Gram had said.

"No," she finally admitted. "But sometimes at supper—especially when he's really tired—he gets this look. Kind of defeated, I don't know. I used to think he missed his ex-wife—"

Trey snorted a dry laugh. "Trust me, he doesn't. She was a total psycho."

"Then why?"

"It's my fault. Partly, anyway." All traces of good humor faded from Trey's eyes. He glared at his lap and brushed cookie crumbs onto the floor. "Because of me, he can't ever enlist again."

"Why would he want to?" Luke had said he hated taking orders, which made perfect sense, considering what a control freak he'd always been as a kid.

"He loved it. I swear to God, June, being a soldier was like a calling to him or something."

"What happened?"

Trey's glance flicked up and then back down just as quickly. He shook his head. "He doesn't like people knowing, and I don't blame him. Hey, don't tell him I said he can't reenlist. I shouldn't have told you that."

June nodded, more confused than ever. She didn't know much about the military, but it must've taken a pretty serious offense to bar Luke from ever serving again. And how was Trey involved? Only one thing made sense: June now understood the occasional hardness in Luke's eyes, as if his old, mischievous spark had been snuffed out. That look made June's stomach sink, like she'd swallowed a pound of lead. June was more determined than ever to help Luke finish his investment property. For whatever reason, he'd already lost his dream career. She wouldn't let him lose the Gallagher land too.

"Oh, Luke. It's beautiful." June gazed up at the charming, two-story Tudor home set against a backdrop of ancient oaks and maples. Vacant window boxes contrasted against the clean, white stucco and begged to be filled with colorful pansies. The exposed dark wood beams gave the structure an historic European feel. Gently rolling green hills filled the landscape as far as she could see. Surely, it would be developed someday, but in the meantime, it made Luke's house seem more like a sprawling estate than a typical suburban plot. She thought she heard the babble of a creek nearby. No wonder he already had several families interested. "I wasn't expecting anything like this."

"Don't get too excited. You haven't seen the inside yet. The last owner had five dogs, seven cats, and somehow, a rodent problem. Damn cats must've been lazier than Karl."

"*Had* a rodent problem? Like, past tense?"

"Why?" Luke wriggled his fingers up the back of her leg, making her squeal.

"Very funny. Seriously?"

"I sleep here, Junebug. Of course I got rid of the vermin." He tipped back his ball cap and smiled down at her—a real, no-holds-barred Luke smile that knocked the breath from her lungs. "Come on. I'll give you the tour."

The interior still needed work, but most of it seemed cosmetic. Instead of wayward animals, the home smelled like fresh pine dust and plaster. Luke had removed a few walls to open the floor plan, and he was halfway through renovating the kitchen. In the upcoming weeks, they would need to refinish the wood floors, lay new carpet, paint the bedrooms, tile the bathrooms, and landscape the yard. A tall order, but doable, if they worked hard.

Finally, they stopped in the master bedroom, the cleanest space in the house. A king-sized air mattress covered in rumpled, blue cotton sheets lay against the back wall. June pictured Luke snoring there, sleeping on his stomach with his mouth partly open and one arm reaching out to the side like the bronze man atop the Heisman trophy. He'd always slept that way, but in his smaller bed at Grammy's, his arm had flopped over the edge of the mattress.

"So, what's the plan?" she asked, pulling her hair into a sloppy ponytail.

"You take the upstairs bedrooms, and I'll be in the

kitchen if you need me." Luke reached out and cupped her cheek, then bent down to give her a pointed look. "And be careful."

For the next two hours, June pulled up the ugliest, Pepto-Bismol-pink shag carpeting she'd ever seen. Then she rolled it up, dragged it down the stairs, and heaved it halfway into the Dumpster, before tackling the mint-julep-green carpet in the next bedroom. Afterward, she vacuumed and mopped the wood floors underneath, and wiped down the walls to prep them for painting.

When she met Luke in the kitchen, her face felt flushed and swollen, and a plump bead of sweat tickled its way down her back. She wiped her face against the shoulder of her T-shirt and opened the refrigerator to linger in the frosty air awhile. The abrupt chill swept the sides of her neck and gave her goose bumps.

Luke's firm body pressed into her from behind, and he reached beyond her to grab a cold Mountain Dew. His other hand lingered at her waist a moment while he en-joyed the cool air, and June wondered what he would do if she leaned her head back against his chest. Just as she began to cover his hand with her own, he moved away.

"Grab that bag on the counter," Luke said, unfolding a tattered patchwork quilt and spreading it on the dining room floor. "Pru packed dessert."

He returned to the kitchen and turned on the sink. Then, tugging off his cap, he dipped his head under the faucet and sighed loudly, using one hand to splash water onto the back of his neck. When he finished, Luke shook his head like a wet dog and rejoined her.

June set out paper plates and handed the bag to Luke, and they both sat cross-legged on the blanket. Tendrils of red-brown hair dripped down the sides of his throat and soaked the collar of his thin, white T-shirt, and she half wished he'd take it off. No, strike that. It was a whole wish, not half. His shoulder didn't seem to bother him anymore, not that she'd mind massaging those strong muscles again. The way he'd rested his head on her stomach had felt so intimate, and God help her when he'd used that low gritty voice to call her name—

"Mmm," he said, slipping two fingers into his mouth and sucking them off with a smack. "That's so good."

Heat rushed into June's face, and she used an extra paper plate to fan herself. The last time she'd seen Luke do that, he'd just dipped those same fingers inside her—

"Pie?" he offered. "It's peach." He used a plastic fork to push one slice onto her paper plate.

Sweet mercy, she needed to get her mind out of the gutter. June glanced down at her plate and something caught her eye. The quilt. It looked familiar, mismatched swatches of multi-colored fabric connected in uneven hand-stitching. After a few minutes, it finally sank in. This was *the* quilt—the one she'd spread in the cool, shaded grass at Gallagher pond nearly a decade earlier. The same quilt where Luke had laid her down and made love to her so sweetly, right before he'd crushed her heart in his fist, the way a cruel child crushed insects between his fingers.

But after all these years, she couldn't be angry with him for his reaction that day. Luke hadn't swindled her out of her virginity. He hadn't made any false promises or seduced her—quite the opposite. He still didn't know it, but she'd planned everything that day, from making sure Gram was occupied all afternoon to tucking a condom inside the quilt just in case Luke hadn't had one in his wallet, which he had, of course. No, she'd shed her bikini bottoms of her own free will and suffered the consequences for it.

"Hey." Luke had finished his pie and started eyeing hers. "You gonna eat that?"

June pushed her plate across the blanket and tried to think of something else—anything else. "I went to visit Trey today."

Luke lowered his brows and asked in a clipped tone, "Why?"

"What do you mean, *why*?"

"Never mind. How'd he look? I haven't seen him in a couple days. He says he's doing okay, but I can't tell if he's lying on the phone."

"A lot better. He's going home soon." June took her hair down and put it back into a fresh ponytail. "We talked about you."

Luke's mouth was full of pie, so he just flashed his *and…?* face.

"Trey wouldn't say much, but he thinks all your problems are his fault."

For several minutes, the only sounds in the empty dining room were the distant hum of the refrigerator and Luke's chewing. June started to worry she'd said too much, that maybe he'd be angry with Trey for revealing anything at all.

"That's bullshit," Luke said. "And I've told him so a hundred times. I make my own choices, and if I have problems, they're my fault. Nobody else's." Then he licked his fork and clumsily turned the subject away from himself. "How'd you wind up in the bar business? I thought you wanted to study psychology."

"I did. But I found something I liked better."

After hightailing it out of Sultry County with her heart in pieces, June had distracted herself from the pain by enjoying all the freedoms Grammy hadn't allowed back home: dancing, listening to the devil's music, wearing makeup, and drinking. A lot. But she'd grown tired of chugging cheap beer through funnels and swilling trash can punch with the masses. That's when she'd truly learned to appreciate alcohol—not drinking it, but experimenting with new recipes and combinations. She'd dropped out to study bartending more seriously, learning the difference between single malt and blended scotch, between a pilsner and a lager, and serving drinks as a cocktail waitress until she was old enough to tend bar. Grammy'd had a fit, and it had been the final nail in their relationship's coffin.

June sighed, thinking of her bar and hoping Esteban was monitoring the pH levels inside the tanks. Twenty majestic, orange-striped lion fish would arrive tomorrow to fill the side wall aquarium, and she didn't want them going belly-up.

"You should come out for opening night," she said. "Luquos is one of a kind. Peaceful, romantic, dim. The kind of place where you can sit and have a conversation without shouting over the band, know what I mean?"

Luke swallowed his last bite of pie and smirked. "Sounds kinda boring."

Before June knew what she was doing, she bunched up one knuckle and slugged him in the bicep.

Luke gasped in shock, then a purely wicked grin curled his lips. He rubbed his upper arm. "Did you just frog me, Junebug?"

"No! No, no, no!" Oh, sugar. She hadn't meant to do it. Luke had never hit back, but he'd always done something much, much worse in retaliation: tickled her until she'd nearly wet herself, and then administered a nasty wet-willy. Extra wet. "We're even! You called my bar boring!" She started crawling backward, tensing her body to spring away, if he attacked.

"Oh, we're not even." His green eyes practically glowed with mischief as he inched forward and licked his index finger, preparing to stick it in her ear. God, that was so gross, and he knew how much she'd always hated it. "Yet." And then he launched forward to grab her ankle.

But June was faster. She scrambled on her hands and feet, slipping momentarily on the quilt, until she righted herself and barreled into the kitchen. The rubber soles of her sneakers squeaked against the wood floor as she ran. When she didn't hear Luke's heavy boots clomping behind her, she glanced over her shoulder. He wasn't there. Instantly, she halted. He'd probably circled through the other doorway in the dining room to ambush her.

She backed behind the kitchen island, using it as a barrier, but making sure not to corner herself. The house was too quiet, and her frantic breaths would give her away. She held the air inside her lungs and tiptoed silently back into the dining room. He'd never expect her to return there.

The backs of her thighs tingled the way they always did when she was nervous, and June peeked around the room, seeing nothing except the disheveled blanket and scattered paper plates on the wood floor. There was nowhere to hide, and she could only avoid Luke for so long. She needed a plan. If she made it to the front door, she could bolt outside and lock herself inside his truck until he promised amnesty. June crept forward into the dark living room more carefully than a soldier navigating a minefield. Her shuddering breaths seemed amplified, but she couldn't hold them inside any longer.

The front door was within sight, and a burst of adrenaline propelled her into a sprint for freedom. But then two strong arms flashed from the shadows, snagging her around the waist and pulling her backward. June released a primal scream, and then before she knew it, Luke had her pressed against the foyer wall. She writhed against his enormous body in a futile attempt to escape, but it was like trying to move a boulder. Finally, she resigned herself to defeat, and he used one hand to pin both her wrists above her head.

"If I remember correctly," he said against her temple, sliding one hand down the length of her rib cage. "There's a little spot right here…" He yanked her T-shirt up and brushed his fingertips across her belly.

Darn it, he had a really good memory. "No," she pleaded. Then his fingers started wiggling against that one weak spot right behind her waist, and she burst out in hysterical laughter. "Please," she managed with a gasp. But he was relentless. The sounds of her uproarious torture reverberated through the vacant foyer.

"You know what to say," he taunted.

"Uncle! Uncle!"

"Unh-uh. Not that."

"Okay!" June tried to stop giggling long enough

to get a sentence out. "Luke Gallagher is..."—she laughed, more from remembering the old words than the tickling—"the only Master of the Universe."

"Stronger than?" he prompted, playing her ribs like a piano.

"Stronger than He-Man and twice as good-looking!" she shouted in a rush.

Mercifully, his fingers paused, and he curled his large, warm hand around her waist. "That's a good girl." Then he eliminated the sliver of air between them and pressed harder against the length of her body. Soon his lips were at her ear. "You know what comes next."

"Oh, come on, that's disgusting."

She felt his chest rumble with low, quiet laughter. "If you mess with the bull..." he whispered. But instead of a cold, wet finger, the tip of his soft tongue swept the inside swirl of her ear, and her knees buckled with pleasure. When he used his body to lift her up, his chest brushed against her nipples, and her heart pounded so hard it seemed to shake the whole house.

Luke pulled back and gave her a look that would melt a snowman at ten paces. His throat bobbed as he glanced down at her mouth. The silence, interrupted only by their short, quick breaths, was maddening, and the waiting was nothing short of torture.

"You gonna kiss me?" she whispered, feeling suddenly bold.

Luke lifted his lips to her forehead and brushed them back and forth against her skin. "Is that what you want?" Then he moved in an agonizingly slow trail down the side of her face, kissing her temple, her cheek, the edge of her jaw, finally lingering at the corner of her mouth.

"You asked me to kiss you once before. Remember what happened after that?"

June couldn't make words yet. Instead, she whimpered from the back of her throat.

"Mmm-hmm," he murmured, licking and sucking his way down the side of her neck and driving her crazy. "Me too."

With one hand still beneath her shirt, Luke skimmed his palm higher, until he brushed the outside swell of her breast with his thumb. June couldn't think, couldn't breathe. Part of her—one part in particular—wanted him to keep going, but something from deep inside caused her to hesitate. Perhaps that's what forced the words in a shaky voice off the tip of her tongue.

"I remember you rolling off me like I had a flesh-eating disease."

Everything stopped: Luke's mouth, his hand, his breath. It was probably the last thing he expected her to say, and he held still for several long seconds. Heat flooded June's cheeks. She wished she could rewind time and take it back. Why on earth had she mentioned it in the first place? She'd had nine years to get over what he did. Bringing it up now made her feel like a petulant child.

With a long, slow sigh, Luke released her wrists and stepped back. He stood there, watching her with an expression she couldn't quite read, somewhere between solemn and frustrated, but stopping just shy of angry. Similar to the look in Gram's eyes when June had refused to attend the local Bible College and instead applied to a school six hours away.

"I tried to apologize," he said. "Did you read any of my letters?"

June shrugged one shoulder. She'd read them. Right up until his wedding invitation arrived, and then she began marking the envelopes *return to sender* and replacing them in the mailbox. "Didn't change anything."

Placing his hands on his hips, Luke hung his head and then gave a tight nod. "Awful long time to hold a grudge. I didn't take you for that kind of girl."

She started to object, but as much as June wanted to tell him there was no grudge, she couldn't say it aloud. Because maybe he was right. Maybe she *had* held on to that pain and anger too long. The fact that she'd let nine years pass without reaching out to Luke pretty much proved it.

After another minute of charged silence, Luke gestured to the kitchen. "Let me get another hour in before I drive you home."

Nodding her head, June cleared her throat and said, "Sure. I need to finish that third bedroom."

Chapter 10

LUKE TORE ANOTHER CHUNK FROM THE SIDE OF HIS empty foam coffee cup and glanced at the clock above the hospital admissions desk. Four-thirty. While he'd waited around for Trey's doctor to discharge him, one perfectly good hour of daylight had burned away.

"'Scuse me," he called to the receptionist, leaning forward in his chair. "How much longer?"

She shrugged and flashed an apologetic grin. "Things move a little slower on the weekends. Shouldn't be too much longer, though." She bit her bottom lip and slid her eyes to the side in an unmistakable invitation, but Luke thanked her and turned away.

There was only one woman on his mind that day— hell, for the last week and a half—and that was June. When he'd learned she still hadn't forgiven him, it had felt like a kick to the beanbags. Luke didn't know why he was so surprised, though, since he'd never really forgiven himself either. Hell, even at eighteen, he should've known better.

Ever since Luke had discovered how to get a girl into the backseat of his Camaro, he'd been careful to make his intentions known. To the point of brutal honesty, he'd made it clear he wasn't offering anything beyond an hour or two of fogging up his windows. He'd never had a steady girl, and he'd never wanted one. When June had come on to him that day at the pond, he should've turned her down. Luke had always known about her little crush on him, and he'd been a fool not to realize sex would mean something completely different to her. Especially for her first time. Being young and horny and undeniably stupid was no excuse for what he'd done to June.

Luke leaned back in his seat and closed his eyes. Ever since she'd come back to town, the memories of that afternoon had pressed the walls of his mind like water against a breaking dam. And like the little Dutch boy, Luke didn't have enough fingers to plug the leaks. Every sweet and bitter detail of their final day together came rushing forth in a deluge.

They'd just graduated high school on that fateful morning, and the ceremony had dragged until lunch-time. Pru had been so proud of him and June that she was practically glowing. She'd served cold sandwiches and leftover cherry pie and then gone into town to buy ingredients for a special supper. Luke had finished his meal and walked half a mile to his family's pond, while June stayed behind to pack for college. It was late May, and the temperature had already broken ninety-five that afternoon, so he'd peeled off his Sunday clothes, hung them over a low tree branch, and tossed his wallet into the grass before wading naked into the cool water. The air was thick with the scents of algae and cedar, and Luke let his body float on the water's filmy surface while he listened to wind stir the leaves high in the trees.

He'd been swimming less than half an hour when the crunch of twigs and the rustle of underbrush sounded from the nearby path. Then, like a model in one of the Victoria's Secret catalogs he kept under his mattress,

June stepped into the clearing, wearing her little black bikini. Pru obviously hadn't known June owned the thing, because those miniature triangles didn't do much to cover her bouncing, full breasts, and God bless America, when June turned around to spread a quilt in the shade, the crack of that glorious, broad ass peeked out from the top of her swimsuit bottoms. Sometimes he wondered if June enjoyed torturing him. Luke already had a semi from watching her move around for ten seconds, and he was grateful to be waist-deep in the dark water. Just to be safe, though, he swam out until the water concealed most of his chest too.

June pointed to his clothes, which flapped gently in the breeze. "You skinny-dipping?"

"Well, duh."

"Maybe I will too."

Luke laughed and called her bluff. "Go ahead. Get naked." But she never would. Pru kept that girl under her thumb so tightly she probably couldn't even *say* the word naked.

"You think I won't do it," she said with a sideways grin.

The way she looked at him—all cocky and smiling—he should've known something was up. She sauntered toward the water, slowly trailing one hand up the side of her ribs to the back of her neck. Then, even more slowly, she pulled the string that fastened her bikini top until it came loose. He'd expected her to whirl around and face the other way, to tease him and hold the material against her chest and then run into the water to hide, but she didn't. With all the confidence of a Playboy centerfold, she pulled off her flimsy top and extended one arm to let it drop to the ground.

"Ho-o-ly shit," he whispered, going from semi to hard as titanium in an instant.

Luke knew his mouth was hanging open like a fly trap, but there wasn't a damn thing he could do about it. He'd imagined June naked a time or two. Or a hundred. But this put every one of his fantasies to shame. Her brazenly exposed, pink-tipped breasts swayed along with her body as she stepped nearer to the water, and he couldn't have looked away for a million dollars.

"Still think I won't do it?" June hooked her thumbs under the fabric around her hips.

If there was one thing that could tear his gaze away from her magnificent breasts, it was *that*. Part of him screamed, *Don't do it!* But another, much more influential part, begged her not to stop.

June paused, waiting until he glanced directly into her warm, brown eyes. Then, watching him the whole time, she peeled the stretchy black fabric down over her thighs, shimmied it to her feet, and kicked it aside. Again, he expected her to hide behind her hands or rush into the water, and again, he was dead wrong. She stood completely naked before him and just let him look. And he did look. Her body—especially the drastic flare of her hips and those little dimples in front—was almost too feminine, if such a thing were possible, and his hands grasped at the water in an overpowering urge to touch her. The skin between her long, fair legs was totally bare, something he'd never seen before, except in dirty magazines.

"Jesus, Junebug," he whispered, completely stupefied.

Finally, she stepped into the pond, wading forward until she was waist-deep, and then dove in headfirst.

When she surfaced several seconds later, she was right behind him.

"Guess you don't know me as well as you thought," she said, gasping for air and slipping her arms around his shoulders. When the firm tips of her nipples brushed against his back, Luke had to press his lips together to keep from groaning out loud.

He cleared his throat and tried to sound casual. "I'll consider that my graduation present."

"I don't know," she said, still trying to catch her breath. She pulled herself around to face him and then wrapped her smooth legs around his waist. When the inside of her thigh skimmed his erection, he gasped and held her still. "I think," she continued, "such a momentous occasion calls for more."

"Christ," he hissed, pushing away. "Stop. You can't do that."

For the first time that afternoon, he saw her confidence falter as her coy little smile drooped into a frown. She peered through wide eyes and asked, "You really want me to stop?"

Luke held his breath for a long moment then let it out real slow. "No. But you don't understand about guys, Junebug. I'm already too—"

"I know plenty." Cupping one hand against his cheek, she pulled his head lower, until they were eye-level. "I know I want you to kiss me. And I won't ask you to stop, whatever happens after that."

Oh, god. How many times had he abused himself beneath his bedspread, imagining this very situation? But this wasn't just any girl. This was June. His Junebug. The only person in the world who'd never turned her back on him or let him down, and for all practical purposes, his best friend. If they had sex, there'd be consequences. They'd go their separate ways for now—him to basic training and her to university—but what about when they came back to Pru's at Christmastime? Would this ruin everything?

"Don't think," she whispered, tightening her legs and pulling their bodies together. "Just kiss me."

So he did. He took June's face in his hands and he kissed her, brushing his lips lightly against hers, and then taking her bottom lip between his teeth. Her mouth was soft and wet, and she tasted like cherry pie. When Luke deepened the kiss and felt her warm tongue sweep against his, a jolt of pleasure struck directly between his legs. Kissing June was different than his experiences with other girls—not a dull, mechanical exchange of tongues or a stepping stone to second base. With June, he felt that kiss deep inside his chest, as if his lungs were balloons inflating bigger and bigger, until they might pop. And she kissed him like he was the only man on earth, fisting her little hands in his hair and pulling his mouth harder against hers, trying to consume him. He wanted to consider the consequences more, but his mind grew foggier with each soft swirl of her tongue.

The noises that came from the back of her throat caused his heart to skip ahead a few beats, and then she started exploring his body, smoothing her fingertips along the tops of his shoulders, down his back, over his ass. Then she grabbed both cheeks and pulled herself closer to strain against his erection.

"Shit," he whispered, clenching his eyes shut and tilting their foreheads together. Did she understand what she was doing? He wanted her to stop rubbing up against him, but he wanted her to keep going even more. Gripping the bottoms of her thighs, he shifted her higher, away from his groin, and then pulled her face up for another slow kiss.

June moved one hand over his, tugging it away from her cheek and guiding it to her firm breast, and then, keeping her legs wrapped tightly around his waist, she leaned back into the water, bringing her nipples right to his mouth. God damn, it was like a wet dream.

Luke cupped one breast and sucked the satiny nipple into his mouth like a greedy child, feeling a surge of pride when June moaned loudly in response. Then he moved to her other breast, using the seam of his lips to brush lightly back and forth across the tight pink bud, teasing her into a frenzy before drawing it deep into his mouth.

She whispered things he'd never heard her say before—filthy words that would make a porn star blush, and it made him want to drive her further, to see how she'd react when he pushed her over the edge. Skimming one hand along her round bottom, he lifted his lips from her nipple long enough to ask, "You kiss your Gram with that mouth?"

Instead of answering, she dug her nails into his shoulders and pulled herself back up. Then, heaven help him, she started grinding again. But this time, she angled her hips so the tip of his shaft pressed right against her warm, slick opening. She attacked his mouth, kissing him with animal ferocity, and lowered onto his erection just a tiny bit. Just enough to make his breath catch. Just enough to get her pregnant if they weren't careful. Luke

SULTRY WITH A TWIST

was out of his mind with need, but not so far gone that he'd take that risk.

Luke wasn't sure how he managed it, but he grabbed June's thighs and carried her across the uneven, silt-covered pond floor, out of the water, and onto dry land without dropping her in the process, and then laid her on the quilt in the shade.

When he lowered his mouth to hers, water droplets from his hair fell onto her cheeks and trailed down the side of her face like tears, and it reminded him this was her first time. It would hurt. He'd never had a virgin be-fore, and he wondered if she'd cry. Suddenly he wasn't sure if he could do this. He couldn't bear the thought of hurting June.

"We don't have to," he whispered against her lips. "We can do other things instead." And he trailed one hand down over her slippery, wet breasts, over her flat belly, all the way between her thighs. He swept his knuckles lighter than a dragonfly's wing across the soft folds of skin there, and when she opened her legs, he skimmed his thumb across her slick, sensitive flesh, until she whimpered and arched her hips for more pres-sure. "See?" he said. "This is just as good." It was a lie, but she didn't need to know that.

"Please." She cupped his cheek and pleaded with heavily lidded eyes. "I want you to be the first. Not some frat boy."

Luke's gut clenched into a knot so tight he thought he'd get sick. The thought of some preppy college prick touching her—sliding his dirty hands across her nipples, settling his thumbs in the dimples at the front of her hips that were made for him, slamming into her without a care for her discomfort—enraged him to the point of madness.

June was his girl. All his. And he'd take this gift she offered and treasure it. No matter how far apart life scattered them, no other man would have what she'd given him today.

"Okay," he said. "But only if you're sure."

"I'm ready." She wrapped one leg around his waist and tugged down on his shoulders.

He was ready too—had been since the moment she'd slipped off her bikini—but he wanted to give June pleasure before the pain. The only problem was how she might react. Some girls were squeamish about it. He reached between her thighs to stroke her again and said, "I want to kiss you here first."

"You can *do* that?" When June's mouth popped open and her eyebrows shot up, it took every ounce of Luke's dwindling self-control not to smile. But he remained stoic, refusing to laugh at her innocence. It just made her that much more beautiful. "But," she objected, "isn't that kind of gross?"

"Unh-uh." He shook his head and continued moving his thumb in slow, lazy circles. Then he slipped his index finger inside where she was warm and snug. Though it took a Herculean effort, he tried not to imagine how it would feel around his painfully hard shaft. This part was just for her; he needed to focus on her. Then he brought that same glistening finger to his mouth and sucked it clean right in front of her astonished eyes. "You're delicious, and I want to taste you again. Just say yes."

"Yes."

Starting with her forehead, Luke kissed his way down

June's body, pausing at the strawberry birthmark on her neck that had always taunted him. Her sweet, salty skin smelled like coconut lotion, and when he bit her, she gasped and pulled his head down, urging him to bite her again, harder.

He lingered at her breasts awhile, and then kissed down the length of her stomach to her hips, stopping to kiss each luscious indent. When he finally reached the apex between her thighs, Luke settled one hand beneath her bottom and angled her toward his face. Then, slower than molasses going uphill, he licked her salty, wet flesh and waited for her reaction.

June gasped and clutched the quilt with both hands. Her thighs closed an inch, but she didn't ask him to stop. He continued using the tip of his tongue for a few minutes, and then flattened it against her with more pressure. When she moaned and let her knees fall open, he did it again, but faster, and holy shit, the noises she made were the most erotic sounds he'd ever heard. He used his other hand to dip one finger inside her, then two, and he used gentle suction to draw her most sensitive spot into his mouth, alternating between firm suction and shallow penetration. He repeated the pattern again and again until she fisted his hair and arched her hips off the ground. All her moans and cries of *oh God* and *Luke* and *yes!* incinerated his last shreds of control, and he climaxed right there on the blanket. But when her slippery muscles clenched and shuddered around his fingers and she cried his name, he was hard again in an instant.

Luke lifted his face and watched her legs tremble. Then he reached across the grass for his wallet, found a condom, and rolled it on. He settled between her legs and lowered himself onto June's warm body, gazing at her flushed face. When she smiled up at him like he'd just shown her heaven, he thought his heart might burst. This *was* his girl. And from somewhere deep in his brain, he knew if he could only be inside her, he'd tie them together forever. He needed to make them one person, and then everything would be all right.

He kissed her ear and whispered, "Relax," and gently nudged her thighs wider apart. Then he curled his fingers around one hip, letting his thumb settle into the small dimple there, and he eased into her as slowly as he could stand, pulled back, and then slid an inch deeper. He couldn't think about how good she felt. Because if he focused on her snug, warm fit or how absurdly slick she was, he might ram into her like a jackhammer. Instead, he concentrated on her eyes, soft and overflowing with emotion. When he pushed all the way inside, he saw pain flash in those brown eyes, but she didn't make a sound. So brave, just like always.

"I'm sorry," he whispered, stroking her cheek and brushing back her brown curls. He lowered his mouth to hers again and tried to ignore the mounting tension deep in his belly, tried to ignore the urge to thrust harder. He wanted to slow things down—it was too soon to come, too soon to let it end—but the tension mounted and grew and built, until his fingers trembled against June's face. Then, with one final stroke, he buried himself completely inside her and convulsed in the hottest release of his life. He tried to muffle his cry against June's shoulder, but it echoed across the pond.

That should've been the moment when they cuddled and shared quiet kisses, but while he lay there fighting for oxygen, June said the three ugliest words in the English language. Useless, hurtful words that people tossed around like used bottle caps. They were the same three words his mama had said before walking out of his life without a backward glance. They meant nothing.

"I love you." She ran her fingers through his hair and said it again. "I love you, Luke. I love you so much." Then she wouldn't stop—she kept whispering it again and again, like verbal vomit.

A few other girls had let the L word slip during orgasm, but it had never bothered him before. He knew most people couldn't control their mouths at a time like that. But for some senseless reason, June's fevered, emotional declarations turned his belly to ice. Cold fingers snaked around his chest, and he fought the urge to run away. He pulled out of her and moved quickly to the other side of the blanket.

"Don't say that," he ordered in a voice harsher than he'd intended. "You don't mean it."

"What? Of course I do." She sat up and touched his shoulder, but he flinched away.

"Just stop, damn it."

And then the shit really hit the fan. As luck would have it, Deputy Jenks had chosen that particular day to spend his lunch hour fishing, and he'd caught them buck naked and guilty as sin. He didn't arrest them. Instead, he'd done something far worse: driven them home to Pru and told her everything.

June had run up the stairs crying and locked herself in her bedroom, and then Pru had turned to Luke and yelled so hard he'd worried she might have a stroke. *Is this the thanks I get for taking you into my home?*

she'd said. *I raised you like my own, and you defiled my grandbaby! You ruined her!* After Pru was done making him feel like the world's biggest pervert, she'd given him five minutes to dash upstairs and collect everything he could grab before she kicked him out of the house. He'd driven to the recruiter's office, slept in his car, and then shipped out for basic training the next morning.

Luke had never told anyone, but he'd asked the army shrink about what had happened that day at the pond—why had he reacted that way?—and supposedly, it was linked to his "abandonment issues," whatever that meant. Either way, it didn't change anything. He'd written June dozens of letters apologizing, but she'd never responded. And just when he'd thought they'd mended their friendship, he'd learned she was still holding it against him.

There had to be a way to earn her forgiveness.

"Hey, get me the hell outta here." Trey's voice brought Luke to attention. "I want a greasy burger and a cold beer. How about we get an early supper and then head over to Shooters?"

Luke stood and pointed to the cast that shackled Trey from hip to toe. "You sure?"

"You bet your sweet ass I am." Trey tipped his wooden cane in the air like a crotchety old man yelling for kids to get off his lawn. "I can sit down at the bar as well as I can sit down at home."

"Sounds good to me," Luke said with a shrug. "I could use a drink."

Chapter 11

JUNE WAS NO FEATHERWEIGHT—SHE'D WORKED IN dive bars before. But none of them held a candle to Shooters. She glanced at the faded wood floor, coated with some layer of gritty material that slipped beneath her sneakers. Sawdust? Seriously? A cocktail of unpleasant scents—stale beer, cigarette smoke, sweat, and cheap cologne—stung the inside of her nose, and she tried not to imagine how the heat from hundreds of bodies would amplify that odor later tonight.

Pausing to let her eyes adjust to the dim surroundings, June rested her palm on a tall, wooden bar stool. "Ah, gross," she whispered to herself, yanking free of the mystery-glue that bound her skin to the seat. She hoped to God it was just dried beer. As much as June was tempted to sniff her hand, she resisted and pulled a wet-wipe from her purse. Sometimes ignorance really was bliss.

A few seconds later, she could finally see all the way to the back, where six coin-operated pool tables competed for light beneath a single green, hanging lamp shade. Empty racks lined the wall, while the cues that should've hung there lay haphazardly across tables, leaned against the jukebox, and littered the pathway to the restroom. If Shooters looked like this at five o'clock, she shuddered to imagine the devastation at closing time.

Taking a mental inventory, she counted the tables

outlining the main room's perimeter—thirty, each with four chairs—and then turned her attention to the long, maple bar, where she spotted another forty seats, only two of which were occupied at this early hour. Shooters had a halfway decent capacity, and as the only bar between two dry counties, June assumed it stayed busy.

Collecting stray blue chalk cubes along the way, June walked to the far end of the bar, where a stout, gray-haired man with pockmarked cheeks dried shot glasses and chatted in a low voice with his patrons. When the bartender glanced at her, June set the cubes down in a pile and flashed the confident smile she'd rehearsed in the mirror that morning.

"What can I getcha?" he asked in a slow drawl.

June decided to get right to the point. "A job."

"Sorry, hun. We already got a waitress."

"I'm a TABC-certified bartender, not a waitress, and my next few Saturdays are free, if you need the help."

His furry, gray eyebrows rose in appreciation, and he seemed to consider her offer seriously. "License current?"

"Yes, sir."

"You handle a tough crowd? Things get hectic, and folks don't like to wait."

"Why don't you let me show you what I can do? Then decide."

"Okay. My last guy quit on me, so you're in luck." He nodded slowly, as if still mulling it over. "Tonight's the one-dollar, well-drink special. If you can survive that, you're hired."

June groaned inwardly, giving a mental eye roll. Nothing in her world was more blasphemous than cheap, gut liquor, and she had a feeling well-drink night would become her own personal hell. Damn her clunky, old hatchback and its costly engine parts.

"I'll warn ya, though," he said. "Cheap crowd on dollar nights. You won't make much."

June laughed and reached across the bar to shake his hand. "Don't worry. I know how to make tips."

———

A wall of stench smacked Luke in the face, and he tried to breathe through his mouth while navigating the thick crowd of bodies backed up against the bar.

"Smells like ass in here," Trey shouted while wrinkling his nose. He hobbled closely behind Luke, leaning on his cane, and then hauling his cast forward a few inches at a time.

"No worse than the field barracks."

"What?" Trey yelled. The noise of laughter, clacking cue balls, and a hundred simultaneous conversations competed against Lyle Lovett on the jukebox. "Can't hear a damn thing."

"Never mind."

Luke spotted Trish balancing a tray of drinks in the crook of her left arm, while holding another fully loaded tray in her right hand. By the look of all those clear plastic cups, it was dollar night, the friggin' bane of his existence. The cheap drunks came out in droves and took up all the seats. Bastards always puked in the urinals too. Trish caught his eye, and she nodded toward an open, quiet table near the back corner. Luke waved a silent thank you.

Once they were settled, Trish circled back around and pulled an order pad from her black apron. She pointed her pencil at the sticky tabletop.

"I held this one when I saw y'all pull up," Trish said, mostly talking to Trey. Everyone knew she was sweet on him. "Don't want you standin' on that leg, sugar."

"Aren't you a darlin'?" Trey took the back of her hand and kissed it. "Bring us a pitcher of Bud, and I'm yours forever."

Trish blushed and disappeared into the crowd.

"You ever gonna pull the trigger with that one?" Luke asked. "Seems cruel to keep leading her on."

Trey used his hand like a telephone and pretended to answer a call. "Hello? Yeah, Pot's right here." Then he handed the "phone" across to Luke and said, "It's Kettle. He wants you to quit calling him black."

"How hard did you hit your head when you fell off that roof?"

"Not so hard I don't notice how you look at *Joooonbug*, you hypocrite." Trey picked up a round cardboard coaster and flicked it at Luke. "Or the way *she* looks when she talks about you."

Luke caught the coaster in one hand and shook his head. "Maybe you're still high on painkillers. June hates me. She thinks I'm trash just like everyone else around here does." He spun the coaster like a coin across the tabletop and remembered the way she'd looked at him last night, all hurt and angry. A knot lodged in his stomach, and Luke had a feeling all the beer in the world wouldn't wash it away.

"Who thinks you're trash? I've been here four years and never heard anyone say—"

"Common knowledge. I ever tell you how my dad made his living?" When Trey shook his head, Luke continued. "Moonshiner. And it was no secret, either. When

I was seven, he cooked up a bad batch, and it killed him, along with a few other guys."

"Shit." Trey's face contorted like he'd just sucked a lime. "But that's got nothing to do with you."

Luke shrugged a shoulder. "June can do better, and I'm sure she knows it."

"Buddy, no offense, but you've got your head shoved so far up your own—"

"Here ya go, sugar." Trish plunked a heavy glass pitcher onto the table, and amber liquid sloshed over the rim. Then she handed them each a frosty mug. Luke knew Shooters didn't freeze their glasses, so she must've kept these in the back just for Trey. God, she had it bad.

"Thanks, beautiful," Trey said.

A chant broke out from the crowd of people huddled around the bar, but they were too far away and too drunk for Luke to understand their words.

"What's going on up there?" Luke asked Trish.

"Oh, Jiminy Christmas." She placed one hand on her hip and rolled her eyes. "The new bartender's showin' off again. Makin' one of them fancy drinks that you set on fire. It's not safe. Plus, we don't have time for that crap. Not on dollar night. I don't think Burl should allow it, but nobody listens to me."

Whoever the new bartender was, Trish sure didn't like him.

"And don't even get me started on that outfit she's wearin'," Trish said with pure poison in her voice. "Showin' off her"—she held two hands in front of her chest, cupping an imaginary pair of honeydews—"just for tips. Back home, we have a name for women like that."

Luke laughed harder than he had in a week. He had an

appreciation for *women like that*, but he held his tongue. No use pissing off the lady who freezes your beer mugs.

"Oh, sorry Luke. I didn't mean it that way. Sometimes I get to rambling, and I—"

"What're you talking about?" he interrupted.

"I forgot June's a friend of yours."

It was a good thing he hadn't taken a mouthful of beer yet, or he'd have sprayed it all over Trish. This was the last place he'd expected to find June—she couldn't leave Sultry County. The seed of a wicked idea took root in his mind. If Judge Bea found out she'd violated her agreement, maybe he'd make her stay longer. The thought appealed to Luke much more than it should have.

Before Trish left to take more orders, Trey crooked his index finger at her. "After this cast comes off, I want to take you dancing. What do you say?"

Trish's face lit up like she'd just opened her front door and found the Prize Patrol standing there with an oversized check. Apparently, she couldn't speak, so she nodded and backed away.

Trey filled both their mugs and held his up in a toast. "Here's to pulling the trigger. Now it's your turn." He didn't bother clinking Luke's glass before taking a long, deep drink.

Luke downed his beer and wiped foam from his upper lip. "I'll be right back."

"Take your time, buddy," Trey said with a knowing smile.

The closer Luke moved to the bar, the louder and more tightly packed it became. While passing the jukebox, he heard someone say, *That hot bartender Trixie wants to hear some Stevie Ray Vaughan*, and it relieved him to know June wasn't giving out her real name. Dollar night brought the sludge of three counties out to play, not the kind of people you wanted looking up your address in the phone book or on the web.

Luke squeezed through one last row of sweaty drunks and wedged himself into position at the bar. Finally, he understood why half of Shooters had gravitated to that spot, and he didn't like it one damned bit. June had her hair up in a twist that left a few curls dangling around her glistening, flushed face, but that's not what drew the crowd's lecherous gaze. She wore a low-cut tank top tied in a knot right below her breasts, exposing her slender waist and flat tummy. And, if that wasn't bad enough, a lacy, hot-pink thong peeked out from beneath the waistband of her jeans when she bent over to grab a clean dish towel from under the counter. If he'd worn a button-down over his T-shirt that night, he'd have taken it off, hopped over the counter, and wrapped it around her.

But appearances aside, June was in her element. Luke watched her line up a dozen plastic cups, load 'em with ice, tip a bottle of booze upside down over each one, and then top them with Coke from the fountain, all in less than twenty seconds. She pushed the cups forward, money exchanged hands, and her tip jar overflowed with wet, crumpled dollar bills. When Stevie Ray's "Cold Shot" sounded from the jukebox, June closed her eyes for a few seconds and smiled to herself before singing along and lining up a dozen more cups.

"Bud," Luke said.

"Bottle or draft?" she asked in a rush, and then sang on. She must've been too deep in her zone to recognize his voice.

"Draft."

Stevie and June sang about letting love go bad while she tilted a glass mug beneath the tap. Luke listened to the lyrics and wondered if June had any feelings left for him now. He could tell she was attracted to him, but anything beyond that? He didn't know why he cared because it didn't matter anyway. She'd be gone in a couple weeks. And besides, what did he have to offer a woman like June? But still, that didn't ease his curiosity.

"That'll be three-fif—" June froze, eyes wider than silver dollars. Then she knocked Luke's mug over, flooding the counter with beer and foam. For an instant, the cool, fresh scent of Bud replaced the reek of sweat and chewing tobacco from the men around him.

"Son of a biscuit-eater," June mumbled, snatching a handful of rags and mopping up the mess.

Luke let a smile pull the corners of his mouth, and he tossed a five dollar bill onto a dry patch of wood. "What kind of self-respecting bartender uses a swear like that?" He leaned close enough to smell her warm, orangey shampoo. "I've heard you use words that would make a sailor faint. And I've met plenty of sailors, so I'd know."

"Cussing's not professional." June ignored his teasing, filled another mug, and set it on the counter with exaggerated care. Then she pushed his money away. "This one's on me."

Luke took the five and shoved it into her tip jar. When she started to object, he shook his head and shoved the money farther down.

"Thanks." She nodded at his Bud. "I'm surprised you still drink American beer after living in Germany. I'd have ordered a nice Hofbrau lager, not that Burl stocks it."

"Maybe I don't like the taste of those memories."

"Ever gonna tell me why?"

"Nope."

"Hey, listen." June twirled her finger around one of her curls and studied a thin crack along the surface of the bar. "I want to talk to you, but it's too crazy right now. Sleep at Gram's tonight, okay? Then in the morning—"

A familiar voice shouted from across the bar, and Luke glanced up in time to see his best crew member slide off a bar stool. "How long's he been here?"

June looked over her shoulder and then shrugged. "Pauly? I don't know. Awhile."

"What's he been drinking?"

"It's dollar night. What do you think?"

"Shit." Wasn't Pauly supposed to be spending the weekend at his daughter's house? He'd been writing to her for months trying to patch things up, and she'd finally invited him to visit. He'd gabbed nonstop about it yesterday morning. Things must not have gone very well. "He can't drink. Parole violation. I've gotta get him sobered up before he goes back to the halfway house."

Luke considered his untouched beer and sighed. Then he looked up at his half-naked Junebug and sighed again. "Be careful when you leave tonight, you hear me? Ask Burl to walk you to your car. And make sure it actually starts before he goes back inside."

"I've done this before, Luke." She flashed a condescending grin and tossed a wet dish towel under the bar. Then she was back in her zone: filling cups, taking money, flirting with drunk and dangerous men.

Luke hated to leave her there, but he couldn't let Pauly go back to prison. After arranging for Trish to drive Trey home, Luke helped Pauly into the truck, and they went in search of some late-night coffee.

―∿∿―

Once, when June was thirteen, Luke had found a stash of firecrackers left over from the Memorial Day parade. Together, they'd spent the afternoon lighting hundreds of bangers, and when it was over, her ears had rung for two days. Her ears rang like that now. She'd forgotten how loud a dive bar could get, and when her ears had finally adjusted to the clamor, Burl had announced last call and then the place cleared out. Now the silence almost hurt. But not quite as much as June's lower back. Closing time didn't mean the work was over. She'd just finished scrubbing down the bar and loading all the glassware in the back room dishwasher.

June pulled aside the cleanest looking chair she could find and plopped down next to Burl at a table in the back. "Ah," she groaned loudly, as pinpricks of relief stung her spine. "It feels so good to sit down."

Burl grinned and continued counting his loot. Tidy stacks of bills bound with rubber bands were heaped in front of him, and when he stopped and added another stack of twenties to the pile, the greedy cash-lust in his gaze reminded June of the old Scrooge McDuck cartoons she used to watch as a kid.

Not that June had anything against making money. She'd pulled in more than enough tips that night to repay Luke for fixing her engine. And, if he refused the money, like he'd said he would, she'd mail it to him when she returned to Austin.

Austin. When she imagined returning home, her chest

tightened as if a blood pressure cuff were squeezing her ribs. Maybe she shouldn't think about that right now.

"You did real good," Burl said. "See ya next Saturday?"

June nodded and covered her mouth to yawn. "Actually, I have a proposition for you."

"Let's hear it."

"Monday's Labor Day. Do you have a permit to sell at the fair?"

"You betcha." Burl finished rolling a stack of quarters and folded down the brown paper tabs. "Lookin' for an extra shift?"

"I'll work for free." That got his attention. His head snapped up and his brows reached for the sky. "I'll even mix a batch of my famous sangria—I noticed you've got some fruit in the back room."

"What's the catch?"

"Here's the deal." June began helping Burl sort coins, starting with the dimes. "I'll work the whole day—all shifts by myself—if you'll donate half the profits."

Burl made a face like he smelled something rotten. "Oh, I dunno—"

She cut him off with a raised hand. "Just hear me out. First off, you'll save money on labor, because I'll do everything myself. Second, you can write off the donation on your taxes. In the end, you'll actually make *more* this way."

Pursing his lips, Burl considered her offer. "I'll think about it and let you know tomorrow."

June shook her head. Nine times out of ten, *I'll think about it* was just a preemptive *no* in disguise. The only way to get out of manning the church booth—a chore she'd always hated as a kid—was to raise a sizable

donation from Shooters. "I need to know now. My
sangria takes a full day to marinate." She stared him
down over a pile of cash and added, "If I can't clear at
least what you made last year, you can take it out of my
tips next week." If that didn't sway the old tightwad,
nothing would.

"Deal."

June thanked him and then dragged her sore, throbbing body into the storage room, where she had just
enough energy to mix a cooler full of what she called
"cheater's sangria," using extra juice, one bag of oranges, a couple of apples, and a bag of frozen fruit she'd
add right before serving. She'd told Burl a small fib—
this wasn't her famous blend, but she didn't have much
to work with, and the indiscriminate crowd at the fair
would hardly notice.

About half an hour later, she grabbed her purse and
rejoined Burl at the table. In six short hours, she'd have
to wake up for church, so if she left now, maybe she'd
manage five hours of sleep. "Walk me out?" she asked.

"Sure thing. Lemme get my Louisville Slugger."

That sounded like a wise move. While she'd rummaged behind the bar for her purse, June had peeked
out the front window and noticed some stragglers in
the parking lot. Stragglers always made her nervous.
Nobody had a good reason for hanging around two
hours after closing time. By then, all the patrons should
have either found a ride home or found a new friend
to take them someplace discreet. Anyone still lingering
beyond that point was looking for trouble. Or planning
to follow her home. June's heartbeat quickened, and she
wondered if she could lose a tail on these open back

roads. Probably not. Feeble old Bruiser couldn't outrun a deer, let alone another vehicle.

"Ready?" Burl held the back doorknob in one hand and a baseball bat in the other.

"Yep."

Together, they crept into the dark parking lot, scanning the nearly empty space for anything—or any*one*—suspicious. At first, nothing seemed amiss, but then male voices and barking laughter erupted from the side of the building, and from the corner of her eye, she noticed Burl stiffen and take a defensive stance. Tingles burned along the backs of her thighs. As much as she wanted to pretend the danger was all in her imagination, Burl's reaction proved otherwise.

Just when she was about to suggest they go back inside and lock the door, red and blue flashing lights pierced the darkness, and a Sultry County Sheriff's cruiser pulled to a stop beside June's car. She placed one hand over her thumping heart and exhaled a shaky sigh of relief.

When the sheriff swaggered toward them, June recognized him immediately. If she lived to be a hundred, she'd never forget the look on Deputy Jenks's face when he'd stumbled upon her and Luke naked as the truth on Gram's patchwork quilt nine years ago. Obviously, he'd earned a promotion since then.

"Hello there, Mae-June." Sheriff Jenks hitched up his pants and pulled a long, black Maglite from his utility belt.

"It's just June."

"Good to see you again." He clicked on the Maglite and pointed it at her bare midriff. "Though it'd be nice to see a little *less* of you for a change."

Burl relaxed and slung his baseball bat over one shoulder. "Trouble, Sheriff?"

"Not at all. Got a call from Luke Gallagher a couple hours ago. Said Mae-June requested a shadow home tonight."

Like baking bread, June's heart warmed, puffing up until it nearly bumped her ribs. Hot tears prickled behind her eyelids. No one had ever summoned the sheriff to escort her safely home. Heck, no one had even called to see if she'd made it there alive. One teardrop escaped, rolling down her cheek, and June brushed it away before either man noticed.

Resting his hand on the butt of his pistol, Jenks strolled to the other side of the building. June couldn't see the men loitering there, but she heard the sheriff's loud, firm voice.

"Which-a-you boys is fit to drive?"—then some indistinct muttering, followed by—"Best be on your way then."

An engine started, and seconds later, the low rumble of a bad muffler began to fade into the distance.

She watched to make sure Burl made it back inside, then climbed into her car. The sheriff flashed his lights, and she pulled out onto the road with a smile tugging the corners of her mouth.

After June arrived at Grammy's house, she waved a thank-you to Sheriff Jenks and crept upstairs to Luke's bedroom. The digital clock beside his vacant bed read three in the morning, so either he'd driven back to his investment home, or he was still helping Pauly sober up. And based on his chivalrous actions that night, her money was on the latter.

June skimmed her fingers across Luke's cool, cotton pillowcase. He'd changed. This wasn't Luke-the-boy, who'd taken whatever he wanted without a care for anyone else. This was Luke-the-man, who gave second chances to downtrodden men and went out of his way to keep his friends—even the estranged ones—safe and protected.

Though June tried to block it out, Gram's voice repeated inside her head: *He needs someone to teach him to love. Think on that.* Maybe June needed to learn a thing or two as well.

Chapter 12

JUNE AWOKE WITH A GASP AND BOLTED UPRIGHT IN bed. Then, as the slow, dizzying fog of slumber began to lift, she relaxed against her headboard and realized it was only a dream. Luke wasn't really dead at the bottom of Gallagher pond. Just a dream. She checked the clock and then turned away from the window's soft, early glow to catch one more hour of sleep.

But a few minutes later, the same persistent cloud of dread needled her stomach, refusing to dissipate. June glanced into the dim hallway. If she could see Luke in the flesh—know beyond a doubt he was all right— maybe she could relax enough to fall asleep.

June padded carefully on the balls of her feet, avoiding the creakiest floorboards. Only Gram's gentle snores and a distant ticking from the grandfather clock disrupted the silence. Stealthy as a thief, June pushed Luke's door open one quiet inch at a time, before slipping inside.

There he was, safe and sound, sprawled on his bare belly across the double bed with one arm dangling off the side of the mattress. June couldn't help smiling— some things never changed. Long, red-brown locks of hair swept over his eyes, and he'd curled one leg out from beneath the comforter. He looked so peaceful, and June felt a little tug at her stomach. She knew she should return to her room, but she wasn't tired anymore, so instead, she crouched down and knelt on the wood floor beside Luke's bed to watch him sleep.

Before long, June realized she'd unconsciously matched her breathing to his deep, slow rhythm. Leaning forward, she pressed her cheek lightly against his shoulder and closed her eyes to savor his warmth, his smell. She wanted to pull back the covers and slip inside with him, to share his body heat and surround herself with the scents of leather and soap and Luke. What if she did? Would he pull her tightly against him and bury his face in the curve of her neck? Would he smooth his hot palms up the length of her thighs and make love to her with Grammy in the next room? June had a feeling he would, and although she grew warm and aching just thinking about it, she'd lose the last bit of her heart to him that way. So, for now, she felt content to watch. And maybe to touch, just a little.

Using one finger to lift a section of hair away from Luke's face, she cupped his cheek in her palm, smiling at the scratchy tickle of his whiskers against her skin. God help her, he was so magnificent. Sometimes the sight of his face made her breath catch, even after all these years. And now, when he seemed so childlike and innocent, she wondered if his mother had watched him sleep like this. How could she have left such a spirited, beautiful boy behind? June simply couldn't comprehend it. She wanted to gather him against her breast and hold him there forever.

Luke's bedroom window faced east, and the rising sun cast a pink radiance over the skin along his upper back. June knew she'd stayed too long, but she couldn't make herself return to her empty bed yet. She peeled down the black comforter a few inches and rested her palm against Luke's strong, broad back.

"Harder, and to the left," Luke mumbled.

June gasped and yanked her hand away like she'd touched a hot stove. Then she placed that hand over her pounding heart. "You scared the sugar out of me," she whispered.

Luke's quiet laughter shook the mattress. "I bet you still taste plenty sweet." He rolled onto his back and stretched his body like a lean tomcat, drawing her attention to his steely, lithe torso. *Hot buttered biscuits.* Then he rested one arm behind his head and blinked at June with sleepy eyes. "Here to take advantage of me?"

"I had a bad dream." She pushed against the mattress and stood to leave, but he curled his long fingers around her wrist and tugged her down to sit on the edge of his bed.

"Tell me about it." He took a handful of her white nightgown and rubbed the fabric between his fingers, whispering to himself, "This thing's sexy as hell."

Pulling her gown away, June scooted to the foot of his bed, out of his reach. "It's no big deal. I didn't mean to wake you. But since you're up—"

"You have no idea how *up* I am, Junebug."

"Stop thinking about sex for a second and listen."

"Says the woman feeling me up in my sleep."

"You called the sheriff last night," she said softly.

"Ah, hell." Luke groaned and pushed into a sitting position. "You're not pissed about that, are you?"

"Thank you." June touched his leg through the blanket and gave the side of his calf a gentle squeeze. "That's the nicest thing anyone's ever done for me."

For a long moment, Luke said nothing. Then he raked

his fingers through his hair and glanced across the room at the window shade. "Then you need nicer friends."

"And I made enough to pay you back for all those parts."

Luke's brows lowered over his drowsy, green eyes. "That better not be why you took the job. I told you not to worry about—"

"If you don't want the cash," June said with a shrug, "put it in the offering."

"What offering?"

"Since you're awake, you can come to church with us."

"Oh, no, no, no, no." Luke held up one palm and laughed, shaking his head frantically, like a kid who didn't want to take his medicine. "Since when do you go to church?"

"Since you kicked me off the Jenkins project." She took his large, rough hand in both of hers and tried to pull him out of bed. "Come on, it's not that bad."

"Yeah, it is. My ass twitches when I see those hard pews."

"But think how happy it'll make Gram." June lifted the back of his hand against her cheek and made her best pleading, pouty face, the one she hadn't used since high school. "It'll be just like old times."

"In that case, I should expect Pru to beat my ass with the wooden spoon before lunch."

"Only if you make rude noises with your armpit during the sermon again. Or reach under Beth Caldwell's skirt. Or flop on the ground and pretend to speak in tongues." A series of giggles bubbled up from June's chest, and she squeezed Luke's fingers while struggling to get the next sentence out. "Or steal the letter *S* off the sign in the lobby, so it says, 'Ushers will eat latecomers.'"

An impish grin brightened Luke's face. "God only knows how many years I shaved off your grandma's life. Fine, I'll go." When he freed his hand and threw back the covers, June caught a fleeting glimpse of *everything*, before she gasped and turned away. And he wasn't lying about being *up*. "What?" he asked in a teasing voice. "Think you're the only one who sleeps commando?" Then his warm breath tickled the back of her neck. "Unless you plan on leading me into temptation, get out of here so I can get dressed."

June scurried out the door and pulled it closed behind her as Luke shouted, "And don't use all the hot water!"

Thirty minutes later, when Gram was out of the bathroom and dressed, June indulged in an extra long, hot bath, refilling the tub twice and making sure to drain the water heater. She grinned to herself, figuring a cold shower would do Luke some good.

Instead of singing the opening hymn—"Brethren, We Have Come to Worship"—June shivered and rubbed her palms briskly over her upper arms to generate some heat. Maybe God was punishing her for that cold shower incident, because within ten minutes of leaving the house, the outside temperature had dropped twenty degrees. Not exactly sleeveless dress weather. And since fall's abrupt arrival also took the church custodian by surprise, he'd run the air conditioner all night long in anticipation of another scorching Texas morning.

"I should let you suffer," Luke whispered, while shaking out of his suit jacket and then shoving it in June's lap. "Lucky for you, I'm full of Christian charity today."

"You're full of something, all right," June whispered back, sliding her arms into the warm, satiny-lined sleeves and surrounding herself in his scent. Without thinking, she lifted the suit lapel to her nose and inhaled Luke's spicy aftershave, then caught herself, and tried to pretend she was just scratching her cheek.

When the song ended and the shiny, silver collection plate came around, Luke tossed a bulging envelope inside—all June's tip money from last night. Grammy pressed her lips together like she might cry from pride, and June mused at the irony of donating cash she'd earned in a bar to a church vehemently opposed to alcohol consumption. But like her daddy had once said, all money was green, and it all spent the same way. June had served most of her hours in God's Cupboard, a food donation program, and she knew they needed the cash.

Before gearing up for the sermon, Pastor McMahon reminded his congregation to join the Labor Day Celebration at the tri-county fairgrounds tomorrow. "Bring a lawn chair and a smile," he said. "There's on-site camping for those who'd like to join our revival bonfire and make a night of it."

Luke squirmed on the hard wooden pew and folded his arms across his chest, trying to hide a shiver. A bonfire probably sounded great to him right about now. From time to time, he'd glance over at his jacket with a longing expression, but June knew he'd stand naked in the snow before asking her to return it.

June pulled off the jacket and scooted over a few inches until her bare arm brushed Luke's starched, white shirt sleeve. He stiffened and gave her a questioning glance. Linking her arm through his, she whispered,

"Here, take this side," and reached over to tuck the heavy, lined jacket over both of them like a blanket. When Luke tugged his arm free, June thought he would object, but instead, he wrapped it around her shoulder and pulled their bodies close. June's heart lurched inside her chest. He'd never held her like this, not even after they'd made love. She relaxed into his warmth and rested her head against the side of his solid chest. It felt so good that for the first time in June's life, she wanted the sermon to last forever.

From her peripheral vision, June noticed Grammy watching them with a discreet smile on her face. *He needs someone to teach him to love. Think on that.*

And then, as if God Himself were conspiring against her, the pastor began to preach about love. "The Lord's plan for you, my brothers and sisters," he said in his slow drawl, "is to love one another. And that love must start in the home…"

Is that what Grammy had meant when she'd said Luke's mama had set a poor example? Had Luke struggled with emotions because there'd been no love in his home, until he'd come to live with Gram? June reflected on their childhood and realized Luke had never used the word. He'd avoided saying "love" like it was the granddaddy of all swears. When they'd exchanged Christmas or birthday cards, he'd signed them simply, "Luke," or if he was feeling particularly generous, "Your friend, Luke." And, of course, he'd practically bolted into the next county when she'd said "I love you" at the pond all those years ago.

With his strong arm wrapped protectively around her shoulder, it was so easy to pretend Luke already cherished her, and June wanted it to be true so badly it hurt to breathe. Could she really teach him to love? And, more importantly, was she brave enough to try? She'd never shied away from risks before. Heck, she'd invested her entire life's savings in Luquos—she'd even sold her home to bring that dream to fruition. But with Luke, she'd be risking more than just money. Cash lost could always be earned again, but the pain of heartbreak lingered for years.

June nestled deeper against Luke's chest and placed her palm lightly on his thigh. When he covered her hand with his own and rested his cheek atop her head, June made up her mind right then. To hell with the risks. If there was even the slightest chance Luke could hold her like this for the rest of her life, it was worth it. Somehow, in the next two weeks, she'd teach him to love her, and they'd work out the logistics of a long-distance relationship, until one of them could relocate. And since Luke didn't respond to words, she'd have to use actions. Desperate for ideas, she tuned back in to Pastor McMahon's sermon.

"...that love isn't a feeling, it's a choice, an action, a show of goodwill. It's about serving our brother, listening to him and supporting him without benefit to ourselves. It's believing the best about someone who's wronged us. And love never quits, never abandons in a time of need..."

Pretty vague, but it was a good start.

—∞—

Luke tore at the silk knot squeezing his windpipe and then ripped the tie from around his neck and flung it to the bedroom floor. He yanked his arms free of his jacket with so much force the sleeves turned inside out. Then, right as he tensed his shoulder to hurl the coat through the air, he hesitated and brought it to his nose. The collar still smelled like June's sweet, floral perfume, and Luke's stomach knotted like a pretzel. He fisted the material and threw it against the wall, where it thudded softly and swished to the floor beside his tie.

It had felt so good—too damned good—to pull June's warm, soft body against him and hold her close through the whole sermon, feeling her deep breaths and the tickle of her hair against his cheek. But when she'd rested her little head against his chest and held his hand, he'd done something really stupid—closed his eyes and imagined she belonged to him.

The images his mind conjured were so vivid, he could almost feel his palm smooth across June's tight, round belly, swollen with his child. He could almost hear the rustling of their other children fidgeting on the hard pew beside them. And when the daydream ended, the force of loss knocked his breath loose like he'd taken a soccer ball to the gut. He had no right to fantasize about a family with June—or anyone else for that matter. Like his parents before him, Luke would just ruin a child. And if all that weren't bad enough, he'd been forced to listen to the pastor drone on about love for another half hour. The old guy got one thing right: *I love you* were the most overused words on earth, and most people didn't understand or mean them.

Now what could've been a fine day was ruined by his pissy mood. Luke changed into jeans and a gray, long-sleeved T-shirt. Maybe he'd head over to get some work done on his house. A little physical labor might lift his spirits. Besides, time was getting away from him, and he needed to get the place sold. Maybe he'd never have June or a family of his own, but at least he'd have his land—something solid and secure that nobody could ever take away.

Pru called from downstairs, and Luke pulled his boots on and shoved his wallet in his back pocket. She'd probably give him hell for skipping out before supper, but he'd make it up to her another time. When he rushed into the kitchen and opened his mouth to say good-bye, he had to stop short to keep from knocking June over.

"For you," she said with a smile, holding out a steaming mug.

The tangy scent of spiced cider wafted up, making his mouth water. He accepted her gift, taking a reluctant sip while scanning her over the top of his cup. She'd changed into skintight jeans that hugged those wide hips for dear life, paired with a thin, pink sweater unbuttoned low enough that Luke could see cleavage if he looked at just the right angle. Which he did.

"To celebrate your first Sunday without getting the wooden spoon," she said, padding on bare feet to the kitchen table. She lifted the lid on Pru's wicker picnic basket and stuffed a handful of napkins inside.

"Thanks," he said, "but I'm on my way—"

"I packed lunch. We can eat by the pond." She slipped her little feet into a pair of flip-flops and nodded at the counter. "Grab that blanket, will you?"

Before Luke could say no, Pru walked in and waved two white envelopes in the air.

"You coming, Grammy?" June asked.

Pru shook her head. "I'm headin' back to the church hall. We're makin' pies and cookies to sell at the fair tomorrow." She handed both envelopes to Luke and patted his shoulder with her big, bony hand. "But take these with you."

He recognized his name scrawled in his own clumsy handwriting on one, and June's name in loopy cursive on the other.

"It's still a little early," Pru explained. "I wasn't s'posed to give you these till spring. But with June goin' back home in a couple weeks, heaven knows when we'll see her again. Thought you might like to open these together."

"Oh, no." June's shoulders drooped an inch or two, and her brown curls shook right along with her head. "I don't want mine. I already know what it says."

"What's in here?" Luke asked.

"Don't you remember?" June asked. "In senior English, Mrs. Moore made us write letters to ourselves ten years into the future. We had to predict where we'd be and all that."

"Junebug, I can't even remember what I ate for break-fast yesterday." He folded the letters in half and tucked them behind his wallet. "Sounds like fun though."

"Well, you have a blast. I'm throwing mine out."

"Must be some juicy stuff in there." He had no inten-tion of trashing it, at least not until he'd read it first. To hell with work, he'd play hooky with June the rest of the day. Like Pru had said, June would leave soon, and who knew when she'd come to visit again? He flipped the blanket around his neck and held the door open for her.

In Luke's perfect world, every day would feel exactly like this one—cool and crisp with the gentle sun barely warming the tops of his shoulders. It was that perfect, narrow window between seasons when he could spend all day outside and never feel uncomfortable. He'd been away from the pond too long and forgotten how much he missed the scents of wet earth and stagnant water. The smell of carefree youth. He pulled a deep breath through his nose and sighed slowly.

With the new chill in the air, Luke decided to spread the blanket in a patch of sunlight beside the tall reeds. While June knelt down and unpacked the picnic basket, he pulled his envelope out and tore it open. He didn't recall the assignment, but Luke had a feeling he'd written the bare minimum, and he didn't expect a long letter from his eighteen-year-old self. Once he unfolded the paper, he snickered. One short paragraph, just as he thought.

"*Hey there, you good-looking son of a bitch,*" Luke read. An immediate grin formed on his lips. That sounded a lot like him back then. "*Right now, you're bored as hell writing a dumb-ass letter to yourself. But since the teacher's watching, and you need this credit to graduate, I'll go ahead and tell your future. You're a Green Beret squadron leader, traveling the world to kick ass and take names. Your elite team of men has just been assigned a top secret mission to rescue a yacht-load of naked supermodels…*"—Luke laughed, while he crumpled the paper and tossed it into the wicker basket—"I'll spare you the rest. Jesus, was I really that much of an idiot?"

"No." June uncovered a plate of cold fried chicken. She snatched a drumstick and pointed it at him. "You were worse."

Luke scoffed, pretending she'd offended him, and

then stretched out on the blanket and dangled June's envelope in front of her face. "Let's read yours now."

"No! Give it here." She dove over a plastic bowl of potato salad and landed on top of him, before straddling his chest and making a frantic grab at the letter. "Mine's embarrassing."

"Sweet! I can't wait." Luke kept it out of her reach and laughed, while trying to find the leverage to flip her over. It didn't take long to roll June onto her back, and unfortunately, right into the potato salad.

She gasped like he'd just tossed her into a tub full of ice cubes. "My hair!" Mustard-yellow clumps matted June's curls against one side of her head, and Luke tried—swear to God, he really did—to keep a straight face. But he could only take so much, and eventually, he convulsed into hysterical laughter, flopping onto his back and holding his sides.

June reached beside her head and grabbed a handful of goop, then smeared it across the side of his face. "Not so funny now, is it?" But it still was, and he chuckled while using one finger to push a creamy bite into his mouth. She leaned over him to make another grab at the letter. "Gimme!"

Luke fisted the envelope and rolled to his feet before she could get a good grip on it. Then he backed away from the blanket a few paces. "No way. I let you listen to mine. Now it's your turn."

June groaned and started picking potato chunks from her hair. "You're so mean." She threw one glob in his direction, and it landed on his boot.

"Okay," Luke said, sliding his finger along the seal, "the moment of truth." He pulled June's stationery out and unfolded it, then cleared his throat and began. "*Dear June, if you're reading this, then ten years have passed. I hope you had fun in college and made some new friends...*" Luke rolled his eyes and shook his head. "Sounds just like a girl." He continued reading aloud. "*By now, you've earned your doctoral degree, and you're practicing psychology as Dr. Gallagher, PhD—*" Luke's eyes widened, frozen on the page. He glanced at June, whose face flushed ten shades of crimson. She looked like she wanted to crawl into a mud hole and die. He read the next few sentences in silence, which detailed their wedding—a casual ceremony at the pond in which she'd worn her mother's dress—and went on to describe each of their three children, all boys who looked exactly like him. June had predicted he'd leave the army after his first enlistment and then earn a living as a civil engineer.

Luke's throat tightened, and he swallowed a cherry-sized lump. No wonder she hadn't wanted him to read her letter. "Don't feel bad, Junebug," he said, trying to lighten the mood. "I didn't get what I wanted either."

Judging from the look of mortification in her wide, brown eyes, that wasn't what she'd wanted to hear, so he tried again. "You dodged a bullet. If this came true"—he held up the letter—"I'd've dragged you down with me, and trust me when I say it was a damned hard fall." Luke knelt on the blanket in front of June and laid the letter in her lap. "You deserve better than that. Wait for the right guy, and don't settle." The words burned his throat like bleach.

June tilted her head to the side. "You don't think very highly of yourself. Why is that?"

It seemed obvious to Luke, since he'd felt like a reject

his whole life. Hell, his own mama couldn't even stand him. He shrugged a shoulder. "I'm a screw-up, Junebug. Always have been."

"Well, I don't see it." June pushed the picnic basket into the grass and crawled forward until their knees touched. She took one of his hands in hers. "You could've done anything with the money Morris Howard left you, but you started a charity—"

"Nonprofit. And how'd you know about the money?"

"Grammy told me. And look at all the good you do, not just for people who need help with their homes, but for those guys who need a second chance. Look at what you did for Pauly last night. And you must have the patience of a saint to put up with Karl. I couldn't even stand him for one day."

"A lot of people do more good than me."

"But most people do less." She linked their fingers and gazed at him intently, despite the globs of potato salad beginning to dry in her hair.

As much as it warmed his heart to see June cared, Luke didn't appreciate people blowing sunshine up his butt crack. He knew who and what he was, and he was okay with it. "Stop trying to make me out to be some kind of hero. I'm still the same horse's ass I was when I wrote that letter."

"Hey." She leaned in and took his face firmly between her palms. "Nobody talks about my best friend like that." With fire burning behind her gaze, she inched forward, until Luke felt her warm breath on his skin. "Take it back."

Luke's stomach flashed hot and lurched against his ribs. June's eyes were on his mouth, while her hands and quickening breaths caressed his face. "What're you doing, Junebug?" His mind clogged with warring emotions, part of him needing her to pull back and an even larger part needing to gather her close and never let go.

"Take it back."

"Okay, I take it back."

The sliver of air between them crackled with electric tension. June eliminated the space, until her lips whispered against his, "Repeat after me. Luke Gallagher is a good man."

With his heart thundering inside his chest, he swallowed hard and stammered, "Luke Galla—"

And then she kissed him in one tender, simple motion that shook him to the soles of his feet. The touch of her lips was just as soft and sweet as he remembered, one gentle graze, and then another and another. Her fingertips tangled in his hair, grasping little handfuls and angling his face to deepen the kiss, and then her warm tongue swept across his lower lip more delicately than a water strider gliding along the surface of the pond. June's heady scent caught in his lungs, and before Luke could stop himself, he crushed her body against his chest, fisting her sweater in one hand and stroking her cheek with the other.

But he couldn't let this go too far, both for his sake and hers. The taste of June's wet mouth, her scent filling his nostrils, taunted him as things he could never have. And if her childhood crush was still burning, it wasn't fair to add kindling to the fire. Luke forced his hands to cup June's face, and he pushed her gently away, breaking the kiss.

"We'd better stop," he whispered in a shaky breath.

Her eyes fluttered open, and her lips, still glistening from their kiss, parted into a wide smile. She practically glowed from the inside out, so damn beautiful it made him ache. "I don't want to ruin things again," he said.

June's glow dimmed, and her smile faltered a moment, but she bit her lip and nodded. "Right." She remained in his arms a few seconds longer before backing up to dish out their lunch on white paper plates.

For the next several minutes, they ate in awkward silence, dining on cold chicken, leftover biscuits from breakfast, and coleslaw. A bullfrog croaked to announce his presence before splashing into the pond, and June brought a startled hand to her breast. That's when Luke knew he needed to break the ice.

"What'd you want to talk about last night?" he asked around a mouthful of chicken.

"Hmm?"

"Last night at Shooters. You said you wanted to talk."

"Oh, right." June lowered her bite of coleslaw and chewed the inside of her cheek instead. Clearing her throat, she began idly lifting containers and putting them back down.

"Spit it out, Junebug. There's nothing you can't say to me."

With a smirk, she opened her mouth to reply, but pressed her lips together, biting short whatever smart-ass barb she'd intended to launch. He wished she wouldn't bottle it up. He liked her sharp tongue, her biting remarks. Strange as it was, he liked her anger.

"It's no big deal," she said, avoiding his gaze. "But, about the other night at your house, before we almost... well, I want you to know there's no grudge. I'm not mad about what happened here." She gestured to the shady patch of grass where they'd had sex all those years ago. "But you were right when you said I hadn't really forgiven you yet. I worked through it though, and I can forgive you now."

"Oh." Luke glanced down and pushed a fork across his empty paper plate. "Well, I'm sorry, all the same."

"Me too." She rose to her knees and packed the clear, plastic containers inside Pru's basket. "I wasted almost ten years feeling hurt and angry, and it was selfish. But I want to start over. A clean slate, okay?"

Luke nodded, still focused on his plate. He'd been waiting for June's forgiveness nearly a decade, so why did his chest feel heavy all of a sudden? Why did his stomach feel knotted like a pretzel again? It made no sense, but Luke almost preferred June's passive-aggressive anger to her offer of a new beginning. It had been easy spending time with her knowing he'd never stood a chance, but now…somehow he felt uneasy. Afraid. But of what, he didn't know.

What in the name of Sam Hill was wrong with him?

Chapter 13

JUNE GAZED HIGH ABOVE THE SINK, WHERE THE wooden spoon hung from a weathered loop of twine attached to its handle. She caught herself unconsciously rubbing her bottom and grinned, marveling at the power that unholy torture device still held over her. Standing on tiptoe, she pulled it down and then used its blunt edge to scrape the inside of Gram's food processor.

She'd never made salsa from scratch before, let alone using freshly plucked garden chilies and tomatoes, but if the spicy, mouthwatering scent was any indication, she'd done a halfway decent job on her first try. She sprinkled a pinch of chopped cilantro into the bowl and dumped the mixture into a saucepan to let it simmer in a little olive oil.

She'd resolved to teach Luke how to love, and nothing said *I love you* like breakfast in bed—huevos rancheros, his favorite. It had taken some epic guilt-tripping for Gram to convince Luke to spend the night, and June didn't intend to waste this rare opportunity.

While the salsa bubbled, she coated Gram's skillet in butter and heated a flour tortilla for two minutes on each side, then slid the lightly browned flatbread onto a warming plate in the oven. After adding another hefty pat of butter to the skillet, she fried three eggs over easy, the way Luke had always liked them. She ladled some steaming salsa onto a plate, topped it with the warm tortilla, then added three flawlessly fried eggs. Another spoonful of sauce and a sprinkle of shredded cheddar, and the dish was complete. She even garnished it with a tiny bluebell from the backyard.

With a mug of piping hot black coffee in one hand and the world's most perfect breakfast in the other, June made her way to Luke's bedroom. Luckily, he hadn't closed his door completely, so she bumped it open with her hip.

"Oh, sugar." His room was empty. Seconds later, the squealing pipes in the hall bathroom told her he'd turned on the shower. So much for breakfast in bed. She could set her watch by Luke's showers—exactly ten minutes. Hoping the stewed salsa would keep his eggs warm, she placed the meal on Luke's nightstand and scrawled a short note on the back of a gas station receipt: *Happy Labor Day!* ~*June*

Since she'd already checked in with Esteban, June returned to her bedroom to dress, choosing a pair of jeans that covered the stings on her legs. Most days she didn't bother hiding them, but who'd want to buy food and drinks from someone who looked poxed? She slipped on her fitted, black Shooters T-shirt, pulled her hair into a ponytail, and then padded downstairs to the kitchen.

Gram had come in from the garden, and she stood behind the sink washing dishes while Lucky mewed and brushed against her calves.

"Come here, sweet kitty." June made kissing noises and crouched down to scratch behind Lucky's ears, but he hopped forward, rejecting her touch in favor of kneading Gram's house shoes with his front claws.

"I think I've been replaced." June grabbed a dish

towel and began drying. "Maybe I should leave him with you when I go back to Austin."

Because they stood so closely, June felt Gram's shoulder tense at the words. "Plenty 'a time to talk about that later," Gram said, clearly not ready to face June's return home. Truth be told, June wasn't ready to face it either. "I need a favor."

"What's that?" June asked.

"Can you take a couple hours off this week? I gotta have a procedure done, and I can't drive myself—"

"*What?*" June interrupted, fisting her dish towel. *Procedure* sounded so clinical and serious. "Are you okay?"

Gram waved her soapy hand. "I'm fine. Just somethin' Doc Benton orders once a year since my surgery."

"Surgery?" Taking a step back, June scanned Grammy from the top of her gray head to the tips of her fuzzy, blue slippers, checking for dull skin or bowed posture, anything that might indicate Gram was unwell. "When did you have surgery?"

"Hmm." Gram glanced out the window into the yard. "Goin' on seven years, I s'pose. Had some intestinal blockage."

"Wh—" The word died on June's tongue, choked out by disbelief. Grammy had gone under the knife, and nobody had bothered to tell her? Heat flushed June's cheeks—first in anger at her fellow townsfolk, and then at herself, because ultimately, she'd been the one to cut ties with Gram. Had Grammy been scared, or in a lot of pain? Who'd stood by her bedside to pray with her before the operation? Who'd brought flowers and cards afterward and driven her home to make sure she hadn't overdone it?

"It was nothin' serious," Gram reassured her, but June knew better. Competent physicians didn't recommend surgery without good cause. "So can you?" Gram asked. "Drive me?"

"Of course." June finished drying a cereal bowl, then set it on the counter. "But do you promise you're okay? Tell the truth." She'd always seen Gram as unshakable—a six-foot-tall pillar of fortitude—but maybe this giant of a woman wasn't as strong as she'd assumed. Maybe Gram was mortal after all.

"I'm fine, June," she said in her signature, stern tone. "I swear it on the Good Book."

June let out a breath. "Okay." Since both hands were wet, she leaned against Gram, giving her a side hug. "I'm glad. And I'm sorry I wasn't here for you, Grammy." But she *would* be here the next time her grandmother needed her.

"Psh!" She bumped June's hip. "Now, don't start that mess."

June smiled. The old Gram was back. "Yes, ma'am."

"You workin' Burl's booth today?"

"Yeah. I told him I'd run the booth for free, if he'd donate half the profits. Wasn't easy convincing him." She dried the wooden spoon and reached up to restore it to its proper place above the sink. "I thought I was tightfisted, but he pinches pennies so hard they bleed copper."

Gram grunted softly, her version of a snicker. "Where's the money goin'?"

"I figured I'd split it between God's Pantry and Helping Hands."

They worked quietly for the next few minutes,

letting the scratch of steel wool and the gentle slosh of water fill the silence. June peered out the window, taking in the clear, indigo sky and the morning sun playing across golden cornstalks. From her earlier visit to the garden, it seemed fall had decided to unpack its bags and stay awhile.

She looked forward to spending the day outdoors at the fair, even if it meant working. Maybe she'd abandon her post long enough to enjoy some cotton candy and ride the bumper cars. Too bad she couldn't convince Luke to take the afternoon off and play, but he intended to celebrate Labor Day by laboring. No surprise there.

"What about you?" June asked. "Are you selling pumpkin butter, or making the sandwiches?" Gram's church was famous for their five-alarm barbeque beef sandwiches. Their banner hadn't changed since June's childhood: *Come for the Brimstone BBQ, stay to be saved! Because your mouth should burn, not your soul!* June smiled to herself, realizing Burl's booth-o-wickedness would probably face the church tent from the opposite side of the field, where the county lines changed from dry to wet. A showdown between sinners and saints.

"Well, I'm not rightly sure." Gram drained the sink, shook her wet hands, and then wiped them on the front of her checkered, blue apron. "I'd kinda thought about—"

"Hey," Luke interrupted, clomping into the kitchen in his heavy work boots. His damp hair dripped down the side of his neck, and he seemed more rested than she'd seen him in a week—skin bright and freshly shaven, his clear, green eyes free from the weight of exhaustion. He held the empty breakfast plate in one hand while sipping his coffee. "I'm heading out." And then he walked right past her, set the plate in the sink, and turned to go without another word.

June's heart sank an inch. He didn't even mention the breakfast. He'd obviously eaten it, and there was no way he'd missed her note.

"Did you like it?" she asked in a voice much more fragile than she'd intended. "I got up at six to start making the sals—"

"Sorry." Still facing away, his back stiffened, the wide muscles of his shoulders stretching that thin white T-shirt tight enough to bust a seam. "I didn't thank you for the eggs."

"Well, you still haven't." Heat flushed June's face again, heart thumping as hurt morphed into anger. But just as June geared up to say, *See if I ever make huevos rancheros for you again, dillhole*, she remembered the pastor's words. This would take time. And patience.

Luke turned and made a grand, faux gesture of gratitude, flourishing his hand and bowing low like a knight in shining Timberlands. "A thousand pardons, your grace." The hint of a smile played on his lips, and it was the only thing holding her back from flicking his face with the dish towel. "From the bottom of my soul, thank you for the eggs."

"You're welcome, jerk."

"Uh, Lucas," Grammy began, pausing to untie her apron. "What're your plans for the day?"

"Same as the last time you asked. Installing granite countertops in the kitchen."

Grammy froze, then jabbed one finger in the air. "You gettin' smart with me?"

"No, ma'am." Shaking his head, Luke leaned against the refrigerator and tried to hide a smirk.

"I gotta favor to ask." She draped her apron over the back of a chair, then slowly lowered onto the wood seat with a groan. Bringing one hand to her hip, she massaged in circles, while her face contorted in pain. June gasped, remembering the conversation they'd had a few minutes earlier, but just as she opened her mouth to ask what was wrong, Gram locked eyes with her and winked. *Grammy actually winked?* "Need your help today," she continued, "at the church tent."

"Oh, no, no, no. I can't, Pru. I already wasted one day—"

"It's this hip-a-mine," she interrupted. "Actin' up again. It's never been right since that time you left the floor wet an' I slipped 'n fell. Remember?" She groaned again and nodded at Luke. "You dropped them ice cubes, never cleaned 'em up."

Luke heaved a sigh, his shoulders rounding forward as he deflated like an old beach ball. "That was a million years ago, but yeah, I remember."

"Sure would be nice to stay home 'n rest. Workin' the fair's tough on my back, and now, with this hip—"

"Jesu—uh, I mean, jeeze, Pru." Luke squeezed the bridge of his nose, and June wondered if she should tell him he was being played like a royal flush. "Can't you get someone from church to fill in for you?"

"We're spread mighty thin, Lucas. There's the bake sale, cookin' up all that beef, collectin' money, the mission work…"

"What about you?" Luke said, glancing at June with his brows raised in hope. "Come on, Junebug. Do me a solid here."

June pointed to her T-shirt, where *Shooters Tavern* looped across her chest in red embroidery. "I'm selling the devil's brew today. Sorry." But she wasn't sorry, not at the prospect of sharing another day with Luke. Her time in Sultry Springs was limited, and she'd make the most of the opportunity Gram had just tossed into her lap. Maybe she could even drag him to the bumper cars. No, the Ferris wheel—that sounded more romantic. Plus, he couldn't run away when belted in a seat and suspended sixty feet above the ground. "But, hey," she said. "If you're sticking around, can I get a ride? I need to pick up a ton of stuff from Shooters, and it won't fit in my car. I'd planned on borrowing Trey's truck, but this way I won't have to."

Luke closed his eyes and locked his thumb and forefinger around his temples. "What time's your shift, Pru?"

Grammy glanced at the digital time display on the microwave, and June could practically see the wheels turning in her grandmother's wily mind as she calculated how long it would take Luke to drive to Hallover and back. "Noon to six."

Well done, Grammy, you evil genius. It was ten o'clock now, not enough time to make the round-trip and get any work done at his house before twelve. June felt a distant pinprick of guilt as she watched Luke hang his head in defeat, but she vowed to increase her efforts and get his property on the market in plenty of time. Besides, in the grand scheme of things, what difference would one day make?

"Fine," Luke grumbled. "But I'm gettin' a free sandwich out of this." Pointing to June, he added, "Beer too. I'm gonna need it."

"Deal. Let's go." June grabbed her purse and planted a kiss on Gram's cheek. "Hope you feel better, Grammy. Call Luke's cell if you need anything. Mine doesn't get service out here."

"Mmm-hmm." Gram gave another conspiratorial wink. "You kids behave yourselves. Y'hear?"

Pressing her shoulder against the back door, June heaved forward with all her weight, while simultaneously jiggling the rusted key inside its lock. "Burl needs to replace this dead bolt," she complained. There was a trick to getting the door open, but she hadn't mastered it yet.

"Burl needs to replace a hell of a lot more than that. Here, move over." Luke nudged her aside and took hold of the doorknob, then lifted hard and pulled back. "Now try."

The bolt slid aside easily, and they stepped inside the veritable minefield that was Shooters. June kicked aside a fallen pool stick and wrinkled her nose at the foul potpourri of odors emanating from the men's room.

"God bless," she said, regarding dozens of unwashed beer mugs—some still half full—that covered the back tables. "There'll be rings all over the wood now." The staff wasn't supposed to leave before cleaning the glassware and tidying the place. She did her part Saturday night, but nobody else seemed to give half a darn, least of all the owner. What a waste.

"This place is a dump. Looks even worse in the daytime." Luke flipped on the lights, then inspected a few chairs until he found one clean enough for his jean-clad backside. "It's a good thing Burl doesn't have any competition around here."

"You know, he's not a bad guy. I actually like him a lot, but he's a terrible businessman." She swept her hand toward the pool tables, covered in a dusting of peanut shells and blue chalk. "He tries to save money by not hiring a cleaning crew, but it hurts him in the end."

"I dunno, Junebug. This place stays packed."

"Right, but not with the kind of clientele I'd want." She steered around stray chairs and hopped over an errant eight ball, until she reached the bar. "If he spruced this place up, he could draw a more upscale crowd and raise his drink prices. That's what I'd do."

"Uh-huh." Luke snorted a laugh. "You'd fill the joint with jellyfish and classical music. Maybe add a library off to the side and make everyone wear dinner jackets."

"Don't knock my jellies. Luquos'll be the hottest bar in Austin, you'll see." Ignoring his teasing, June fished around under the bar until she found the supply of plastic cups. Someone had moved them. God, were these people allergic to organization?

She carried the boxes to the front door and then paused, feeling an odd tingling along her scalp, an intuition of being watched. The hairs on her forearms stood, and chills puckered the surface of her skin. June didn't need to turn around to confirm it; she felt Luke's gaze on her body like a physical touch brushing her skin. When she glanced over her shoulder, he'd dipped his head low, studying her beneath his lashes with a simmering intensity that didn't seem at all friendly. Something had shifted in him, a change so abrupt that she replayed their conversation to make sure she hadn't said anything offensive.

"Are you mad at me?" she asked.

An invisible hypnotist snapped his fingers and awakened Luke, restoring his cheer. Well, maybe cheer was too strong a word. Restoring his regular cynical attitude. Lifting his chin and masking whatever emotion had just played across his features, he said, "No. Why would I be?"

"I don't know. You were glaring at me just now."

"Nope. Just thinking." And then he kicked his boots onto the table, folded his hands behind his head, and flagrantly changed the subject. "So, what would you do with this place?"

Luke's behavior made as much sense as advanced trigonometry, but June let it go and scanned the room. She'd actually given this subject some thought, so it didn't take long to form a reply. "Well, first I'd close down for a month to refinish the floors and all the table-tops. Then put a few coats of fresh paint on the walls and ceiling, new toilets—they overflowed all Saturday night—and I'd remodel the bathrooms. Reconfigure the table layout to clear space for a dance floor. And I *would* add a room, but not a library. Something to draw more income, like poker machines or a mechanical bull—"

"*A what?*"

"Sure. Make people sign a waiver, then charge them ten dollars a ride. I'll bet that'd even draw a crowd in Austin. Of course, it's not right for Luquos, but it's perfect for Shooters." June shrugged and trekked toward the back room, calling over her shoulder, "Doesn't matter though. Burl's too much of a tight-ass—oops, I mean tightwad—to consider it."

She unlocked the door to the storage room and then rifled through the cabinets and drawers until she found a steel ladle. Luke joined her, leaning one hip against the chipped, Formica countertop that had once been white, now darkened with age and neglect.

Luke nodded at the industrial-sized, walk-in refrigerator and the adjoining freezer. "So this is where Trish freezes Trey's beer mugs."

Opening the heavy refrigerator door, June laughed and walked inside to check the sangria that had been marinating since Saturday night. The cool air made her shiver. "From what I hear, she freezes a lot of guys' mugs, if you catch my drift." June typically didn't judge, but she liked Trey and didn't want to see him hurt. Not emotionally, anyway. June had already banged him up physically.

"Huh. I'd've never guessed it." He cleared away a stack of old pizza boxes and hopped up to sit on the counter. "What're you doing in there?"

"Checking my sangria." She flipped open the cooler's lid, dipped the ladle inside, and poured a sample into her plastic cup.

"That sounds naughty."

"You would think so." She took a small sip and swirled the cool wine over her tongue, considering the citrus flavor, the sweetness. The fruit juices had mingled nicely, especially the berries, but she preferred a bit more tang. "Look in that cabinet and hand me a can of pineapple juice." She pointed above Luke's head. "I don't usually take shortcuts like this, but there's not enough time to do it right."

After he handed it over, she popped the lid and poured it into the cooler, then stirred the whole batch. The next sip was just right, or at least as good as it would get using Burl's cheap house Shiraz and frozen fruit.

"Can I ask you something?" Luke said, examining her again, but with less severity.

"Sure. Hey, try this." June extended her cup, and Luke wrinkled his lips in suspicion.

"It looks like a frou-frou, girly drink."

"I promise you won't grow boobs. But even if you did, just imagine how much fun you'd have with your new toys."

He scooted off the counter and joined her, peering into the cup like it might contain one of those spring-loaded, foam snakes that popped out of novelty prank cans. "What's in it?"

"Let's see." She ticked off an itemized list on her fingers. "Eye of newt, toe of frog, scale of dragon, hair of dog. Oh, and ginger ale." She palmed the hard contours of his chest and gave a playful push, but it didn't budge him, and she lingered there a moment, enjoying the thrill that charged her fingertips. "Basically, it's fruit, wine, and a little brandy. Don't be such a baby."

She moved forward, advancing slowly until Luke's breath stirred the loose tendrils of hair framing her forehead. She took his warm, rough hand and curled it around the drink, peering into his widened eyes and stroking the soft, furry skin of his forearm. It felt so good to touch him again, like stepping into the sun's heated embrace after a long, frigid winter. Since their kiss yesterday, he'd stayed well out of reach, and she'd felt the abrupt loss like a blanket ripped away on an icy morning.

The scents of shaving cream, soap, and Luke mingled together and dizzied her mind. He glanced at her mouth and swallowed, his tanned throat bobbing visibly above his white T-shirt collar. When his tongue darted between his lips, June's blood boiled and rushed through her veins. She rose onto her toes, lifting her face to meet his, hungry for the taste of his mouth. Just one taste…

"Junebug," he whispered and closed his eyes. Then he shook his head and stepped back, gently tugging free of her grasp and restoring the boundary he'd set yesterday. "No."

The air left her lungs in a whoosh, and she sank back onto her heels, trying to conceal the heat of embarrassment flushing her cheeks. Luke was a shadowboxer, guarding his heart and delivering a sucker punch right to June's sternum. Willing her pulse to slow, she cleared her throat and knelt beside her batch of sangria. She recalled Pastor McMahon's words: *Love never quits, never abandons*…but replaying them in her mind didn't ease the sting of rejection.

"Try the drink." She stirred the mixture absently, watching apple and orange slices bob to the surface. "I think you'll like it, if you give it a chance." She was talking about more than just the wine, and he probably knew it.

Though facing away, she heard him drain the cup. "It's good," he said softly. "Just not right for me."

Luke's own veiled message brought moisture to her eyes, and she spoke in a rush, before her throat thickened any further. "What did you want to ask me?"

"Why do you do this?" When she glanced up in alarm, he added, "The alcohol, I mean."

After hooking the ladle over the edge of the cooler, she closed the lid. Another shiver danced over her flesh, and she stepped out of the fridge and then shut the thick, metal door behind her. "Burl's donating half the proceeds today. The more I sell, the more—"

"No. I mean why'd you choose this line of work? The way you talk about your bar—Luquos this and Luquos that—it's like religion to you. I know you said you liked bartending better than psychology, but considering what happened to your parents..." He trailed off, his tone growing apologetic, almost backpedaling. "I know the rumors aren't true, but still."

"*Do* you know the rumors aren't true?" June grabbed her hips and took a defensive stance. Of all the people in this town talking shit—oops, sugar—about her mama and daddy, she hadn't expected hearing this from her best friend. "The accident was just that—an accident. I've seen their death certificates."

"Hey," he held his palm forward in an obvious attempt at damage control. "I'm not trying to say—"

"You ever seen a Texas death certificate?"

Luke mirrored her pose and shook his head.

"There's a little box," she said as she demonstrated with her hands, "that asks if alcohol caused the death. And you know what it says on both their forms?" Without giving him a chance to reply, she spat, "It says no!"

"Jesus, Junebug, I believe you. I'm just sayin'—"

"Why would I follow in their sinful footsteps? Is that what you're just sayin'?"

"No...well, kind of, but I wouldn't put it that way. It's just, with your grandma and how she raised you, and with all the talk about your folks...Ah, shit." He waved a hand dismissively and then raked it through his shaggy, brown hair. "I'm makin' a mess of this." After a heavy sigh, he reached for her fingers and then pulled back, seeming to think better of it. "Look. We both know what the name Gallagher means around here.

Both my parents were trash, and there's no point trying to deny it. I don't care what people think, but at the same time, I…" Shaking his head, he went silent.

"You do care," she answered for him, feeling her anger soften. "A little."

"Maybe." He shrugged. "So, it made me wonder why you'd go into the bar business, all things considered."

When he put it that way, the question didn't seem so offensive. Perhaps she'd overreacted. She relaxed her posture, slipping her hands into her back pockets. "Well, first of all, I'm good at it. Everyone needs to feel like they're good at something. Look at you—building houses and running a charity."

"Nonprofit."

"Whatever. Using your hands to create a home, that's your talent. Maybe I'll never build a house or be a legendary cook like Grammy, but you know what? When people get married in Austin, they come see *me* before they visit the florist or the bakery. Because they know I'll come up with a special drink for their wedding that people won't stop talking about for years. You know how that makes me feel?"

Luke nodded, a sympathetic grin curving the edges of his mouth. "I can imagine."

"And you gotta love the magic of a good drink. There's power in alcohol—it boosts your confidence, helps you relax, makes you more affectionate—and I like harnessing that power. Show me something else, well, something *legal*, that can do all those things." Luke started to reply, but she cut him off with one important clarification. "But I don't condone getting wasted, and I can't stand sloppy drunks. That's one of the reasons I'm passionate about Luquos. It's a classy place for people to enjoy one or two cocktails, not some pit stop along the bar crawl."

"Yeah." His gaze flickered away, and he studied the staffing schedule taped to the cabinet near his head. He trailed his index finger down the spreadsheet, but he didn't seem to read the words printed there. "I can tell it means a lot to you." A fog settled over him, shifting the mood once again. Abruptly, he turned and brushed his hands together as if preparing for hard work. "Well, that answers my question. What needs to go? That cooler, right?"

Like a kick to the head, June realized what had been eating Luke. It was Luquos—the common denominator in his changing moods. She'd mentioned it while digging for cups behind the bar, and again, just now, resulting in a Jekyll and Snide reaction. "Uh-huh. And two kegs, plus ten gallons of hard iced tea. There's a dolly behind the door." She wanted to ask why he resented her dream, but he'd only deny it. Could he fear losing her when she returned home? That didn't make sense, because Austin was only a six-hour drive.

"Hey, did you hear me?"

"Hmm?"

Luke had the refrigerator door open, and he pointed to an army of shiny kegs lining the inside wall. "Coors or Bud?"

"Bud."

"Okay. Let's load up and get the hell outta here. The sooner we get to the fairgrounds, the sooner that 'magical' Bud"—he made sarcastic air quotes—"can transform me into a brave, relaxed, lovable saint."

—∿∿—

When Luke turned twenty-one, his friends had taken him out for a night of carousing, the standard rite of passage for any guy that age. They'd done Grape Granstaff shots all night long until he'd passed out in the bar bathroom, and then he'd spent the next twenty-four hours spewing like a geyser. To this day, the scent of Grape Pucker turned his stomach and gave him the dry heaves.

He was beginning to feel the same disdain for the reek of stewed tomatoes, chili powder, and scorched cow.

He'd suffered the last few hours in assembly line hell, and before that, roasted right along with the giant slab of beef on the rotisserie. Since most of the church members were busy scouring the crowd for souls to save, he was the only man in the tent, and apparently, possession of a penis qualified him for grill duty. Even worse, old Ms. Bicknocker had made him tuck his hair under a shower cap while basting and braising, so the fire's heat had soaked into his body and traveled right to his head, where the plastic trapped it inside. He'd felt like a giant condom.

And sweet Jesus, the preaching. Those little church ladies thumped a mean Bible. Praise the Almighty for Trey. He hadn't done a lick of work, but Luke was glad for the company of someone who didn't want to dunk him in water and scrub away his sins. Luke preferred his sins intact, thank you kindly.

He glanced at his buddy, who'd kicked back on a folding chair in the shade with his bad leg resting on a crate of paper plates. Trey held a sandwich between his palms and shook his head in awe, gazing at the bread lovingly like he was about to plunge his face between a woman's thighs, instead of his supper. He sank into the bun and groaned with pleasure.

"Hey, man," Luke said. "You and that sandwich want a little privacy?"

"God *day-uum*, that's hot!" Trey slapped his cast, leaving behind a brown, greasy handprint. "But tastier than a motherfu—" He shut his pie hole when Ms. Bicknocker whipped her head around and pruned her mouth in disgust.

"Beg your pardon, ma'am." Removing his straw cowboy hat, Trey dipped his head and smiled in contrition, bringing out those deceptively innocent dimples. "I'll repent later. Promise." Then he added a little wink, and the stodgy broad blushed and went back to dishing out plates.

"You make me sick, you know that?" If Luke was ever reincarnated, he hoped to come back with a pair of get-out-of-jail-free cards built into his cheeks.

Trey ignored him, returning his full attention to the lover between his hands, and Luke tossed his steel serving tongs aside, figuring he'd earned a few minutes of rest. He reached up, stretching his aching back, and thought of poor Pru. As much as he hated being here, he was glad she wasn't on her feet all day.

After collapsing onto the grass beside Trey's chair, Luke pulled on his ball cap, leaned back on his elbows, and watched the Miss Sultry County contestants parade by in sparkly, rhinestone-studded pageant gowns that probably outweighed the girls wearing them. No doubt heading to the stage on the other side of the field, they hitched up their skirts and teetered across the muddy terrain, bits of loose straw sticking to their high heels. Seemed like a lot of trouble to go through for a shot at a cheap sash and a silly crown.

The blaring, amplified twang of a steel guitar came to an end as the live band wrapped up a song and took five, and now Luke could hear the distant screams coming from the Tilt-A-Whirl. If he peered at an angle, he could just make out the Ferris wheel's twinkling lights circling above the treetops.

Come take a break, June had said earlier. *Let's go on some rides. The Ferris wheel!*

Luke wanted a ride, all right, but not here at the fair. His favorite attraction had soft curves and wide, brown eyes that burned everywhere they touched. But no safety bar could keep him from free-falling if he succumbed to that quick thrill. He knew a few minutes inside June's funhouse would leave him with whiplash—shaken, hurt, and, in the end, alone.

Saying no to her sucked so hard he had a hickey on his soul, but it wasn't fair to lead her on when he didn't have anything to offer. He only wished she weren't so sweet to him. It'd be a whole lot easier rejecting her advances that way. Rolling to the side, he reached into his back pocket and pulled out the crumpled, withered bluebell she'd given him with breakfast.

Even cold, those had been the best damn Mexican eggs he'd ever eaten, but when he'd gone downstairs to thank her, something had happened he couldn't explain. He'd stood there outside the kitchen and watched her absently drying dishes while gazing out the window. She'd looked so pretty and relaxed, at home in her ponytail and little bare feet, that his breath had caught. The words he'd prepared evaporated off his tongue, just like that.

"Hey." Trey pointed at the keepsake in Luke's hand. "What's that? A *flower*?"

Luke shoved it back in his pocket. "It's nothing." Before Trey had a chance to give him hell, Luke stood and peered across the main thoroughfare about thirty yards away, where June manned the Shooters tent. A few curls had come loose from her hair elastic, stirring against her cheeks with the breeze. He couldn't hear her tinkling laugh, but he watched as she gabbed and giggled with a group of guys. Narrowing his eyes, he identified one of them as the douche she used to date in high school, Tom something-or-other. That tool had always tried getting in her pants, and it looked like he'd decided to give it another shot.

"No effing way," he muttered. The son of a bitch was doing *the lean*, curling his hand around the tent pole behind June's head and angling his body until it practically covered hers. It was universal male body language for: *Back off, all you bastards, this one's coming home with me tonight.*

"Trey, stand up a minute." From behind him, Luke heard his buddy grunt, hoist out of his chair, and limp over. "Do me a favor."

"What?"

"Take your folding chair and gimp on over there." He pointed to the Shooter's banner. "Hang out with June awhile and keep an eye on her."

Trey tipped his hat back and shielded his eyes, gazing across the crowd. "Who're those guys?"

"Some assholes from high school." One of the men swayed in place, and Luke wondered how much they'd had to drink. "Probably tanked."

"Looks like they're havin' a little rendez-booze." Trey clapped him on the back and grinned. "Never fear, buddy. I'll watch out for *Joooonbug*."

"Thanks, man. Tell her your beer's on me."

"I'd already planned to."

Luke observed Trey as the near-cripple limped across the field, folding chair in one hand and wooden cane in the other. A couple minutes later, he reached June's booth, where he spoke animatedly with the group of men, waving his hands and pointing to God-knows-what. He wrapped one arm around June's shoulders, pulling her tightly against his chest and kissing the top of her head. Luke's gut clenched at the sight, but he knew what his friend was doing—sending a message for her admirers to back off. Then Trey lowered onto his seat and propped his leg on an empty keg that had fallen on its side. After a few minutes, the mini reunion broke up, and the guys wandered off. Luke gave Trey a thankful wave and got back to work.

Before his break ended, Luke made his way to the Porta-John encampment. He passed the dart game, smirking at the stuffed snakes and knockoff Scooby-Doo prizes that cost less than what the carnie charged for one play. When the petting zoo and pony rides came into view, he veered away, figuring he'd suffered enough foul smells for one day, and instead, paused at the fried dough stand to buy a funnel cake.

By the time Luke arrived at the "restrooms," he'd just sucked the last bit of powdered sugar from his fingers.

He took his place in line behind a few pot-bellied red-necks, wishing he could just take a leak in the woods the way God intended.

A few moments later, a nearby voice caught his attention.

"You get a load of Mae-June?"

"I'd like to shoot a load *in* Mae-June."

Luke's vision went black for a split second, and then he scanned the crowd to identify the man he was about to pummel six feet into the ground.

"Dude, I've got dibs on that tail. We've got unfin-ished business from senior year." It was that wanker, Tom what's-his-name, and he was about to freaking die. "And you know what they say—the best way to get over one woman is to get under a new one."

That's right, he'd heard something about Tom's wife dumping his ass for a chick. Luke couldn't blame her. He'd rather switch teams than join DNA with a buck-toothed dickhead like that. He left his place in line and stalked across the straw-covered mud to where Tom and two friends—one tall and lanky, the other built like a tank—huddled beside a corn dog stand. Luke's heart pounded so hard he felt it in his teeth, and his vision tunneled, blocking out everything but his enemy's pale face, the arrogant set of his lips, his shifty eyes.

"Never happening, man." The tank shook his head and laughed.

"A few shots of tequila turn a *no* into a *yes* real fast." Tom elbowed the tall man. "Besides, the acorn doesn't fall far from the tree. If she's anything like her drunk whore of a mama, I'll be tappin' that fat ass three ways from Tuesd—"

"Hey, asshole!" Luke marched close enough to make out Tom's acne scars. He grabbed a handful of the man's plaid, button-down shirt and slammed him hard against the corn dog trailer's tin wall. As much as he'd love to sucker punch the prick, that was how sissies fought. Luke wanted the satisfaction of beating Tom senseless like a man, fair and square.

"What the fu—" The jerk's brows lowered, and the smell of stale beer rushed Luke's face as all the wind left Tom's lungs. Then he recovered enough to ask, "Luke Gallagher?"

"That's right." He released his grip and backed up a pace. "We're gonna go over there"—pointing to a freshly mown field used for overflow parking—"and I'm gonna put my foot so far up your ass, you'll taste leather for a month."

Tom held two palms forward in preemptive surrender. "Dude, what the hell?"

Snatching Tom's elbow, Luke towed him toward the fight zone. "You won't touch June! Don't even look at her, you hear me?" He spun around and grabbed Tom's cheeks in a vise between his fingers and thumb, driving his point home. "You won't be talkin' shit about her when I'm done with you."

Before Luke could take another step, Tom's buddies bum-rushed him, grabbing his arms and dragging him backward, while their friend wriggled free. But these meddling jerks weren't trying to break up the fight—they intended to hold him, so Tom could have a free go. Luke yanked his arms, but the tank holding him tightened his grip, digging steely fingers into his biceps, and the tall one was stronger than he looked. Tom took his time straightening his shirt, emboldened by this new turn of events. With a cocky grin, he glanced at the crowd beginning to draw.

"You want some-a-this?" The pansy swept his hands along his own body. "I got somethin' for your punk ass, Gallagher." Then he made a fist and pulled back, winding up like a baseball pitcher to deliver an epic blow to Luke's face.

In a flash, Luke leaned into the guys behind him and hoisted his legs off the ground. Kicking out with all his strength, he landed the heels of his heavy work boots right into Tom's gut. The bastard bent at the waist, making a cartoonish "oof" noise while his eyes went so wide they nearly popped out.

As Tom crumpled to his knees and started retching half-digested beer onto the grass, Luke threw his head to the side, clocking the tank in the bottom lip with his skull. The guy's grip slackened just enough for Luke to wrench one arm free and use it for an uppercut to the kidney. Without wasting a second, he turned to the tall man, but not quickly enough to avoid the fist that caught him under the jaw.

Luke's head snapped back, his ball cap flew off, and he saw a flash of light as bolts of pain shot up his temples like bottle rockets. The tall guy gasped and drew his fist to his chest, cradling it in pain, and Luke took full advantage, twisting his upper body for maximum impact and punching the fool in the belly. Unlike his opponent, Luke knew to hit the soft parts—it did just as much damage without the risk of breaking a hand. Luke glanced up at the tank and lunged, barely missing a jab intended for his nose. The guy's hand connected with a spectator's cheek, and then a few new bodies joined the brawl as the stranger's friends jumped in.

The sounds of cussing, grunts, and flesh smacking flesh filled the tight space. Luke ducked his head and backed away from the chaos. He'd accomplished his goal of shutting Tom down and had no interest in recreational ass-whooping. He was too old for that shit. Scanning the ground for his ball cap, he spotted it beneath someone's sneaker, halfway between a patch of mud and a puddle of vomit. To hell with it, he had three more at home.

As he strolled back to the Baptist tent, Luke glanced over his shoulder, just in time to see a body fly into a Porta-John. It teetered over, and dozens of men scurried away, as if the plastic walls had loosed a herd of bulls.

Luke shook his head and stroked his throbbing jaw. Leave it to June to wreak havoc from a quarter of a mile away.

Chapter 14

AUTUMN'S COOL KISS TEASED SULTRY SPRINGS FOR A few fleeting days before buckling under summer's last stand, and once again, temperatures soared into the upper nineties. With a heavy sigh, June pulled the bottom of her tank top up over her face to blot away the last hour's worth of perspiration. She closed her eyes and imagined the cool, air-conditioned office back at church, where she'd balanced donation ledgers two days ago, and a shiver rolled down her spine. Actually, that was sweat, not a shiver. Lovely. What, exactly, had possessed her to get back on the Jenkins project?

"Hey, *Joooonbug*," Trey called from his reclining lawn chair in the shade. He held his glass in the air and shook it so the ice tinkled inside. "Can I get a refill?"

Oh, that's right. She'd insisted on serving as Trey's right-hand-woman, so he could supervise the Jenkins crew, allowing Luke to spend his days on his investment property. How very thoughtful of her, not that anyone noticed. Certainly not Luke.

For the past several days, June had tried to follow Pastor McMahon's advice on demonstrating love: listening patiently to Luke as he detailed problems with rotted baseboards and stubborn inspectors, supporting Luke by scrubbing and painting his home, and most of all, forgiving him for the past and believing the best about him. But if anything, he'd only become more distant, declining to join her for supper and going out of his way to avoid any physical contact between them. She hadn't expected instant results, but some little sign of progress would've been nice.

When June reached out to take Trey's glass, he yanked it back playfully. But after spending all afternoon staining the new deck, June's shoulders ached, her skin burned, and she wasn't in the mood to play.

"You want that drink or not?" she snapped, rolling her shoulders to release the tension. The odds of Luke reciprocating that massage she'd given him last week were about a trillion to one.

Trey let out a long, low whistle and tapped his fingers against his plaster cast, which had darkened to a grubby gray with dust and sweat. "I can wait." Then he smiled and flashed those adorable dimples, and June felt like the biggest shrew alive for getting snippy with a virtual cripple…especially since she'd had a hand in his fall.

"Sorry, I'm just cranky today." She took his glass, and this time he released it without a fight. "Tea or Coke?"

"You heading over to Luke's tonight?" he asked, ignoring her question. "He's been in a sour mood too."

"I noticed." June sat down in the grass beside Trey and held his cold, wet glass to the back of her neck. "His family's land means a lot to him. Maybe he's getting nervous about the auction."

"Oh, I know he is. But that's not what's bugging him." Trey picked up his clipboard and flipped through the pages. "I think he's in love."

June's stomach jumped into her throat. She wanted to believe Trey, but she knew from experience how dangerous it was to get her hopes up.

"With," he continued, pulling her time sheet from the stack, "a woman he thinks is too good for him. Someone unattainable."

"What?" June's backbone locked. "That's ridiculous."

Trey shrugged and gave a *you're-preaching-to-the-converted* look. "I think you should spend more time over there. During the day. You know, before you get all hot and cranky."

"I can't. My service hours have to come from charity or nonprofit work. Besides, who'll help you out here?"

"Karl's an imbecile, but even he can fetch me a glass of Coke now and then." He clicked his pen and scrawled something on her time sheet. "And lookie here. You've already served eighty hours over the next two weeks. Doesn't that fulfill your requirement? I guess that frees up your days."

For a few stunned seconds, June stared into Trey's smiling blue eyes and couldn't say a word. He was willing to falsify a court document—total forgery—so she could get closer to Luke. "Why're you doing this? I don't know what the penalty is, but—"

"He's my friend. And I'd like to see him quit acting like a dickweed."

"Well…" June trailed off. Could this really work? She'd just met with the judge yesterday, so she didn't have to worry about her time sheet looking suspicious until their next appointment, and then she could claim to have left it at home. It was dishonest, illegal, and probably a bad idea. Anything for love, right? And, heck, she could make up for it working on the church newsletter at night. "Thanks, Trey! I owe you one."

———

Two hours later, after June had stopped home to shower, change into clean work clothes, and pack Luke's favorite lunch, she stood on the front stoop of the Hallover house and admired the brand-new door Luke had installed. Solid cherry with stained glass panels, a nice touch. She rang the doorbell three times in quick succession and let herself in.

"Back here," Luke called over the radio in the kitchen. "I want the estimate for the four bedrooms upstairs." Then he went back to singing "Rock You Like a Hurricane" with the Scorpions.

"I'm not the carpet guy." June tossed her bag next to a power sander on the glossy granite countertop.

With a cordless drill in one hand and a cabinet door in the other, Luke glanced up from the floor in shock. For one nearly invisible split second, June saw excitement flash in his eyes, but then his expression hardened just as quickly, and he turned back to the cabinet base. "What're you doing here? You're supposed to be helping Trey." He picked up a few screws and held them between his lips.

"Well, hello to you too." She pulled a foil-wrapped sandwich from her bag and waved it in the air. "I made your favorite. Peanut butter and molasses."

Luke said nothing while he drilled each screw into the hinge. From the radio, a heavy metal song she'd never heard before blared out, and the screeching guitar riffs were more pleasing to her ears than Luke's silence. It went on and on, and June wondered if she should simply go upstairs and get to work. Then he opened and closed the cabinet door until he seemed satisfied it was level and muttered, "I already ate." He started to elaborate, but changed his mind and moved on to the next set of hinges.

Pulling a deep, steady breath into her lungs, June counted backward from ten to zero and reminded herself to be patient. "Okay," she said, trying to manufacture some cheer. "I'll just leave it here for later."

"You didn't answer my question," Luke said with one screw dangling from the corner of his mouth.

June tiptoed over tools and cords to join him on the floor. She scooped up some screws and handed them to Luke one at a time. He shot her an unappreciative glance that said he'd much rather do it himself, but she insisted. "Trey didn't need me around," she said, "so he sent me out here."

"And you left him?"

"He's fine. I wouldn't have come otherwise."

"Trey shouldn't have done that." Luke snatched a screw from her fingers with exaggerated force. "He doesn't have the authority."

"Well, he did anyway. And he fudged my time sheet, so I can spend all my days helping you around here. Won't that be *fun*?" Then she flipped her hand over, slamming the silvery hardware back against the floor. "I'm going upstairs to get a first coat done in the master bedroom." *Call me when you pull the stick out of your ass.* June wrangled her tongue and managed to keep that last comment to herself.

While June spread a plastic tarp over the bare wood floor in the master bedroom, she tried to figure out what was going on inside Luke's thick skull. Last Sunday, he'd held her close and shown more intimacy than ever before, only to push her away after their kiss. She knew he didn't want her to stop—his body's reaction had told her in no uncertain terms—but since then, he'd held her at an arm's length, and a very long arm, at that. A psychology degree would've come in handy right about now.

She pried the lid off the paint can and poured thick "Caribbean Sand" into a plastic tray. While June rolled the color onto the walls, she tried to dust off her memory of introductory psych for anything that might prove useful.

June didn't remember much about Luke's mother, but when she'd left him behind and chosen to keep his sister, that had obviously left Luke feeling inadequate, insecure, and probably a little misogynistic. Which explained why he thought so little of himself, and maybe also clarified his wild behavior when he'd come to live with Grammy at age twelve. Luke had tested her to see if she'd shuffle him to another family. When Gram had responded with firm discipline and refused to give up on him, Luke had finally calmed down. Maybe he was testing June now to see if she'd stay in his life or run away like his mother had. June was no professional, but that made sense. If Luke was sabotaging their relationship and annoying the shit—oops, sugar—out of her because he was afraid she'd leave, then she needed to show him nothing could drive her away—a tall order considering June *was* leaving in less than two weeks. Maybe that was part of the problem too. Was Luke afraid to get close, knowing she'd return to Austin?

Throbbing heat from June's shoulder interrupted her

musings. She reached across to massage her knotted muscles, wondering how Luke, Trey, and the rest of the crew did this stuff every day.

And then, speak of the devil, Luke's boots crinkled across the plastic tarp behind her. "That's the color you picked?" From the dark tone of his voice, she could tell he wasn't pleased.

June swallowed her sarcastic reply and said, "Mmmhmm" instead.

"I don't like it. When I flip a house, I paint everything white."

June tightened her grip on the paint roller before resting it against the tray. Taking a deep breath, she turned around slowly. "Remember what I said about staging? You'll make more money if you—"

"Screw staging. I want it white. Wait till that dries, then prime it again." He lowered his chin and folded his arms across his chest, every bit as defiant as the brokenhearted boy who'd smashed Grammy's figurine against the wall when he'd learned his mama wasn't coming back to get him.

Instead of focusing on Luke's words, June peered right into his cool, green eyes and remembered the different ways those eyes had regarded her during the past weeks—with tenderness, warmth, and sometimes blazing hunger. This coldness wouldn't last forever. She had to remember that. June strode forward, noticing more hesitation in Luke's gaze with each step she took. When she moved close enough to let her breasts brush the front of his dampened T-shirt, she poked her index finger into his stone chest.

"I'm not leaving," she said firmly. *I'm not your mother*.

Luke backed up a pace and furrowed one brow in confusion. "I didn't ask you to."

"Keep pushing my buttons. I'm not turning my back on you. But this'll be a lot more fun for both of us if you stop acting like a jerk." Then she turned and marched back to her tray to roll the sandy color onto the white-primed wall. "And I'm keeping this shade. Deal with it."

"Deal with—" Luke sputtered. "This is my house!"

"And this is free labor! So either pick up a roller, or get out of my hair."

For several minutes, he fell silent, and June wondered if he'd finally come to his senses. Maybe he'd close the distance between them and wrap his arms around her waist. Maybe he'd cup her cheek and apologize, then kiss her temple and beg forgiveness. She'd tell him there was nothing to forgive, and he'd sweep her into his arms, Hollywood-style, and carry her off to his bed. Well, his air mattress.

"You're doing it all wrong anyway," he said. "Everyone knows you trim first, then roll out."

Or maybe not. Did she really think it would be that easy?

"And," he went on, "I didn't ask for your help. I don't even want you here."

Either the paint fumes were too thick for her lungs, or Luke's words had made it hard to breathe. Regardless, it wasn't fumes that twisted her heart or turned her belly cold. She swallowed a lump the size of a peach pit and waited to speak until she knew her voice wouldn't shake. In the smoothest motion she could manage, she lifted her paint roller and pushed it against the wall with even strokes.

"I'm not leaving," she repeated in a thick voice and

then cleared her throat. "I want to be here. When I said I wanted to start fresh, I meant it. Even when I go back to Luquos, I want us to stay close. Six hours isn't all that far, and we can meet up—"

"I've gotta finish the cabinets." His retreating footsteps sounded down the hallway.

That hadn't gone as well as she'd expected. The contrast of stark white primer against Caribbean Sand mirrored Luke's new dual personality, and June began to feel a needle of doubt at the back of her mind. What if he was too damaged? What if Grammy was wrong and he couldn't be taught? Or what if he simply didn't want to learn? Taking a deep breath, June steeled herself and pushed aside discouraging thoughts. She had two weeks to do her best, and even then, she could come back to visit and hammer away at him some more. Like the pastor had said, love never quits, never abandons in a time of need.

———

Two hours later, June stood back to admire her work. She'd rolled a thick first coat over the primer and trimmed the ceiling, baseboards, and corners, which meant now she could drive home and soak in a warm bath.

She'd just finished washing her hands in the master bathroom when Luke pushed open the bedroom door. With his hands low on his hips, he stood in the doorway and surveyed the walls in silence. Raising her chin, June prepared for an angry tirade.

"Dried better than I thought," he said, raking his fingers through his hair. "Guess the color's not so bad."

"Warm and neutral. Buyers tend to like that."

"If you say so." He shrugged one shoulder.

"Well," June said, wiping her wet hands on her shorts and moving toward the door, "I'm heading back to Gram's. You coming for supper?" She knew the answer, but had to ask anyway.

"No."

She stepped around him and let her fingers graze the outside curve of his arm, and then he touched her hand once—a touch that was barely a touch at all—and said, "Guess I should thank you for the sandwich. You didn't use enough molasses, but it was still good." Technically, he didn't thank her, and ordinarily, she'd make an issue of it. Not today.

"You're welcome. See you in the morning."

June strolled to her car, smiling the whole way. It wasn't much progress, but she'd take it.

Chapter 15

THE SILKEN GRASS BENEATH HER BARE FEET, COOL morning dew soaking the hem of her nightgown, the absence of all sound aside from tranquil bird calls and the whisper of wind through leaves—these were the things June had never realized she'd missed until now.

Turning one flawless tomato over in her hands, she stood on tiptoe in the soft soil of Gram's garden and peered over a row of tall cornstalks to the Gallagher land beyond the backyard. Soon Luke would make his home there, but she couldn't picture it. In June's mind, his home was in Grammy's house, with her. Perhaps because she didn't want to, June couldn't imagine him dwelling any place where she wasn't. They'd almost always lived together, aside from one short decade that now seemed like a mere hiccup in their lives, and she wondered if it could be that way again. But she had a life in Austin. Assuming Luke got over his sudden aversion to her, would he be willing to abandon his land and join her in the city?

Esteban had called, faithfully as always, that morning, and they'd discussed June's idea of negotiating a lower cab fare for Luquos patrons who might overindulge and need a ride home or to the nearest hotel. Maybe she'd haggle over a lower room rate too. But as June had paced the creaky wood floorboards with the phone pressed to one ear, her thoughts had drifted two counties away to a man in threadbare jeans and a white cotton T-shirt. She'd never had to force herself to focus on Luquos before—it had always been her pleasure to brainstorm, design, and plan everything from the wall décor to the soft background music—but June had to admit her heart wasn't really in it. She told herself she'd simply been away too long. Once she stepped through the front door of her very own bar, once she saw her jellies floating delicately in their tanks, she'd feel that swell of excitement in her breast again. But then June quit lying to herself and admitted how much she'd miss home. She'd miss Grammy and Judge Bea and especially Luke. Could she really have it all? There had to be a way.

After June hosed off her feet and padded into the kitchen for breakfast, Gram placed a steaming platter of scrambled eggs on the table. Nodding at two cardboard boxes near the back door, Gram said, "I'm donatin' those old Christmas decorations to the church rummage sale, so if there's somethin' special you wanna keep, go through and take it."

"Oh." June rolled a tomato onto the counter. "Is Mama's angel in there?" She couldn't imagine Grammy parting with the porcelain tree-topper Mama'd made in high school, but better to be safe than sorry.

"No. I'm keepin' that."

"What about the advent calendar tree?" Grammy had crafted a felt evergreen tree with twenty-five fabric pouches sewn to the front, which June and Luke would open each morning in December. Gram had stuffed the pouches with candies or coins, and the last one always contained an extra-special treat, like homemade fudge or divinity with nuts. June had taken their simple family tradition for granted until her first December away from home, when she'd had nothing to look forward to each morning. That's when she'd begun to appreciate the little things Grammy had done to make the season special.

"I'm keepin' that too," Gram said with a firm nod.

"Good. I missed that." She'd spent so many Christmases working double shifts—both to distract herself and to take advantage of the higher wage—that she hadn't given much thought to how Gram had spent her holidays. "Before Luke moved back home, who'd you spend Christmas with?"

"Oh, I don't rightly know." She turned to the refrigerator and pulled out a carton of orange juice. "I ate supper with Bea once, the year his wife passed, but after that, he started spendin' holidays with his kids in Oklahoma."

"What about the other years?"

Gram shrugged one bony shoulder. "Most folks my age got kin to cook for. Didn't feel right addin' to their burden by invitin' myself over."

"Oh." *She was alone, just like me.* First the surgery, and now this. June wished she could redo the last decade of her life. There was so much she'd change.

Their thoughts must have traveled on the same wavelength, because instead of pulling out her Sudoku book, Gram sat down and folded her hands in her lap. "Let's talk a minute," she said.

"Sure." June brought two plates and forks to the table. "What's on your mind?" Though she had a good idea.

"You'll be goin' back soon." Gram seemed to hesitate, something she didn't do often. Holding her tongue had never been Gram's style. She spooned a serving of eggs onto each plate before saying in a rush, "I don't want another nine years to pass 'fore you come home again."

Before June could get a single word out, Gram held up a palm and cut her off.

"Just listen," Gram said, and paused to glance down at her lap. She fidgeted with the simple gold band she'd worn every day since Grandpa passed away twenty years earlier. "I know I was hard on you growin' up. But when your mama died—" She shook her head and went silent awhile. "You can't know that pain, June. Not till you're a mama yourself. I kept thinkin' if I'd raised her right, she wouldn'a come up so wild. Maybe she'd still be with us."

"Grammy, you can't blame yourself for—"

"Don't interrupt. I gotta say this, and it ain't easy." June nodded and fought to keep silent while Gram went on. "I couldn't make the same mistake with you. I vowed to bring you up proper. To be strict and…maybe I went too far sometimes. But I did my best." Though Gram's bun gripped her hair into tight submission, she smoothed an imaginary stray lock back into place. "Took a long time to admit to myself I drove you away. But things'll be different now. You're all grown, and I'm mighty proud of you. You don't have to stay away, June."

June took Grammy's large hands and smoothed a palm over her spotted, paper-thin skin. These were strong hands—the hands of a woman who'd buried her only child alongside her husband and then pushed down her grief to take in two energetic, young children and raise them as her own. Growing up, June had always resented Grammy's rigid control, never understanding the motivation behind it. Maybe it was a good thing June

had abandoned psychology after all, since she seemed
blind to the obvious. Of course Gram had been afraid
June would turn out like her mother. Gram had lost everyone and couldn't bear to lose her too.

"Nothing can keep me away." June looked directly
into Gram's watery blue eyes. "Not even if you bring
out the wooden spoon." Then she wrapped her arms
around Gram's shoulders and buried her nose in her
neck, inhaling her scent of lavender soap and arthritis
cream. "I love you, Grammy. And I'm sorry. For Mama
and for everything else."

They hugged and cried and hugged again, while the
eggs and coffee grew cold. Then, after wiping their
faces, they reheated breakfast and worked a Sudoku
puzzle together; and when Lucky meowed loudly and
crept into the kitchen, he hopped into Gram's lap instead of June's. She'd never seen him so relaxed or
content. It was surreal to discover the woman June had
feared her entire life had, herself, acted out of fear.
June only wished she'd known sooner. They'd wasted
so much time.

—∿∿—

Over the next two days, June and Luke settled into a
companionable silence that was neither hostile nor
friendly. He no longer snapped and criticized, but there
were no jokes or casual touches, either. Though Luke
still hadn't thanked her, he seemed to have accepted
June's help, or at least resigned himself to it. June supposed it was progress, but she missed the old Luke.
Sure, his teasing had tied her belly in knots and driven
her half-mad sometimes, but it had reflected their years

together—it proved they'd been close once and could be again if they tried.

From the other side of the quilt, Luke grunted with his mouth full of sandwich. "Too much molasses." A complaint, but at least they were eating lunch together again.

"Covers up the taste of spit." June tipped back her water bottle and took a long pull, feeling the icy liquid slide clear down to her stomach. "The more you whine about my sandwich-making skills, the more I'm tempted to put surprises in there."

That earned an elusive smile, and June wished she were as unaffected by it as she pretended to be. She crawled across the dining room floor to the radio and turned the dial until she found a station that wasn't playing heavy metal or country, which didn't leave many options.

"I bought a present for Gram," June said over the soft music. She doubted Luke cared, but she craved conversation, even the superficial kind. "A large-screen Sudoku game, so she can play anywhere."

"Sudo-what?"

"Sudoku. It's a math puzzle. Totally addictive. We've been playing every morning while we eat breakfast."

"Hmm." Luke shoved one last bite of sandwich in his mouth and stretched out on his back, folding his arms behind his head and closing his eyes. "I thought you sucked at math."

"It's just simple addition." Keeping a safe distance, June curled onto her side and propped up on one elbow. "You'll never guess what happened the other morning."

He didn't try.

"Gram apologized to me."

Luke opened one eye and lifted the brow above it. "No shit?"

"No sugar." She noticed the corners of his lips twitch into a grin, probably in response to her non-swear. "Said she was sorry for being so controlling. She was afraid I wasn't coming back after my month's up." When Luke closed his eyes again and pressed his mouth into a line, June spoke in a rush. "But I am coming back. The first year at Luquos'll be hectic, but I'll make time. And once I get a place, Gram can come visit. You can too."

Only the tight set of Luke's jaw told her he wasn't sleeping. Otherwise, he was totally unresponsive. For a few minutes, June listened to nondescript elevator music and worked up the courage to ask a question that would either be met with anger masquerading as nonchalance or just outright anger.

"Hey, Luke? Did you ever track down your mama?"

His body tensed visibly. Slower than a broken clock, Luke turned his head and glanced at her with pure caution guarding his eyes. "Random question, isn't it?"

"Not really." June traced her index finger around and around one misshapen, square quilt patch. "I was thinking about how Gram and I mended our relationship, and it reminded me of you and—"

"No, I didn't." His eyes were still on her, but something new flashed there. Not anger, like she'd expected, but a softer emotion. If she didn't know better, June would have thought it was trust. "She died," he said.

"Oh, Luke. I'm sorry." There went all hope of reuniting mother and son and possibly healing old wounds. She wondered how he'd reacted when he'd learned the news. How much time had passed since then?

"But I found my sister."

"*What?*" June's voice rose three octaves, and she sat upright. "And you never told me?"

Luke gave a casual shrug and then closed his eyes again. "I'm telling you now."

"Well?"

"She's a junior at UCLA, journalism major. A really good kid—I'm surprised she turned out so well, considering. Pretty girl too."

"Oh!" June remembered the young woman from the photo in Luke's desk drawer, and everything snapped into place. That wasn't his wife; it was his sister. Relief flooded her chest, so much that June lifted her hand to hold it all inside. "Short blond hair and really tan?"

"Yeah, how'd you know?" It didn't take two seconds for him to figure it out. "You went through my stuff. Why am I not surprised?"

"Because you know me. I played with your Snake Eyes doll too."

"Hey," he said, pointing a finger at her, "it's not a doll. It's an action figure. There's a difference."

"Sure there is." June rolled her eyes. She wondered how much Luke's sister had known about him before they'd reunited, but then "Under the Boardwalk" came on the radio before she had the chance to ask. It brought back a deluge of sweet memories: the stiff swish of a taffeta gown, the taste of lime punch, the feel of Luke's powerful hands around her waist. "It's our song," she said, unable to contain a smile.

"We have a song?" Luke leaned up on one elbow.

"Well, no. But we danced to this at prom. Remember?" The theme had been Underwater Enchantment, and since Gram hadn't allowed dancing, June and Luke had pretended to go to a baseball game and then changed into their formal clothes in the school locker room.

"Junebug, I can't even remember what I ate—"

"Yeah, yeah, for breakfast." Still smiling at the memory, she folded her legs and leaned toward him. "You took me to the prom after Tommy Boyd broke up with me and asked Joy Giggliano instead. It was so sweet of you."

She'd cried for days over Tommy's rejection, but when prom night had finally arrived, June had been over the moon when Luke held her close and danced with her in front of everyone. For the first time since they'd been friends, he'd treated her like a real lady, bringing her punch and pulling out her chair to help her sit down. He'd even told her how pretty she'd looked in the dress she'd found at a secondhand store. She hadn't given Tommy Boyd a second thought after that. Funny, she'd just seen Tommy for the first time since graduation, at the fair. He hadn't aged well, a fact that shouldn't have pleased her, but it did. June sighed contently and rested her chin in her palm, humming along with the Drifters.

"Uh, about that…" Luke glanced over with a sheepish expression on his face—the same look he'd given her after he'd dropped her CD player in the pond. The one she'd saved a year's babysitting wages to buy. "I have a confession."

"About?"

"I may have…discouraged…Tom from taking you as his date."

"You're joking, right?"

"No, but here's the thing." Luke sat up and held one

palm forward, speaking in a hurry, as if she might bolt at the news. "I overheard him talking about you during gym. He had *plans*, Junebug."

"Is that code for something?"

"He wanted inside your panties."

"And?"

"I took him behind the dugout and threatened to beat the shit out of him if he laid a finger on you. I had a good six inches and thirty pounds on the guy, so…" Luke shrugged as if the rest was obvious. "And believe me, he's a total ass wipe now. I did you a favor."

It took a few seconds for the reality of his words to penetrate the reminiscent haze June had worked herself into, but then a hot ember blazed to life inside her belly. She remembered the moment when Tommy had dumped her, and how her face had flushed with mortification. In the world of a teenage girl, there was no fate worse than being jilted right before the prom. She'd walked around school with her head hung low for a week. And why? Because Luke had thought she might get lucky?

"You…I can't believe—" In her furious stupor, June couldn't quite get the words out.

"And then you came home crying and carrying on, and I felt terrible. I knew you had a little crush on me, so I offered to take you instead."

"How kind of you," June snapped, each word sharper than a snake's fang. "You didn't trust me to keep my dress on, so you chose for me. You sanctimonious son of a bi—"

"Biscuit-eater?" he offered with a cocky grin that enraged her even more.

"No." June clamped her lips together and sucked in

a deep, deep breath through her nose before she said something she'd regret later. But she released it almost immediately, because there was one clarification to make. "And it wasn't a little crush. I loved you."

Luke made a dismissive noise and rolled to his feet. "C'mon. No you didn't. Girls confuse sex and love all the time, especially with their first."

"I think I know my own feelings better than you."

A patronizing shrug was his only reply, and June felt her patience snap like a dried twig.

"I didn't get my psych degree, but I still know ego-centrism when I see it! Don't assume that just because you're incapable of love, the rest of us are too. I loved you harder than I've ever loved any man before or since. Maybe you can't handle hearing that, but it's true, and I won't let you tell me it's not!"

"Hey," he said, raising his voice, "I'm not incapable of anything."

"I would've cut my life short by ten years to make you love me, and then you took everything I wanted and handed it to another woman just three months after I left. That's the real reason I cut you out of my life, Luke. Not because of what happened at the pond. That hurt my pride, but I was getting over it. But I couldn't watch you love someone else. I couldn't watch you touch her face and stroke her hair." June's throat closed, and she fought to keep her voice steady. "So don't tell me it was a crush!"

Pushing off the quilt, she scrambled to her feet and walked—because she refused to run—upstairs to the master bathroom. She knew her hands were too shaky to finish caulking around the new sink, but she needed a quiet space to cry. She could feel the tears coming, and by God, Luke wouldn't see them.

Bracing herself in front of the mirror, June wondered what had possessed her to think she could teach Luke to love. What an idiot she'd been! There was no textbook, no lesson plan to instruct one human to give his heart to another. There was no way this could work. A hollow ache opened so deeply inside her, June imagined she could throw a pebble into her chest and hear it echo for days. Other people fell in and out of love as easily as they changed lanes on the interstate. Why couldn't she be like that? Why couldn't she purge Luke from her system? One plump tear rolled down her cheek, and she scrubbed it away with her fist.

The slow, careful creak of Luke's boots against the hardwood stairs approached, and seconds later, he pushed the bathroom door open. June stared straight into the mirror and watched him settle behind her. For the longest time, he stood in silence, studying her reflection. And then, lighter than a quail's breath, he rested one hand along the curve of her waist. It was the first time he'd touched her in nearly a week, and June's body warmed at the contact against her will.

"I never cared for her," Luke said softly. "It was a green card marriage, and I never cared for her one single minute." His eyes blazed beneath a fringe of dark lashes as he held her gaze in the mirror. The hole inside June's chest began to fill. Luke had never loved his wife. He hadn't given himself to another woman, not in any way that mattered. The words were so glorious, June was almost afraid to believe them.

She noticed Luke hesitate and then bring his fingers

against her cheek to stroke her skin with all the tenderness of a devoted lover. "I never touched her face like this," he whispered, and then he closed the distance so his firm body pressed against her from behind. "I never stroked her hair." Brushing her curls to the side, he slid one more smoldering gaze into the mirror, while lowering his mouth to the top of her shoulder. June closed her eyes and leaned back into his warmth, tipping her head to the side and gasping with pleasure when he bit down. There was no hollow inside her chest now. Heat poured through her; Luke pulsed through her veins until she overflowed with his scent, his touch.

"Open your eyes," he commanded, and she obeyed just in time to watch Luke graze one hot palm over her breast. She felt a tug between her thighs and took his hand to guide it beneath her shirt. When his fingertips found her nipple and rolled it to a tight point, she whimpered and let an obscenity slip off her tongue. She couldn't care less. Even vulgarity was beautiful from within his arms. How was it possible to feel so full when just seconds ago, she'd felt completely vacant?

Luke studied her reflection through heavily lidded eyes. "I've missed your filthy mouth."

So she gave him what he'd missed, turning her face, arching her neck, and grasping a handful of his hair to pull his mouth to hers. The gentle, tentative exploration of their last kiss was gone, replaced by ravenous greed. Something in Luke shifted, and he consumed her like a man who'd eaten, but never truly tasted until that moment. With mindless intensity, he fed from her lips—captured them, nipped them, suckled them—until June broke away, gasping for breath. Then, without hesitation, his mouth was at her ear.

"God, Junebug," he whispered, pulling her back against his firm arousal. When she ground her bottom against him, he released a groan from deep in his throat and hissed her name again. June reached between them and stroked the bulging shaft through his jeans, delighting in the sounds Luke made, the frenzy she worked him into.

Holding her gaze again, Luke trailed one hand down her belly, until it disappeared beneath the loose waistband of her shorts. He halted, asking a silent question that June answered with an arch of her hips, and then his fingers slipped below the thin fabric of her panties.

Parting her sensitive folds, he slid one finger deep inside to gather lubrication before spreading it over her aching pleasure center in whisper-light, teasing circles. He knew just how to touch her, how to bring a moan to her lips, and make her beg with each desperate roll of her hips.

Together, they watched his forearm muscles tighten and bunch, while his fingers moved below the material, stroking her slippery flesh, dipping inside, stretching her in an agonizingly slow rhythm that had her panting for air and swelling with need.

"You feel so good," he whispered against her temple. "So fucking hot. So wet. Did I make you this wet?" His teeth grazed her earlobe, but he never took his eyes off her reflection. "Hmm?"

"Yes, you. Only you."

"Only me? Then I want you to come for me." He

pumped his fingers faster. Harder. So deeply it brought her to her tiptoes. "Right here, so I can watch."

Tipping her head forward, June moaned his name and grasped the countertop with both hands. Her knees turned soft, and the aching pleasure drained her strength with each new stroke.

"Stand up." Luke wrapped one powerful arm around her in support. "Look at what I'm doing to you. Look at how beautiful you are."

Allowing her eyelids to flutter open, June leaned back into his chest and took in all the sensations: Luke's hot breaths quickening against her ear, his scent filling her nostrils, his erotic gaze burning into hers through the mirror, the feel of his iron shaft grinding against her bottom in time with his gifted, pistoning fingers. Each sensation built on the others, multiplying in intensity, until she cried out his name and felt the first wave of ecstasy pulse through her core. His fingers never slowed, never relented, sending her headlong into a sensual chain of spasms that brought a soft cry to her lips.

Before she had a chance to come back down, Luke spun her around to face him and lifted her onto the countertop. Though her limbs were frail and trembling, she wrapped her legs around his waist, feeling instantly aroused again when his erection pressed against her slick center.

"I want you, Luke," she said in a breathy voice that didn't sound like her own. "Make love to me." She wanted to feel Luke's weight, feel his skin inside and out, to be completely enveloped by him.

He shook his head and gave a ragged gasp. "We can't." But even as he refused, he brought his lips back to hers for a nearly savage kiss, claiming her mouth while he tugged her thighs forward and rocked between them, sending another throbbing wave of pleasure washing over her.

"Oh, god," she moaned. "Please."

"I'm out of condoms."

"We don't need one. I'm on—"

"Yes, we do." He moved his hips in slow circles, and June sent half a dozen expletives into the air. "You like that?" he whispered against her lips.

"Yes."

"Tell me how much."

June wanted to tell him, but all she could manage was a string of incoherent four-letter words, so she grabbed his backside and pulled him harder against her, while she arched in wild response.

"God damn," Luke whispered, clenching his eyes shut. He increased the tempo, gyrating in frantic circles while she clutched his jeans and matched his every thrust. They moved together greedily, breathing in urgent gasps, clinging to one another and stealing clumsy kisses during their untamed drive for release.

With one last, deep undulation, June convulsed in an explosive orgasm, crying out against Luke's shoulder, as merciless ripples of jagged pleasure rocked through her. Running her hands over Luke's broad back, she felt his muscles clench and stiffen, and a deep, low groan signaled his own climax. "Oh god, June," he whispered in a ragged breath. And then after a long, shuddering sigh, "Ho-o-ly shit."

For a long minute, they held each other, stroking skin, softly kissing any place their lips met, loving without words. June buried her face in his chest, savoring his warmth, his scent, the feeling of complete contentment and safety within his powerful arms. Knowing it couldn't last forever, she took a handful of his shirt and pulled him closer. It wasn't close enough—it would never be close enough. Then he laughed softly against her temple.

"What?" she said tentatively, afraid to break the spell.

Luke pulled back and smoothed the hair away from her face. There was humor in his eyes, a pure happiness she hadn't seen in years. "Junebug, I haven't come in my pants since I was fifteen and Lori Marsh wouldn't stop freak dancing on me."

Giggling, June hooked her thumbs through his belt loops. "I heard she's a stripper now."

"Oh, yeah? Not surprising. I swear to God it was no accident—she knew what she was doing. After that, the rest of the night was uncomfortable as hell. Sticky and cold." He shuddered at the memory.

"Sorry." She nodded toward his pants. "But we don't need condoms. I'm on the Pill."

"Unh-uh." Luke shook his head and placed a chaste kiss on the tip of her nose. "There's no such thing as too much protection."

June had a feeling he was talking about more than just birth control and STDs.

"Why don't you meet me downstairs?" he said, de-tangling himself from her limbs. "I need to change."

Ten minutes later, he descended the stairs, while looking at the railing, his boots, the spindles, anywhere but at her. Lips that had just made love to her mouth now formed a cold, hard line. The magic was gone, his shields up once again.

Once, when June was ten, Luke had accidentally launched a kick ball right into her midsection at close range. It had seemed to take five minutes before she could breathe again. June felt that way now. She hadn't seen this coming, and as much as she tried to conceal the effects of the blow, her cheeks sagged, and her jaw slackened. She felt the sick tingles along the backs of her thighs that always warned her when trouble was coming.

"Listen," he said, running a hand through his hair while studying her sneakers. "What we just did upstairs…that can't happen again." Finally, he locked eyes with her, which made his message even more devastating. "Nothing's changed. I'm still no good for you."

"We can make it good." June hadn't meant to say it. She'd intended to salvage her self-respect and remind Luke that he'd sought her out and initiated everything. The last thing June wanted to do was plead for something Luke wasn't ready to give, but the words fell off her tongue of their own volition.

Shaking his head a little too firmly, as if trying to convince them both, he said, "I shouldn't have led you on like that. It won't happen again."

"Sure it won't." Scraping some of her pride off the floor, June rolled her eyes and folded her arms beneath her breasts.

"I mean it." But Luke's head still shook back and forth. The war raging inside his mind wasn't a private battle—his inner conflict was obvious. Why did he have to fight her so hard?

"You know what?" June's fists clenched as hurt suddenly gave way to anger. She'd committed herself to teaching Luke to love, but that didn't mean she had to play nice. Maybe he needed tough love. "You're right. It won't happen again. You're an emotional coward, Luke—so afraid I'll let you down that you won't try getting close. But you don't hesitate to let *me* down. You'll throw me right under the bus, if it spares you some pain. You're completely spineless."

He blinked a few times, clearly not expecting the tirade. "What the—"

"Spineless as the jellyfish in my tanks. And you won't lay a hand on me until you grow some stones and go all in."

"Fine." Hands on his hips, Luke clenched his jaw and gave a curt nod. "Then you probably won't be coming around here anymore. I'm okay with that."

"Oh, no. I told you I wasn't leaving. I'm in your life for good, even when I go back to Austin. But you won't share my bed until you grow a backbone."

And then June found her own backbone and marched right past him up the stairs to finish caulking the bathroom sink. It would be a cold day in Hades before she shed another tear for Luke Gallagher.

Chapter 16

"SHE CALLED YOU A JELLYFISH?" TREY SWUNG HIS disgusting, friggin' half-rotted cast forward and then leaned on his cane to hobble into Jenkins's kitchen. Luke wondered how much longer until that nasty thing came off. It was starting to smell, tainting the lemony scent of a freshly mopped floor with the reek of trapped sweat. "Was it the end of the day?" Trey asked. "'Cause she's pretty cranky by then, especially if it's hot."

"Emotional coward. And no, it was lunchtime." Pointing to a misaligned drawer, Luke added, "Have Pauly check the track on that one." The day had come for the final walk-through on the Jenkins home, and Luke couldn't stop thinking about June long enough to focus on his checklist. She had his mind so twisted he'd driven ten miles in the wrong direction that morning before he remembered where he was supposed to be. "Everything pass inspection?"

"Yep." Patting himself down, Trey searched for the paperwork and came up empty-handed. "Karl probably has it."

"Creepy Karl?" Luke tossed his clipboard onto the kitchen table, where it landed with a loud thud. "He's probably smoked it by now." Damn it, driving in circles, falling behind on the Hallover property, and now misplacing paperwork. His personal life was making him sloppy, something he couldn't afford to let happen, not if he stood a chance of finally getting his family's land back.

"You're not gonna believe this," Trey said, lowering himself into a wooden chair, "but Karl's a halfway decent assistant. Keeps all the papers and receipts in this little plastic file box better organized than I ever did."

"Huh, no shit?" Maybe they'd found a use for him after all.

As if they'd called for him, Karl waddled in with the inspector's report folded neatly in his hand. "Hey, boss man. Where's *mamacita*?" With one hairy hand, he stroked his round, even hairier belly and thrust his pelvis into the empty air. "She done blown my mind, and I ain't wantin' it back!"

"You jackass." Luke snatched the report and pointed it at the back door. "Jenkins'll be here in a minute. Put a shirt on, and get back outside to make sure there's no trash on the lawn. I want this property cleaner than a hound's tooth." Decent assistant or not, that man was a canker sore.

"Okaly-dokaly, boss man." Smiling like he'd just finished a cold beer, Karl strode out the door.

Trey chuckled from his chair and shoved a ballpoint pen down the top of his cast. "This thing's itchy as hell," he said, scrubbing at his skin.

"Jesus, remind me not to borrow that pen."

Ignoring him, Trey kept scratching and asked, "So, what'd you do to piss off *Jooonbug*?"

"You automatically assume I did something wrong." But before Luke objected any further, he waved a dismissive hand and owned up to his mistake. "Yeah, okay. I screwed up. We had a fight, and when I went to apologize, I kissed her, and things went a little too far."

"How too far?"

"None of your business." Deciding to fix the faulty drawer himself, Luke pulled it out and lifted it from the track. "Anyway, I told her it couldn't happen again, and she accused me of being emotionally spineless. Said I'd let her down, thrown her under the bus."

"Ouch." Abandoning the pen, Trey reached for a toilet auger. "You think she's right?"

"I swear to God, if you put that thing down your cast…" Luke cocked his head to the side. "What do you mean? Of course she's not right. You think I'm a pansy or somethin'?"

Holding his palm forward like a peace officer, Trey shook his head and—thank God—threw the auger back in his toolbox. "I didn't say that. But think about it. How long have I known you?" Trey thought for a moment. "Nine years? And in all that time, you've never had a steady girl, unless you count the ever-faithful Frau Gallagher."

"I don't!"

"Okay, fine. And you don't date. I mean, have you ever slept with the same woman twice?"

Annoyed, Luke shrugged a shoulder and wished he'd never told Trey about the argument in the first place. He could see where this was going. Feeling along the metal drawer track, he tried to identify the problem, but couldn't concentrate longer than two seconds before his mind wandered back to June, particularly to the way she'd looked when he'd made her come. His heart raced just thinking about her flushed cheeks and how she'd moaned his name.

"I'll take that as a no." Pausing a moment to rifle

through his toolbox, Trey sighed and then added, "Don't you think that's weird? Maybe June has a point." His face lit up when he found a heavy, metal tape measure, and as Trey extended the tip two feet into the foul plaster depths, Luke thought about what he'd said.

Avoiding relationships had saved him a lot of time, which he'd used to build a business and accumulate enough capital to buy the Gallagher land. And by refusing to date local women, he'd saved himself all the awkward headaches that came with a messy breakup. That didn't make him a coward, just practical.

"Either way," Trey said, appearing satisfied and retracting the tape, "you need to figure out what you want. Fish or cut bait, buddy. Do you love her?"

The word *no* was on the tip of Luke's tongue, but it slid backward and lodged inside his throat.

"I've seen the way you look at each other," Trey said with a smug grin. "And didn't you drive to Shooters at closing time a few nights ago to make sure—"

"We grew up together." Luke tightened a screw to adjust the left track. "I care about her."

"I was in love once." Trey leaned back and heaved a sigh. "Mindy Roberts. Couldn't stop thinking about her for five minutes. Damn near drove me insane. But that's not how I knew it was love—just thinking about a woman could mean anything."

"How'd you know?"

"She was the only girl I'd ever pictured having a family with. I could almost see our kids running around in the backyard. And the sex wasn't just sex; it was more. Like I lost part of myself every time. It's hard to explain. And scary as the devil on steroids."

Sliding the drawer back in place and testing it out, Luke wondered why he'd never heard about Mindy Roberts before. Probably for the same reason he'd never mentioned June to Trey. Some things were private. Or too painful to mention aloud. "So what happened?" he asked.

"She met someone else while I was in basic." Then in a softer voice, "Guess she didn't feel the same about me."

Neither of them said a word, choosing instead to let the distant hum of the air conditioner and the whoosh of forced air through the vents fill the silence. After a long minute, Trey recovered his earlier cheer and asked, "So, how many kids have you imagined with *Jooonbug*?"

Three—all boys who looked exactly like him—just like she'd predicted in her high school letter, but Trey didn't need to know that. "Who said I pictured a family with her?"

Hauling himself out of the chair, Trey gave a dry laugh. "Well, unlike me and Mindy, I can tell June's just as crazy about you. As crazy as you pretend not to be."

"I don't know." Luke tossed his screwdriver into the toolbox, satisfied the drawer was level. At least one thing went right that morning. "What would she see in someone like me?"

"Buddy, who gives a shit? If you win the lottery, you don't waste your time asking why. You take your winnings and enjoy the rest of your life." Then he hobbled close enough to infect Luke's space with the wafting scents of sour body oil and plaster. Clapping one hand against Luke's shoulder, Trey warned, "If you don't cash this lottery ticket, someone else will. And you'll kick your own sorry ass every day for the rest of your life if you lose her. You and I both know it. So don't lose her."

After handing the keys over to a very grateful, teary-eyed Will Jenkins, Luke dismissed the crew and told them to meet up at the Hopkins house in two days, which had burned in an electrical fire a month earlier. There was never a shortage of repairs to be done for good people who couldn't afford to pay. There was, however, a shortage of time and money to accommodate them all. And speaking of time, Luke couldn't waste any more of it shooting the breeze with Trey if he wanted to meet his goal of listing the Hallover property by the end of the week. It was time to buckle down and stop letting June distract him.

Rolling down the window in his truck, Luke let the clean morning breeze toss his hair and clear his mind as he barreled down the highway into the next county. For the first time, he looked forward to the thirty-minute drive, which would give him a chance to think about Trey's advice, to decide once and for all what he wanted—to fish or cut bait. Slipping on a pair of sunglasses, Luke asked the most basic question: what did he want? That was easy. He couldn't deny he wanted June; there was no point lying to himself. But that didn't mean he could have her—not forever, anyway. June's time in Sultry Springs was growing shorter, and in the end, she'd return to her bar and to her dirty-minded business partner. And then what? A long-distance relationship? It probably wouldn't last; they never did. Then they'd be back at square one, estranged, their friendship lost. Besides, despite what Trey'd said, Luke just couldn't believe June's feelings went any deeper than an old childhood crush. Which raised the next, more important question: did he love her?

That wasn't as easily answered. He knew June had some sort of power over him, a way of making him feel elation and despair at the same time. He also knew instinctively that to be inside her—to feel her silken warmth, surrounded by her porcelain skin, her arms and legs wrapped around him—would be to lose himself completely to her. That had been the real reason he'd resisted making love to June two days ago, not because he didn't have a condom. Luke had never been without one in the last five years. But was that the power of love, or simply a mixture of attachment and infatuation? He didn't know. Too bad there wasn't a blood test for this kind of thing.

Half an hour later, Luke's mind was still more cluttered than a junkyard, but he'd reached a decision. It was time to let June go. Nothing good could come of a relationship with her—he'd either ruin things, or she'd leave. He'd sit her down right away and calmly explain they'd never be more than friends. Maybe he'd hurt her feelings, but it would spare her in the long run.

When Luke pulled into the Hallover driveway, his breath caught, and his hands tightened around the steering wheel. The very picture of domesticity, June knelt in the front flower bed, tending a variety of bright gold blossoms with her bare hands. Though her face was concealed by the brim of her straw hat, Luke knew she wore a gentle smile. He could tell from the way her fingers swept and caressed the soil. She'd already filled each window box until they overflowed with some kind of delicate purple flower he'd seen before, but couldn't identify. Pansies, maybe. He never would've thought to mix yellow and purple blooms, but the color combination worked. The house finally looked like a real home. Luke could almost hear the joyful shrieks of children playing in the backyard, the sons he and June would never have. He parked the truck, swallowed the lump in his throat, and tried to steel himself for what lay ahead.

"Hey," he said, jogging to the front door. June glanced up and wiped a hand across her brow, leaving a streak of dirt behind, and Luke had to stop himself from brushing his thumb over her forehead to clean it. Instead, he opened the door and nodded inside. "How 'bout you take a break, so we can talk?"

She turned her face to the earth. "Just a minute. I want to finish this last row." Her voice was low and soft, like she knew what was coming. Luke's heart sank into his stomach.

Stepping into the foyer, he reminded himself that he was not in love.

Taking her sweet time, June gathered her trowel and scooped a divot in the ground for the next group of mums. She was in no hurry to hear whatever Luke had to say. There were two kinds of *let's talk*, and she doubted he was eager to share some unexpected good news. The inflection in his voice, the way he wouldn't meet her gaze, the tingles along the backs of her thighs told June this was a *letting you down gently* kind of talk. A pulling away kind of talk. Already, hot tears pressed against her eyelids. She tried to blink them away, but the bright yellow blooms in her palm went blurry and mingled with the deep brown soil. Within seconds, she couldn't even see the new spot she'd dug. Hadn't she vowed a couple days ago not to shed another tear for Luke? So much for that.

She tugged her shirt up to blot her eyes, and everything came back into focus. There were two holes at the tip of her trowel blade, the one she'd dug, and another smaller opening in the ground—something she should've noticed before. The hairs on the back of June's neck stood on end as a sudden movement caught her eye. She instinctively jerked her hand back, but the snake was much faster. Before June had time to gasp, a pair of tiny, white fangs plunged into her forearm and clamped firmly in place beneath a pair of black, expressionless eyes. She unleashed a raw, savage scream and shook her arm wildly, but it wouldn't release her. The tiny jaws compressed her flesh, biting again and again and again. Then fire. She was on fire, skin and muscle burning her up from the inside out, caustic acid melting her veins. Pounding, rushing blood roared inside June's ears as she flailed and smacked her fist against the dirt. And then, as abruptly as the snake had struck, its fangs retracted and it disappeared into the hole in a brilliant flash of colors.

Clenching her eyes shut, June released a sob and rocked forward, clutching her arm to her chest. The bite throbbed like a thunderbolt with each of her rapid heartbeats. Then someone was there, tugging at her wrist and tilting her face up.

"…hear me?" Luke pulled her arm free, revealing two small currents of blood that streamed from the wound. "Shit!" he said. "Did you see what bit you?"

Shock tied her tongue for a moment, and then June could only recite the warning rhyme Grammy had taught her years ago: "Red on yellow, kill a fellow."

"God damn!" With one fluid motion, Luke reached behind his head and tugged off his T-shirt. He ripped it into uneven strips and began wrapping her arm as if she'd sprained it. "Try to calm down," he said. "Your pulse is racing. It's spreading the venom faster."

Unable to speak, she clamped her jaw shut and tried to pull deep breaths through her nose, but damn it, the pain. She still couldn't remember what this snake was called, but she'd once heard its bite wasn't supposed to hurt. What bullshit!

"Calm down!" he shouted, hands trembling as he tied off the makeshift bandage. "I'm sorry." Luke cupped her face, and his green eyes darkened. "Listen. The nearest hospital is half an hour away. It'll take forever for an ambulance to get here, so I'm gonna drive you myself. You keep your arm right here"—he pressed her elbow against her ribs—"and don't move. Not even a muscle, you hear me?"

She nodded, and Luke gathered her into his arms. Someone made a whimpering noise. Was that her? She wanted to relax and slow her sprinting heart, maybe rest her cheek against Luke's chest, but the next thing she knew, her head bobbed and thumped against the back of a hot leather seat. There were noises—an engine roaring, rubber tires whirring over rough asphalt, Luke's repeated, frantic commands to calm down. Then a new pain. "My stomach hurts," she said, bringing her free hand to her belly.

"Don't move!" Quick as the snake that bit her,

Luke's fingers gripped her wrist and held it against her side. "Please, Junebug. You gotta be still." He released her and tapped his cell phone screen. "This is Luke Gallagher," he said, enunciating each word loudly as if speaking to a foreigner. "I'm on my way to the Sultry Memorial emergency room with June Gallagher. She's just been bitten by a coral snake. I'm twenty minutes out. Tell the ER staff to be ready for her when I get there. She's disoriented and in a lot of pain. Make sure they're ready! You hear me?"

"Augustine," she whispered to herself. "My name's June Augustine." Then an unexpected set of giggles shook her chest. "I'm Mae-June July Augustine." What a horrible name. If she died, she'd give her parents a piece of her mind for that. "Oh, coral snake." Instantly, her mind switched gears. The hateful thing that'd bitten her was a coral snake. She remembered reading something in the paper recently. What was it? "Antivenin shortage," she said to Luke. "They stopped making the antivenin."

Luke tossed his cell phone aside and cupped his large, warm hand over hers. He stroked her skin, muttering vile curses under his breath. "It's okay," he said, more to himself than to her. "It's gonna be okay."

A large pair of hands squeezed June's temple, as if juicing an orange. Closing her eyes, she leaned back against the headrest and groaned. Everything seemed to throb—arm, forehead, belly—until June's body felt like one large, pulpy open wound. She tried to say Luke's name, but her words slipped out in a lazy slur. It wasn't supposed to happen this fast. "I love you," she said, using tremendous effort to pronounce each word. "I'm sorry I couldn't teach you how. I really tried."

"Stop that." He gripped her fingers so tightly it hurt. "Don't quit. We're almost there. I swear to God, Junebug, you better not quit. You promised, remember?"

"I'm sorry." Saliva pooled inside her mouth, and she swallowed down bile. Oh, God, please don't let her get sick inside Luke's truck. "I need some air." It came out in half a whisper. "Pull over."

But instead, Luke swore loudly and gunned the engine. Soon, swallowing became more difficult, and each breath took forever to suck into her lungs. June let her heavy eyelids sink, allowed her head to flop and thud against the window. The next thing she knew, her body lurched forward against the seat belt, and then she was in Luke's powerful arms.

There were bright lights and frenzied voices, and June opened her eyes just in time to see Luke's form retreat into the distance. For some reason, he wasn't wearing a shirt, and his eyes were red, his expression so twisted and pained that she tried to reach out one arm and comfort him. But then something scraped inside her throat, gagging her, forcing down deeper into her chest, and the room went dark, the voices faded to silence.

Chapter 17

"SIR? I NEED YOU TO FILL OUT SOME PAPERWORK." The woman's voice pressed. "Sir?"

Luke shook his head and stared blankly at the solid, white double doors that had just closed in his face, shutting him out from June. His last image of her had burned into his retinas, and each time he blinked, he saw those doe eyes brimming with terror, her outstretched arm, still bandaged in the ragged, blood-speckled strips of his old, gray T-shirt. Then a team of medics had shoved June's shoulders down against the gurney and forced a gleaming steel device down her throat. He remembered enough from basic training to understand what that meant. If June needed artificial respiration, her lungs were shutting down. She couldn't breathe. Damn it, she couldn't breathe!

"She needs me." Luke pushed against the immovable doors. "I have to get back there. She needs me!"

A pair of strong arms appeared from nowhere, clutching his bare shoulders and chest, and dragging him back as he pounded his fists against the barrier that separated him from June.

"Whoa, mister, hold on a minute," a voice rougher than three-grit sandpaper said over the top of Luke's head. If the voice belonged to the same arms holding him from behind, this was one powerful son of a bitch. "You gotta stay out here, just like the rest of us."

"Get off me, asshole." Luke struggled in vain, twisting his torso wildly in the stranger's iron grip. "You don't get it—"

"Like hell I don't." The faceless giant dragged him backward, and Luke kicked out helplessly, watching the double doors disappear as blinding sunlight replaced flickering fluorescent bulbs. "Just hold on—stop kicking, you stupid bastard, I'm tryin' to help you. We're only goin' outside a second," the man assured him. "If they call security, they'll ban you from the whole damn place. That what you want?"

"No." The guy was right. He couldn't help June if he got himself handcuffed and booted off Sultry Memorial property. Luke quit fighting, shut his eyes, and tried to slow the adrenaline rush, sucking in deep breaths, and then pushing them out so slowly they burned his lungs. His brain settled down enough to understand that if they'd intubated June, she was still breathing—maybe aided by a machine, but alive. Safe, for now. As the seconds passed, his senses began to return, slowly alerting him to the sun's warming rays on his skin, the distant belch of a car's busted muffler, and the rank, pungent odor of sweat, gasoline, and old cigarettes from the huge guy still wrapped around him.

"Sorry, man," Luke said. "I'm okay now."

The guy's arms dropped. Finally free, Luke turned and craned his neck skyward, where a pair of bloodshot eyes regarded him from beneath the bill of a grubby John Deere cap.

"Chuck," the stranger said with a tight nod.

"Luke," came the equally terse reply. He took a step back to put a little personal space between them and sized up the guy. Judging from Chuck's mud-stained, sleeveless shirt, jean cutoffs, and the grass clippings pasted to his meaty calves, he'd spent the day doing lawn work. Luke wondered if a mowing accident had brought him to the ER.

Chuck seemed to follow Luke's train of thought—or at least the path of his gaze—because he glanced down and swept bits of dried leaves and dirt from the front of his shorts. "Uh, yeah. I was…uh…cuttin' grass when my wife—" He paused, clearing his throat a few times before continuing. "She went into labor and started bleedin' real bad."

"Aw, shit." Luke reached up and gave Chuck an awkward pat on the shoulder. He didn't know the guy, but Luke couldn't imagine anything worse than the threat of losing a wife and a baby in the same day. Heat rose into Luke's face, but not from the fierce Texas sun. He felt like a selfish prick for the scene he'd just caused. "I'm sorry, man. Is she okay?"

Chuck shrugged. "The nurse came out an hour ago to tell me the baby made it." His breath caught and he flashed half a smile. "It's a girl. Our first."

"Congratulations."

"Yeah." His half-smile faded into a thin line. "And probably our last. The nurse said Cindy's still bleedin'— that's my wife—and they wanted to do one of those hysterectomies. Said they needed consent from her next of kin…and that's me."

"So, she'll be all right?"

"I think so." Chuck heaved a sigh and tugged off his cap, then raked a hand through his dampened hair. "Till she wakes up, and I have to tell her she can't have any more babies. And that I'm the one who told the doctors to do it to her." Pulling his cap low over his forehead, he stared off into the parking lot. "She wanted a whole house full of babies, you know?"

They both stood in silence, until Chuck added, "They're real good here. Try not to worry about your wife."

"She's, um…" June's voice echoed in his head. *I love you. I'm sorry I couldn't teach you how. I really tried.* "…not my wife."

"Well, don't say that, or they won't tell you anything. Privacy laws and all. Hey," he said, pointing to something behind Luke, "that your truck?"

"Oh, damn." Luke spun around. He'd forgotten all about the F-250 he'd left idling in front of the emergency room doors. "I'm gonna move it." Backing away, he added, "Thanks for your help back there."

"Sure, bud. Good luck." With a wave, Chuck returned to the waiting room.

Luke fished through his front and back pockets for his keys before realizing they were in the ignition, and then he climbed into the cab and pulled the truck into a space in the visitors' lot. When he cut the engine, a smudge of dried blood on the passenger seat caught his eye, and all the panic he'd just overcome rose again into his throat. His heartbeat quickened as he skimmed his fingertips over the burgundy stain. *I love you. I'm sorry I couldn't teach you how. I really tried.*

God damn it, this was all his fault. If he hadn't accepted June's help—if he'd just done the job himself—she'd be at Pru's right now, probably working one of those math puzzles with the funny name. Or picking vegetables in the garden with her grandma—"Oh, shit!"

Luke had forgotten about Pru! She needed to know what happened, but he didn't want to tell her over the phone. And there was no way in hell he'd leave the hospital, not until he knew June was all right. He grabbed his cell phone and dialed the only person he trusted with something this important.

"Y'ello," Trey answered.

"Thank God you're home!"

"Where else would I be, buddy? With this effing cast, it's not like I can just—"

"Listen," Luke interrupted, "I need a favor. It's an emergency."

Trey's voice darkened. "What's up?"

"Call Pauly, or even that idiot Karl, and ask for a ride to Pru's house."

"Okay…"

"Tell Pru—but be careful, because she's, you know, old and fragile and stuff—that June got bit by a coral snake, and she's at Sultry Memorial. They've got her on a breathing machine, but I don't know anything else."

"Christ," Trey breathed. "I'll do it right now."

The line disconnected, and Luke jogged back into the waiting room—this time with a clear head. He didn't know if the nurse had an update yet, but he'd be ready and waiting when the time came. When he approached the information desk, the receptionist— the same young brunette who'd flirted with him when he'd picked up Trey last week—widened her eyes and pointed to his belly.

"Hey, hon," she said, "you need a shirt, if you want to stay inside." Her playful grin told Luke she'd prefer to see him in even fewer clothes, and then she winked—actually winked at a time like this!—and pushed a clipboard into his hand. "Fill these out please."

"Can you tell me anything about June Augu— uh, Gallagher?"

"Is that the woman you brought in a few minutes ago?"

"Uh-huh. My wife." He yanked his left hand below the counter before she noticed his missing wedding ring. "Anything at all?"

The woman—Heather, according to her name tag— narrowed her eyes, apparently disappointed to learn he was off the market. "I need your wife's insurance card."

Uh-oh, did June even have insurance? "Left it at home."

"Give me her social security number, and I'll try looking her up in the system."

"I don't know it." When Heather rolled her eyes and geared up for a rebuttal, he added, "I was in such a rush to get here that I left my wallet and her purse at home."

She nodded at the clipboard. "Fill those out the best you can, then bring them back."

"What about June? Can't you tell me anything?"

She clicked a few keys on her computer and scanned the screen in silence. "Nope. Nothing yet, sorry." But she didn't sound sorry, and she quit making eye contact. "Don't forget that shirt. There's a gift shop this way"— pointing to her left—"and a lost-and-found bin on the second floor, right outside the elevators."

Luke thanked her and rushed to the second floor. He didn't have his wallet—no lie there—so the gift shop was out. He rummaged through the bins, shoving aside umbrellas, pink jackets, and paperback books, until he identified a man's T-shirt that just might fit. Plucking it from the heap, he charged back to the elevator and then pulled the navy blue, cotton fabric over his head without a care for who'd worn it last, or how many germs infested it.

There was no reason to rush back to the waiting area—still no news about June's condition—but he needed to feel as close to her as possible. Taking the seat nearest the information desk, he leaned forward, resting his forearms against his knees and folding his hands.

An hour later, that's how Pru found him.

"Lucas!" With one mammoth hand clutching her heart, Pru scurried across the lobby, followed closely by Pastor McMahon, the preacher from her church. Hopefully, the old guy had driven her here, because Pru didn't look fit to operate a bicycle, let alone a car. "How is she?"

Luke stood and met her by the information desk. "No word yet. And not for lack of trying, either." He'd bugged the receptionist, each passing doctor and nurse, patients and their families, candy stripers, janitors—anyone who had access beyond those damned double doors—for news of the curly haired snakebite victim, but his efforts were useless. Twice, he nearly stormed the doors himself. Only the threat of being barred from the premises had kept him glued to his seat. That, and the fact that a nurse had to buzz them open. He was beginning to wonder if they'd transported June to another hospital and forgotten to notify him.

"I know the chaplain here," the pastor said in a low voice. He covered his mouth and whispered, "Maybe he can slip back there and let us know what's going on."

"At this point, I'll try anything short of taking hostages." Hell, maybe even that. Luke gave the preacher an enthusiastic pat on the back and watched him hurry away. Then he linked his arm through Pru's and guided her to a cluster of empty chairs by the soda machine.

The late afternoon sun cut through the glass, illuminating Pru's white hair so her bun practically glowed from within. Bathed in the harsh light, each of her lines and wrinkles seemed amplified, and she looked so fragile—a word he'd never, ever used to describe her before now.

"Lucas," she said in a tiny voice. "What happened?"

He pulled his chair closer and held her hand tightly in both of his. "She was gardening. I didn't see it, but I heard her scream, and then I got her here right away." Dropping to one knee, he peered into Pru's watery, blue eyes and lied like the devil. "I know she's gonna be fine."

"I just got her back." Pru pressed her thin lips together, her chin quivering. Tears spilled over her cheeks.

"She's not goin' anywhere," Luke said firmly. He wrapped his arms around Pru's shoulders and pulled her close, feeling her large frame shake with each sob. Swallowing the thickness in his throat, he rubbed her back and repeated, "She's gonna be fine," until several minutes passed, and Pru pulled away, blotting her face with a crumpled tissue from her purse.

When Pastor McMahon returned, Luke had to physically restrain himself from tackling the man and shaking the information out of him like coins from a piggy bank.

"Okay," the pastor said, taking a seat across from Pru, "he said they've given her the antivenin, and they're keeping her asleep until they see how she reacts to it."

"What do you mean 'reacts to it'?" Luke asked. He'd expected the cure to work instantly, neutralizing the snake's venom in June's body the way baking soda neutralized acid.

"Seems some folks are allergic. In that case, the cure's worse than the bite."

"But that's rare, right?"

"No idea, Luke. Sorry, I wish I had more to tell you. Maybe we should find the hospital chapel and put it in the Lord's hands."

Luke chewed the end of his tongue, literally biting back his sarcastic response. Where were "the Lord's hands" when June had needed them earlier? Or when her parents had wrapped their car around an oak tree, leaving her an orphan? How about when his own mama'd abandoned him to a stranger? In Luke's experience, he was better off taking matters into his own hands than leaving them up to God.

"You and Pru go ahead," he told them. "I'm gonna stay here and wait for the doctor."

After they left for the sanctuary, a familiar, dingy John Deere cap caught Luke's eye, and he turned just in time to see Chuck's linebacker form shuffling toward the front entrance.

"Hey," Luke called, rushing to meet him at the automatic doors.

When the giant glanced over, Luke noticed the awful change in him right away. It was his eyes—bloodshot, glassy, their lids swollen half-shut. Bracing himself for the worst, Luke asked, "Any word on Cindy?"

Chuck sputtered and grinned so widely it split his face in two. "Yeah. She's sleeping now—the baby too—but I got to see 'em for a few minutes."

"So the surgery went okay?"

"Uh-huh, just fine. And when I told her the news, she wasn't mad about what I did. Y'know, for letting the doctors operate. Cindy was so relieved the baby was okay that she didn't fret too much about what she'd lost. She said we've got each other, and now our little girl, and that's all that matters. And there's plenty of kids out there needin' a home. We can still have a house full of babies."

"That's great." The tears that had wrecked Chuck's face were of relief then. Luke tried to picture the Goliath in front of him holding a six-pound infant, and the mental image curved his lips. "I'm glad things turned out for you, Chuck."

"Thanks. Any word on your…uh…girl?"

"No, but that's about to change."

"Well, good luck." Nodding toward the parking lot, Chuck waved a quick good-bye. "Gotta put the crib together. The baby came a little sooner than we expected."

Luke watched him walk to his car and stumble over his own feet in obvious exhaustion. A cocktail of happiness and envy blended together and seeped through his body. Damn it, Chuck had closure—his happy ending—and now, it was Luke's turn. He'd waited long enough.

He decided to quit playing nice. People always said the squeaky wheel got the oil, so he decided to squeak like nothing these bastards had ever heard.

Stalking to the information desk, he cleared his throat loudly. When Heather-the-horny-receptionist glanced up, he held her gaze, practically singeing her eyelashes with the intensity of his glare.

"I want to know what's happening to my wife. Right now." Remembering what Chuck had said earlier, he

added, "I'm her next of kin, and I've got the legal right
to make medical decisions for her, if she's unconscious.
So far nobody's asked for my consent, and whatever
they're doing back there might be a violation of my
wishes. Now listen good. Are you listening?" When
she pulled her brows down low, he grasped the counter
with both hands and leaned in close enough to smell
the peanut butter sandwich she'd had for lunch. "I'm
going to wait right over there"—he pointed to the soda
machine—"for exactly ten minutes. If a doctor or nurse
doesn't materialize in front of me during that time, the
next person I talk to will be my lawyer. Got it?"

He didn't wait for her response before charging
away, but when he reached the seating area and turned
around, she was talking animatedly with someone on the
phone. In exactly seven minutes—he checked the clock
above the front entrance—a young man in a lab coat approached him. The kid's baby-smooth cheeks had never
seen the edge of a razor blade, so he wasn't a doctor.
Probably a lab tech, but Luke didn't care, as long as the
guy had news of June.

"Hi, there. Sorry to keep you waiting." He extended
a hand, and Luke shook it, instantly turned off by the
blond stranger's limp-fish grip. You could tell a lot
about a man from his handshake, and this one screamed,
*I'll turn around and take my wedgie now, thanks. Be
gentle when you shove me in your locker.* "You're the
husband, right?"

"Yep."

"I'm Dr. Benton. I've been taking care of Mrs.
Gallagher."

"Ho-o-ly sh—...*you're* her doctor?" Christ, how old

was this guy? He didn't look a day over fourteen. Luke didn't trust the weak-fisted adolescent any farther than he could drop-kick him, and he wanted a hell of a lot more than just news. He wanted visible proof that June was still alive. "I need to see my wife."

"Sure, I can take you back, but only for a few minutes. But I want to prepare you for what you're going to see."

Luke's heart dipped. "That sounds bad."

"No, no, no. She's perfectly stable, but we're keeping her in a medically induced coma overnight, so she's still on the ventilator. Her face is a little puffy, and there's some significant swelling near the bite wound. Sorry, didn't mean to alarm you."

"So she's gonna be all right?"

"I can't make any promises, but I think the prognosis is good. I'll take you back to see her. How does that sound?"

It sounded like the best damn news he'd heard all day. "Lead the way, Doc."

A distant, tiny voice needled Luke's conscience, telling him to wait—to find Pru first, so they could visit June together—but he shook his head and pushed the voice aside. Right or wrong, he wanted this moment all to himself. And besides, all those tubes, wires, and machines hooked up to June might frighten her grandma. So instead of being selfish, he was doing the right thing. Or, at least that's what he kept telling himself as he followed the doctor through the infamous white double doors.

Instantly, the atmosphere changed. The stinging, almost nauseating odor of ammonia replaced the scents of coffee, corn chips, and concerned relatives, and when the doors whispered closed, they blocked the sun's natural light. The same polished, black and white floor tiles he'd paced in the waiting area appeared even gloomier here beneath the yellow glow of a hundred fluorescent ceiling panels.

Luke and the doctor continued down a long corridor lined with open rooms. Nothing but a thin, blue curtain shielded the occupants inside, and if he looked hard enough, he could make out the outlines of bodies curled in their beds. Without the clamor of conversations, crinkling snack bags, and the distant drone of television news, each cough and moan seemed amplified. Sickness and misery closed around Luke like a fog, and he quickened his pace, hoping Doc Benton would do the same.

After so many twists and turns Luke doubted he'd ever make it out again, they finally arrived at June's room. Benton tugged the curtain aside and gestured for Luke to enter.

What he saw stopped him in his tracks and snatched his breath away.

His little Junebug seemed so broken, swallowed up by a sea of white linens, bandages, hoses, and wires. There was no doubt he'd done the right thing by leaving Pru behind—she didn't need to see this. Someone had taped a breathing tube to June's soft, pink lips, and her chest rose and fell with each quiet whoosh and hiss from the machine at her bedside. Stepping forward, Luke lifted her left hand and cradled it in his own.

"Good thing you remembered to take off her wedding ring before the swelling began," Benton said from behind. "Especially if it's platinum. She might have lost a finger."

"Oh, yeah." Luke turned June's arm over, considering the tight, stretched skin puffing from beneath the bandage. "She wasn't wearing it. We were doing yard work."

"Mmm." The doctor moved to the end of June's bed and began flipping through her chart. "Now, keep in mind that all this"—he swept his hand toward her intravenous lines and the wires monitoring her heart rate—"will come off later tonight. We already stopped the medication keeping her asleep, and after it's out of her system, we'll turn off the artificial respiration. Once she's breathing on her own again, I'll remove the tube—probably early tomorrow morning. She should wake up pretty quickly after that. They always do, because the process is a bit painful." Closing her chart and hooking it back in place, he added, "Any questions for me?"

The word "yes" formed on Luke's mouth, but he couldn't summon a single question except, "When can I see her again?"

"When she wakes up, after I remove the breathing tube. How does that sound?"

"It sounds awful." Clearing a spot on the edge of the bed, Luke carefully sat beside June, so their legs touched through the thick blanket. "But I don't really have a choice, do I?"

"Honestly? No." With a grin and a small laugh that puffed out his baby cheeks, he added, "Don't know why I asked. Just a habit, I guess." He stepped out of the room and swept the curtain across the doorway. Not much privacy, but better than nothing. "I'll leave you alone with your wife for a couple minutes, then the nurse will take you back out front."

When Dr. Benton's rubber soles had squeaked down the hall several paces, Luke lifted June's swollen fingers to his lips.

"Damn it, Junebug," he whispered. "This is exactly why I didn't want your help. Chaos follows you like a freaking shadow, and I can't have you hurt on my watch."

June's only reply was a mechanical whisper of breath pulled from her lungs, but had she been awake, he knew how she'd respond. *You can't keep me away. I said I was here to stay, and I meant it. I'm not leaving, so deal with it, you son of a biscuit-eater.*

Caving to June's demands had been easier than standing up to her and seeing the disappointment in her eyes, but look how well that had turned out. What if he hadn't gotten her to the hospital in time? Or if the doctors had run out of antivenin? She could've died today—and for what? So he could get his house on the market a few days sooner? It wasn't worth the risk, not even close. He was done hurting her.

"It ends right here, Junebug."

He'd wait until June's doctor released her, and then he'd make his intentions perfectly clear. It was time to man up and get serious where June was concerned.

Chapter 18

JUNE AWOKE TO THE BITING SCENT OF ANTISEPTIC AND the clinical whisper of voices. *One-ten over eighty* someone said, sounding pleased. Far in the distance, a cell phone chirped, ringing to the tune of a pop song she recognized, but couldn't identify. Where was she? While struggling to recall her last waking memory, she heard a woman's soft voice call, "Paging Dr. Benton," and then everything clicked into place. June remembered now: the vibrant coral snake with steely jaws, Luke's truck thundering down the highway, suffocating pain.

And the pain wasn't done.

Her mouth was so dry, like someone had forced her to gargle with kitty litter. She tried to lick her lips with a thick, arid tongue. *Water*, she wanted to ask. *Just a sip*. Clearing her throat, June tried to speak, but flames scorched her raw, throbbing airway. God Almighty, what had they done to her?

"Mae-June?" a man's soft voice asked. She wanted to correct him and say, "Just June," but it wasn't worth the effort. Instead, she opened her eyes and squinted against the light. The smooth, round face peering down at her was too young to be a real doctor. He must've been a volunteer. "Hi," he said. "I'm Dr. Benton."

Whatever. June didn't care if he was Dr. Pepper, as long as he gave her a drink. "Thirsty," she whispered.

He nodded emphatically, so his limp, blond hair

flapped against his forehead. "We just removed your breathing tube. Turns out you really didn't need it, but better to be safe than sorry, right?"

"Water," she pressed.

"You can have some ice chips in just a few minutes."

She must have given him a look that expressed exactly what he could do with his ice chips, because he straightened and took a defensive tone. "It's procedure. We can't have you throwing up if we need to intubate you again. If you can hold down the ice chips for an hour, then you can have some juice. How does that sound?"

Pulling her eyebrows low, June groaned and held out her hand. Ice chips were better than nothing, and she wanted them now, not in a few minutes. "Please," was all she could manage. Each breath stung her lungs and throat like she was inhaling glass shards. She glanced over the doctor's shoulder and locked eyes with an elderly nurse to silently plead for help. Giving a sympathetic grin, the nurse nodded and left the room.

"The coral that got you must've chewed awhile before he let go." It wasn't a question, but Dr. Benton paused, as if waiting for an answer. June nodded. "Symptoms don't usually present for an hour after contact. You had a lot of venom coursing through those veins. If this ever happens again, try to stay calm and keep your heart rate low, so it doesn't spread so quickly." He gave her thigh a condescending pat through the blanket. "Lucky for you, we still had some antivenin left. Not easy to find anymore. There're so few coral bites that it's not profitable for the drug companies to keep making it." With a casual shrug, he lifted her chart and then scribbled some notes inside. "I think we'll keep you a few days to make sure you don't have a reaction to the antivenin. How does that sound?"

June wondered how Dr. Benton would respond if she said that sounded like a horrible idea, and recommended he produce a tall glass of iced tea and release her immediately. But then she reminded herself this young man had probably saved her life, so she nodded and forced a weak smile.

"Okay, then. If you're up to it, I'll let your family come in. How does that sound?"

If she wasn't in so much pain, June would have laughed. It sounded great. She lifted one hand, shook her IV tube to the side, and gave a thumbs up.

"Okay." Just before reaching the door, the doctor turned and added, "Your husband's been driving everyone crazy. I know he'll be glad to see you're awake."

Her husband. Hearing it felt surprisingly good—like a hot fudge sundae for her ears, with extra nuts and whipped cream. She remembered Luke telling the emergency dispatch "June Gallagher" was coming. He must not have revealed the true nature of their relationship, probably so the hospital staff would keep him informed. June would have corrected Dr. Benton, would have admitted the truth, but her throat was too dry for words. Or at least that's what she told herself.

When her nurse returned with a Styrofoam cup of ice chips, June forgot all about Luke's marital ruse. She tossed back the cup and began working the ice across her parched tongue, then wrapped her hands around the foam to melt the rest as quickly as possible. The cold wetness in her mouth felt so good she groaned aloud. It trickled down the back of her throat and cooled the flames, healed her tender flesh one frigid drop at a time. Who knew a little shaved ice could bring so much relief?

A knock sounded at the door, and then Grammy rushed inside, followed closely by Judge Bea and Pastor McMahon.

"Thank the Lord," Gram said, holding one trembling, oversized hand above her breast. Then her expression hardened, and she shook her head, probably gearing up for a good, old-fashioned scolding. "Girl, you really *are* snakebit."

"Literally," said the judge with a smile. He set a small, plastic vase filled with daisies on her bedside table. "Y'always were a mishap-magnet."

"Probably weren't paying attention," Gram continued without missing a beat. "Your hands in the soil and your head in the clouds. I taught you better than that. What if Lucas hadn't been there? Then what?"

"Now, Sister Pru,"—the pastor wrapped one arm around Gram's shoulders—"our prayers have been answered. Let's not browbeat the poor girl."

"That's right," the judge said. "I reckon she's been fairly punished already. How'd you feel?"

June touched her throat. "Just a little sore," she whispered. "Got any water?"

"I do." Gram reached into her handbag and pulled out a bottle. She held it just out of June's reach and gave it a little shake. "But I won't give y'any. Doc Benton said you might ask, even though he told you no."

Son of a biscuit-eater. If the breathing tube wasn't necessary to begin with, then the odds of needing to shove it down her throat again were slim to none. What was the big deal? She took another mouthful of ice and glowered at her cup.

"Now, Mae-June," the pastor began in a slow drawl. Pausing, he cleared his throat and stared past his round belly to his loafers. "I don't know your, uh, financial situation, but if you need any help with the hospital bill..." He trailed off and cleared his throat again.

"Oh, Pastor Mac." June lifted her hand, and all its tubes, to her swollen heart. The church didn't have that kind of money to spare; she knew from balancing the ledgers. "Thank you, but I'm fine." Luckily, she'd had the forethought to purchase insurance before she tied all her money up in Luquos.

"Well, we can take up a special collection. Just let me know if you need anything."

No one had ever offered to help June financially before, not that she would've accepted, but the gesture brought tears to her eyes. "I will. Thanks."

"We'd best be goin'," the judge said. He leaned over and kissed the top of June's head. "Luke's chompin' at the bit to come in."

"Mmm-hmm," Grammy added. "Never seen him like this—poor boy's tore up." Was that a hint of a smile on Gram's lips? "Besides, you need rest."

When they left, June couldn't see beyond the curtain shielding the door, but she heard Gram order, "Don't give her any-a-that," and then Luke stepped into view holding a jumbo Slurpee. Cherry, her favorite. But unlike the cool drink in his hands, Luke looked like hell.

His typically sturdy shoulders bowed under some invisible weight, stooping him over like Atlas, as he shuffled forward in his heavy work boots. Someone had given him a shirt—New York Yankees and a size too small—something he never would've worn in any other circumstance because he hated the Yankees with the fire of a thousand atom bombs. Faded green peeked from beneath his heavy eyelids with only a hint of the spark that usually flickered there. June wondered how long she'd been asleep. It looked like Luke had gone twelve rounds with the sandman, and the sandman had won by total knockout.

"You nauseous?" he asked. "Doctor Adolescent said you might be."

June shook her head.

"Headache?" Stepping closer, he tilted his head and appraised her face, quirking one brow in suspicion, as if she might be lying. "Stomach hurt?"

"Just a sore throat." June reached for his free hand and then linked their fingers and tugged him closer. Though his warm, rough skin sent a series of tingles up her arm, it was the Slurpee she glanced at with unguarded lust.

"I saw when they"—Luke tugged his hand free and held two fingers to his lips, like he might gag himself— "shoved that tube down there." He sat beside her on the edge of the bed and held the straw to her mouth. "Thought this might feel good."

"Oh God, thank you." Curling her lips around the straw, June took a deep pull and let the frosty slush slide slowly down her throat, savoring the tangy-sweet flavor of cherries and high fructose corn syrup. What a glorious invention. After a few sips, Luke took the cup away.

"Slow down, Junebug." He skimmed his thumb across her palm and flashed a weak smile. "If you puke, we're both busted."

After setting the Slurpee on the table beside Judge Bea's daisies, Luke scooted against June's thigh and began to study her, scanning her body for damage. His fingers brushed lightly over her forehead, then traveled down the side of one cheek, across her jaw, and ever-so-gently down the length of her neck to her collarbone. June's tummy did a double flip, but not from nausea. A series of quickening beep-beep-beeps sounded from her heart monitor, and she tried to steady her breathing, so the elderly nurse wouldn't come running.

Grasping Luke's fingers before they could explore any lower, she whispered, "Thank you. And not just for the drink."

He turned her hand over and trailed his index finger along the bandage that covered her bite wound. "We were lucky."

Luke's choice of words didn't go unnoticed. Not *you* were lucky, but *we*. Hope began to swell inside June's body. Had she gotten through to him after all? She'd been ready to accept defeat, but maybe…

"I can't stay." Luke took her face between his palms and kissed her cheeks. "The rental company's delivering that furniture you insisted on. For staging, or whatever." When he pulled back, he dipped his head and gave a pointed look. "The doctor said he's keeping you a few more days. There's too much stuff to finish at the house, so I can't come back and visit, but I'll pick you up when they release you. Then we're gonna talk."

There it was—the talk, the one he'd wanted to have before he'd rushed her to the hospital. Nothing had changed. All that cruel hope rose into June's throat and threatened to choke her. She grabbed the Slurpee and sucked down three greedy gulps, but all the sweetness in the world couldn't cover the bitter taste in her mouth. If she'd only learn to rein in her excitement, maybe the crashes wouldn't hurt so much. Or maybe, they still would.

"You don't have to," she said in a voice that betrayed every ounce of her disappointment. "Gram can take me home."

"I'll be here." Then he took the cup and left her with one last, soft kiss on the cheek. "Get some sleep."

Luke pulled the curtain shut behind him, and June curled onto her side and stared blankly out the window, until the nurse arrived with a glass of apple juice. She drank without tasting a thing. A flavorless lunch of Jell-O and lumpy cottage cheese followed.

It didn't take long to understand how Grammy and Trey had felt, trapped alone in this sterile shoe box of a hospital room. With no visitors and no work to occupy her mind, time seemed to go backward. If each minute felt like a month, how had Trey survived two weeks here and still maintained his sanity?

And then, speak of the devil—or think of him—the phone rang from her bedside table.

"Hey, *Jooonbug.*" Trey's smiling voice brought a small grin to her lips. She could almost see the dimples dancing in his cheeks. "I heard you were awake," he continued. "How're you feeling?"

"Fine. Just a sore throat. Well, that, and I'm already going crazy."

He laughed, no doubt remembering his own stay at the Sultry Memorial Inn of Misfortune. "That's a good sign. Listen, I can't get a ride today, but I'll come see you tomorrow."

"Thanks. I'd like that."

"If you need a sponge bath, ask for Stephan." Trey snorted a laugh. "He'll hook you up."

"Uh…okay." She decided not to ask for the details behind that joke.

"And just a little tip," he added. "If you're hurting, ask for one of those big, white pills. I dunno what they're called, but they'll make you sleep like a corpse. The days go by a lot faster when you're knocked out."

She said good-bye, deciding the torture of remaining awake was preferable to forcing a "big, white pill" down her lacerated throat. With a lonely sigh, she clicked on the television.

Sleep didn't come easily that night. Finally, at two in the morning with her legs tangled in the starched white sheets, June drifted under. She dreamt again of Luke at his family's pond. Great waves swelled and crashed against the grass, and he stood on Gram's patchwork quilt, trying to catch whitecaps in a paint bucket. But the bottom dropped out before his bucket was ever full, and he finally sank to his knees, cupping his hands in a futile attempt to collect the water. It slipped through his fingers, and then he slumped over, as if resigned to failure, letting the waves carry him away. June ran to him and grabbed his wrist, but he shook her off and disappeared beneath the surface. He didn't want her help anymore.

Chapter 19

"WAKEY-WAKEY," SAID A LOW MASCULINE VOICE. "I need your temperature."

June groaned and opened one eye. The room was still dark, but a sliver of light from the hall sliced through the open door and illuminated the old analog clock on the wall. Four in the morning. She squinted at the nurse's bulky silhouette. "Didn't you just get it five minutes ago?"

"Nope. That was your blood pressure at three-fifteen. I forgot your temp, so I had to come back." He pressed a plastic-covered thermometer to her lips, and June obediently opened her mouth and held it beneath her tongue. Wasn't she supposed to be resting? Who wakes a patient out of a dead sleep for this? She was beginning to understand why people hated hospitals. To heck with lollipops and Care Bear stickers. She wanted a few consecutive hours of slumber.

A soft beep sounded from the nurse's pocket. "Ninety-seven point nine. Okay, go back to sleep."

Sure, until the next time. Over the last three days, a steady rotation of nurses had awakened her for vitals every few hours. By the time she got back to sleep, someone was strapping a Velcro cuff around her arm again. With a sigh, June gathered the blanket beneath her chin and closed her eyes. She focused on the scent of pine disinfectant and the gentle, wet slosh from the hallway as someone mopped the floors. Within minutes, she was out cold.

"Mae-June?" a softer male voice asked. A hand shook her ankle.

"Just June," she said in a cracked voice. Maybe this was all an elaborate prank—*Candid Camera, Hospital Edition*—to see how patients reacted under extreme sleep deprivation. But to June's surprise, she blinked open her eyes and found the room flooded with daylight. It was eight o'clock, and she'd slept for four straight hours. Hallelujah! Doctor Benton stood at the foot of her bed in a clean, pressed, white lab coat with his name tag clipped to the lapel.

"How're we feeling?" He grinned and turned his attention to her chart.

"Fine. My throat's still a little sore, but not as bad."

"Any paralysis or trouble moving around? Psychosis? Hearing voices, anything like that?"

"Nope. Everything's normal." She pushed the button on the bed's control panel and rose into a sitting position. "I've felt fine for a couple days now."

"Great." He sat beside her on the mattress and peeled back the bandage on her arm. "Looks excellent. Still some swelling, but that's normal. Make sure you finish all your antibiotics, and don't miss any doses. Call if you notice any redness or swelling at the site, or if you start running a temperature above one hundred."

"Okay. So I can go home?" *Please say yes. Please!* June was prepared to take a flying leap out the window if the doctor proposed keeping her there for one more day.

"Yep. Let's get some breakfast in you, and then the nurse will be around to take out your IV and go over the discharge paperwork. Any questions?"

"Nope." Breakfast sounded pretty good, even if

it wasn't Grammy's famous egg and ham biscuits. June had been drinking her meals and choking down mushy yogurt and cottage cheese the past two days, so the thought of eating real, solid food again made her mouth water. "Oh, and thanks. For saving my life and everything."

He waved a dismissive hand. "It was my pleasure." Then he backed toward the door and held up her chart in a good-bye gesture. "Take care, and watch out for those snakes."

Over the next hour, June inhaled her bagel and orange juice, then showered and brushed her teeth with toiletries provided by the hospital. She changed into the clean sundress Gram had brought her the day before and then went over a checklist of warning signs with the nurse. Each tick of the clock brought her closer to the dreaded talk with Luke, and she struggled to focus on something positive. Something to look forward to. Aside from a good night's rest, she was coming up empty.

At precisely nine o'clock, Luke knocked on her door and let himself in. Clean-shaven and freshly showered, he seemed refreshed compared to the last time she'd seen him, but his reddened eyes told her he hadn't slept well either. Even in weathered jeans and an old T-shirt, even running on fumes from no sleep, he still took her breath away. It simply wasn't fair.

"Hey," he said, grabbing her plastic bag of personal items in one hand and offering the other to help her out of bed. "Ready?"

Even though she didn't need to, she curled her hand around his firm bicep and leaned against his shoulder while he walked her to his truck. If she only had minutes to cling to him before he gave her the brush-off, she intended to use that time well. She inhaled his after-shave and savored the closeness and warmth, despite the heavy, humid morning air that brought beads of sweat to the surface of her skin.

Once they settled in, Luke reached across her chest and fastened her seat belt. "I can't put this off anymore." June's heart sank like a lead weight, but she nodded for him to continue. "I'm done with your help, Junebug."

"But—" she started to object, and he held a finger to her lips.

"You have two choices: either I drive you to Pru's, or I take you back to my house. But I have to make some-thing clear before you decide. If you come home with me, you won't lift a single paint roller or scrub brush or garden spade. There're three proper beds upstairs now, and if you come home with me," he paused and moved his hand to cup her cheek, "I'm gonna lay you down in one of them."

"I don't need any more rest."

"Good. Because I won't stop making love to you till we're both too weak to move."

A breath caught in the back of June's throat, while heat flushed her cheek beneath Luke's touch. Maybe she hadn't heard him correctly. But when Luke scooted across the bench seat until their thighs touched and pulled her mouth to his, she knew he'd meant every word. His kiss was soft and teasing, a quick taste of things to come, sending the heat from her face downward.

"If that's not what you want," he said against her lips, "then tell me now."

Fighting every instinct, June pushed against his chest

until he backed away. "Wait." She met his gaze, determined not to let him run hot and cold with her again. "You know what that would mean?"

"I remember everything you said."

"All in?" she asked, half expecting a nurse to wake her for vital signs because this couldn't be real.

"I want to try."

"Try?" June shook her head. Tempting as it was, she wanted commitment, not a halfhearted attempt with one foot already out the door. She deserved more. "That's not enough."

"I'm no good at this." Taking her face in his hands, Luke kissed her again and then tipped their foreheads together and pleaded with his eyes. "I don't know what I'm doing, but I want to try. Please? Let me try." June's resolve crumbled beneath the weight of his sincerity. His mouth moved across her jaw to her ear, where his tongue and hot breath mingled and turned her insides to jelly. Then his teeth found the magical spot at the top of her shoulder, and June knew she was helpless. "Just say yes," he whispered.

"Yes."

"Really?" He pulled away, blinking in surprise. Had he actually believed she'd say no? For one brief second, a wide smile curved his lips, and then those lips were on her mouth. June's seat belt released, sliding over her breasts, and then Luke tugged her gently across the leather seat until she was pressed to his side. He pulled the middle lap belt loosely over her thighs and clicked it in place. "Then let's get the hell outta here," he said. The engine roared, the truck lurched forward, and in seconds, they were tearing down the highway.

Still convinced this might be a dream, June curled an arm around Luke's waist and buried her face in the crook of his neck. She breathed in the scents of soap and aftershave and slid her open mouth over his clean, sweet flesh. When he groaned from the back of his throat, the vibration danced across her lips, and she smiled with pride. *This man*, she thought, while smoothing her palm across the hard contours of his chest, *is mine—at least for now—and it's real*. Needing to feel more, she yanked Luke's T-shirt from the waistband of his jeans.

"This needs to go," she said. "I'll take the wheel."

Luke muttered a curse under his breath, but he let her steer the truck while he pulled the shirt off in one fluid motion and tossed it to the floor. For weeks, she'd watched him work bare-chested, and now she could finally touch. Her hands moved greedily everywhere she could reach, and she ached to taste each exposed inch. Starting at Luke's broad shoulders, she kissed her way down his chest, where she flicked her tongue over his nipple. Using her teeth, she grazed the hard bud before drawing it into her mouth with the lightest suction.

"Shit," he hissed, reaching around to stroke her spine.

His heart thumped beneath her fingers as she moved lower to kiss his flat belly. When she unfastened his jeans and pressed her palm against the length of his erection, he gasped and covered her hand with his own.

"What're you doing?" he asked.

Shaking off his hand, she replied, "Mind your own business and drive." She reached inside Luke's boxers and freed him, long and smooth and hard as river rock. Working her thumb over his velvet tip, she spread the bead of moisture there, then stroked the length of him, savoring his groans of pleasure. Lowering further, she used her tongue to lap up each new bead of his arousal, before abruptly plunging him into her mouth. He swore loudly and thrust his hips to meet her. The sweetness of Luke's hot, tight skin, the noises coming from his throat, the tension in his muscles, all sent June's blood rushing between her thighs. She needed to feel him there, thick and full...and soon.

"Stop," he gasped. "Baby, your throat."

Maybe it was a little sore, but she knew how to modify her technique, and she showed him how, using one hand to twist up and down his wet shaft.

"*Christ*." His eager hips contradicted his next words. "Stop, or you'll kill us both."

June didn't want to quit, but he was probably right. Slowly, and with gentle suction, she pulled her lips to the tip of his erection and released him. If she couldn't make love to him yet, at least she could be ready the moment Luke parked his truck in the driveway. Her panties soon joined Luke's boxers on the truck's floor, and she unhooked her bra and slipped each strap over her arms, before pulling it up through the V-neck of her dress.

Taking his eyes away from the road a moment, Luke glanced at the pile of discarded underwear and motioned for her to come closer. "Pull up your dress," he ordered in a husky voice. "And spread those pretty knees."

When she obeyed, he licked his thumb and found her aching, sensitive bud, then began stroking her with a light, teasing touch that puckered her nipples and tore a groan from her chest. Using one finger, he circled her pulsing entrance, until she breathed, "More," and at her command, he slid in and out, pumping her with the same slow, exquisite skill he'd used days ago. He stopped only long enough to tug her knees farther apart, before dipping in again, this time adding a second finger, twisting deep inside to massage erogenous zones she didn't even know she had.

With a loud moan, June tipped her head to rest against his shoulder, unconsciously spreading wider for his luscious touch. Again and again, he took her to the brink and withdrew his fingers before she climaxed, the whole time whispering wicked promises in her ear.

It was sweet torture, withholding her release, as the miles blurred past far too slowly. Leave it to Luke to drive the speed limit, eyes glued to the road, control as rigid as ever. By the time he turned the truck into the driveway, every muscle in her body vibrated like a harp string.

Pulling his fingers away to lick each one, Luke gave her a lust-filled grin that made her heart stutter. "You always tasted so good."

When June launched herself at him and crushed their lips in a frantic kiss, her own salty flavor crossed her tongue. It was more erotic than she ever anticipated. In seconds, Luke cut the engine, opened his door, and gathered her into his arms. God only knows how they made it inside, but June heard the front door slam, and then her body was sandwiched between the cool wall and Luke's firm body.

"Longest drive of my life," he muttered, while tearing at the buttons on her dress. He only managed half of them before sliding the fabric gently down her shoulders, so her arms were pinned at her sides. If not for her wound, she suspected Luke would've been rougher—and the notion of him ripping her clothes off made her head spin.

Glancing from her eyes to her bare breasts, he shook his head in awe. "You're perfect. Just like I remember." He massaged each one with his calloused palms and then bent to draw her nipple deep into his mouth. June felt each tug of suction right between her legs, growing into a hot ache. Needing contact, needing friction, she strained her hips against his and moaned Luke's name. During the entire ride home, he'd tormented her with his fingers, and now, his tongue flicked and circled her nipple to tease again. The dull throb was unbearable.

"Please," she whispered, wriggling her arms free, careful to avoid snagging her bandage, and then pushing her dress to the floor. "Now."

"Not here." Luke backed up and took a second to appreciate her naked body while he shed his boots and jeans. "I'll have you in a real bed for once." After peeling off his boxers, he closed the distance between them, scooped her into his arms like a bride, and carried her up the stairs into the master bedroom. Dark wood furnishings and floral décor passed in June's periphery, but she barely noticed. Her mind shut to all coherent thought outside of Luke's touch.

June wanted to take her time, to slow everything down and savor each sensation, but the second her back hit the comforter, she tugged Luke onto her body and wrapped her legs around him like a vise. "Please. Now," she repeated.

"Just one second." Luke reached into the nightstand drawer and pulled out a condom, and June released him only long enough for him to roll it on. Then she brought him down against her once again, delighting in his weight, in the feel of his heavy, solid body pressing her deep into the mattress.

Luke brushed her hair back and gazed at her beneath heavy lids. He whispered her name and hesitated to say something more. Then he buried his face in the curve of her neck and brought both hands down to grasp her hips, fitting his thumbs to the indents there. "God, I love these dimples," he murmured. "You were made for my hands."

When he settled against her and eased inside, June's eyes rolled back with pleasure. He toyed with her a moment, stoking her desire, teasing her swollen entrance with shallow strokes and pinning her to the bed when she tried bucking her hips to impale herself. Releasing her, he leaned on one elbow, whispering, "Look at me."

She locked eyes with Luke, and at once he rewarded her, pulling back and then driving in to the hilt with one powerful thrust that filled her to bursting and knocked them both against the headboard.

A sharp gasp of ecstasy tore June's lungs, the dull ache at her temple barely registering above the bliss. As she brought her knees up to take him impossibly deeper, Luke pulled back, withdrawing so slowly she felt every ridge and bulge along his hot, distended shaft. His fingers brushed her scalp, eyes searching her face with concern as she writhed beneath him, silently pleading for more.

"Are you okay?"

She trailed her hands down to his backside and took one firm cheek in each hand. "Don't stop." Tugging at his steely buttocks, she rocked forward, guiding him inside once again. He seemed to anticipate her every need, plunging deep and slow, before switching to hard, quick thrusts when her body demanded it. Her hands flitted along his lower back, cupping his muscles as they bunched and flexed with each pump of his hips. The rush of pleasure, the mounting pressure, told her she wouldn't last much longer.

After a sensual kiss, Luke extended his arms and pushed away from her body, holding himself above her so she could watch each long, glistening stroke, but she pulled at his shoulders, needing to feel his weight. She wanted to be crushed, surrounded, engulfed by his warmth, his scent. "Stay here," she whispered in a shuttering breath, wrapping arms and legs tightly around him. *Stay here forever*.

Luke lifted her just long enough to wrap one arm around her back, drawing them even nearer, before covering her with his body. Once again, he knew exactly what she needed, and when he ground against her in a circular motion, June swore loudly and arched her neck off the pillow. The tempo increased as they moved in perfect harmony, sharing the same heaving breaths, both soaring higher and higher toward the peak. With the next slamming thrust, June's inner walls clenched in erotic spasms, and she cried out, feeling him twitch inside her as they both pulsed in hot release. The waves of pleasure continued to crash inside her, one coming and then another and another, until Luke drove himself deep and stiffened, holding there and muffling a cry against her shoulder.

His closeness, all the pleasure he'd given her, caused a swell of emotion to surge up, and June couldn't stop the words leaping off her tongue. "I love you, Luke."

Remembering how those words had caused him to bolt once, she wanted to hold them inside, but she couldn't stop. "I love you. I love you." She fisted his long hair, holding on for life. "God, I love you so much."

"Shhh," he whispered, brushing her cheek with his thumb. He silenced her with a soft kiss, but *I love you* continued to move on her lips. He didn't pull away, didn't flinch. Instead, Luke caressed her face and alternated between gentle kisses and intimate gazes, maybe—hopefully—showing her what he couldn't say.

After a few minutes, June drifted back to reality, once again able to control her tongue. But pressing her lips together to restrain the words didn't make them any less true. She loved Luke Gallagher more than ever. If there'd once been a part of her soul she'd held aside for herself, he possessed it now. She was helpless, vulnerable, but the warmth and safety of his arms staved off the cold shiver of fear inside her belly.

"God, Junebug." Luke's heartbeat began to slow—she felt it against her breast—but he gripped her thigh and rocked against her, and the beats picked up speed. "It's not enough. I don't think it'll ever be enough." His tongue found her nipple, and she felt him grow thick and hard inside her again. "More?" he asked, with a lazy rotation of hips.

"Yes," June whispered, matching each slow stroke. She'd give him more. She'd give him everything.

Chapter 20

A SLIVER OF MOONLIGHT ESCAPED A GAP BETWEEN THE curtains and cast a soft glow over June's curls, picking up a mahogany hue Luke never saw during the day. He propped on one elbow and watched a strand of hair ebb and flow across her lips with each faint snore and exhale of breath. Smiling, he gently pushed it to the side. Shit like that would tickle him awake. She slept like a child, facedown with her mouth wide open, arms tucked beneath her chest. And she sure as hell deserved the rest. True to his word, he'd made love to her until they were both too weak to go on. So what was keeping him up now?

Adrenaline, maybe. Like a kid who gets a sugar buzz from eating a gallon of ice cream in one sitting, he'd gorged himself all day long. How did a guy come down from something like that? God, he wanted her again, right that second—had to restrain himself from waking her with hot kisses on the back of her neck. He felt like a horny teenager with testosterone oozing from every pore. Like that mythical box he'd learned about in school—Pandorama or whatever—he'd opened it, and nothing would ever be the same again. Especially since he'd broken down and allowed himself to feel June without the protective barrier of latex.

Even though she'd insisted they didn't need one, Luke had used a condom each time, until they'd ended up in the shower. June had soaped him up real good, one place in particular, then rinsed him off and dropped to her knees to clamp those full, pouty lips around him. Steadying himself against the tile wall, he'd let her take him almost to the brink, and then stopped her. Something in him had shifted, no longer wanting the extra layer between them. *I don't want to come in your mouth*, he'd said and pulled her to standing. *I want to come here*—and dipped a finger inside—*so you'll feel me later against your thighs and remember everything I'm about to do to you.*

Then he'd settled her facing the bathroom mirror, propped her heel on the countertop, and entered her from behind, so she could watch every hot, wet stroke. He'd touched her where they joined, and she'd peaked again and again and again around his shaft. No sensation in the world had ever felt so good. As he gave, she took, burning a hole in the mirror with her gaze and repeating *I love you* like it was the only thing she knew how to say. It stripped him of all barriers, left him raw inside. And when she collapsed with the pleasure, he'd carried her like a rag doll back to bed and gathered her body against his, until they both fell asleep tangled in each other's limbs.

There was no coming back from that. Nothing else—no other woman—would ever measure up. This realization didn't exactly thrill him, but it was true all the same, and watching her sleep made his tense, knotted abdomen quiver. How could he let her go in a few days? Thinking about it made panic swell into his throat. Compulsively, he wrapped an arm around her waist and touched their foreheads together. Her hair smelled of his shampoo, her body of his sweat, and it brought a smile to his lips. For now, she belonged to him. Luke reminded himself of that fact and drifted back to sleep.

—⁓—

"Oh, sugar!" June's shrill voice knocked him into consciousness, and he bolted upright, glancing around the room for trouble. Finding none, he squinted against the sunlight and turned to her.

"What?"

"I've been here all night! What'll I tell Grammy?" A pink flush stained her cheeks, and the hair on one side of her head bunched above her temple like a bird's nest. She clutched the sheet over her breasts, as if he hadn't seen every inch of her body already.

"Well," Luke said, moving in to nuzzle her shoulder and noticing the mark he'd left there last night, "you sure don't want to tell her what I did to you in the kitchen with the molasses."

"This is serious." She palmed his chest and pushed him back.

Sure it was. A twenty-seven-year-old woman having sex—oh, the horror. Luke tried not to laugh. "Tell you what. I'll call Pru and tell her I was too tired to drive you home last night. It's not a total lie. I just won't mention all the ways you tuckered me out." Hopefully, Pru wouldn't ask about the sleeping arrangements.

"Okay, I guess that—" June sat up straighter, her cheeks darkening from pink to scarlet. Taking her wrist in his hand, Luke felt her pulse quicken and raised one brow as a silent question. "You're um," she said, darkening from scarlet to maroon, "getting what you wanted."

He pulled her palm to his lips, unable to deny he had everything he wanted.

June cleared her throat. "I mean, last night in the shower. When you said I'd feel you later on the skin between my"—cleared her throat again—"and remember what you did to me."

Male pride coursed through Luke's veins and sent a smile in motion across his lips. "Happy memory?"

"Very."

Pulling the sheet away, Luke leaned in and swept kisses along the top of her shoulder. "We should make some more." He trailed a hand over her breast, tightening her nipple to a bud, and continued lower, all the way down. "Memories." But when he eased a finger inside, June gasped and flinched back.

He drew his hand away, feeling like the world's biggest ass. Of course she was sore—he'd ravaged her like a friggin' animal for the last twenty hours. "Sorry, hon." He took her face in his palms and kissed each cheek. "Hop in the shower if you want. I'll put on some coffee and call Pru." And he'd keep his hands to himself, until she made the next move.

—⁓—

Standing back from the steaming shower jets, June hesitated a moment, reluctant to wash Luke's scent from her skin. It was silly, of course. She'd probably heal and feel ready for intimacy again by nightfall, and even if she didn't, he'd wrap her in his arms and his scent again. Maybe a small part of her was afraid he'd run away, and this would be the last time his essence would surround her so completely. Time to be brave, to have some faith.

She moved forward and let the hot water carry away the physical evidence of their lovemaking.

When she stepped out of the shower and dried off, she noticed her clothes neatly folded on the countertop. She smiled, realizing she'd worn them less than an hour yesterday. Technically, they were still clean.

She padded down the stairs and into the kitchen in bare feet, while breathing in the aroma of freshly brewed coffee. Luke used the good stuff, she could tell. When he turned and offered her a mug, June's eyes automatically scanned his face for any signs of regret. He smiled—the signature Luke smile that crinkled his face and sucked the air from her lungs—and she sighed in relief. He kissed the side of her neck and pushed something into her palm.

"Ibuprofen," he said. "I don't keep much food around, but I tried to make you breakfast." He gestured to a sandwich stuffed full of deli meat, and June's stomach rumbled at the sight. She popped the pills into her mouth, washed them down with a swallow of coffee, and attacked the sandwich. Turkey, her favorite.

"Your grandma gave me a tongue lashing for not calling last night, but other than that, everything's fine. She wanted me to give you a message. Your partner called this morning."

"Oh, Esteban?" she said with her mouth full. She'd forgotten all about him.

"I guess." Luke shrugged, pursing his lips in a quick show of disdain. "Said don't worry about anything today, just rest up, and talk to him tomorrow." She wondered if Luke's reaction was fueled by jealousy, or reluctance for her return to Austin. Or both.

"He's just a friend, you know." Setting her breakfast

down, she stepped toward Luke. "And old enough to be my father."

"None of my business."

June smoothed her fingers up and down the length of his bare chest and then wrapped her arms around his waist. "I like to think it is." She rested her chin beneath his shoulder and peered at the stubble darkening his jaw.

His arms tightened around her, and he kissed the top of her head. "We need to get outta here soon. I listed the house while you were in the hospital. Four showings today."

"What?" June's eyes widened to the size of dinner plates. She glanced at the dirty dishes in the sink and the unswept floor. Had anyone finished planting the flowers out front? She hadn't even walked through the rest of the house to see that everything was in order. "How long do we have?"

"Two hours, but you're not lifting a finger. We agreed."

June told him where to shove his agreement, and after a quick and heated exchange of words, Luke relented. He tackled the floors while she washed dishes and made beds. When June suggested picking wildflowers to add to the vase on the kitchen table, Luke volunteered for that chore, probably fearing she'd draw every snake within ten miles with her siren call of rotten luck. The mulch bed along the front walkway had already been finished, lined with mums, and spread with cedar chips. Though she'd wanted to add some evergreen bushes and ground cover, June had to admit the landscaping already had a simplistic, cozy feel.

They walked out to Luke's truck, and he pulled her close. "Let's go fishing," he said. "Just you and me. I don't wanna share you today."

June smiled up at him, not particularly wanting to be shared. "Catch and release, and I'm not baiting my own hook."

"Deal."

Thirty minutes later, they parked in Grammy's driveway and stopped inside to say hello and grab a quilt and picnic basket.

"*There* you are." Gram turned from her place at the kitchen sink, waving a dish towel at them. "Worried me sick!"

"I'm sorry." June paused to yawn. "I fell right into bed and forgot to call." Technically, it was the truth.

"Hey," Luke argued, holding up one defensive hand, "you already yelled at me today. I'm gonna get the fishing gear." He kissed June on the head and scurried out the back door, escaping a lecture in the process.

If the kiss took Gram by surprise, she didn't let it show. Drying her soapy hands, she shook her head and muttered under her breath, "Mm-hmm. Fell right in-ta bed." She made a *come here* motion. "No more bandage? Lemme see."

June obeyed, and after Grammy had inspected the wound to her satisfaction, she held out her arms for a quick hug.

"Good to have ya home," Gram said, nodding at the back door. "Now go on, and catch up with Lucas, but remember"—she lifted one finger in warning—"you're sleepin' in your own bed tonight. Y'understand me?"

June suppressed a smile. "Yes, ma'am."

~~~

She met Luke at the shed, and they walked hand-in-hand

to the pond. A slight chill on the breeze hinted of fall's arrival, but the sun warmed the back of June's neck. The scents of freshly mown grass, cedar trees, and Luke's aftershave swirled inside her head, and she wished she could bottle the smell and breathe it in on cold, dark days when life seemed bleak. It was more soothing than any drink she'd ever mixed.

Luke wasn't really interested in fishing. June could tell from his choice of bait: a pair of discarded rubber worms coated in faded pink glitter that looked less appetizing than pond sludge. Had he been serious, he'd dig for night crawlers in the rich soil beside the pond, or trap a few crickets in the underbrush. But that suited her just fine. She wasn't really interested in fishing either. While he cast their lines into the water and situated the poles between two heavy rocks near the cattails, June spread the patchwork quilt in the shaded grass.

Soon, they cuddled together on the blanket, Luke on his back with one arm folded beneath his head, and June snuggled beside him, wrapped in his other arm. She rested her palm on his chest and felt his heart beat slow and steady, and for several minutes, they said nothing. At one point, he claimed her arm, studied what remained of her bite wound, and brushed a kiss over the two tiny scabs there. Some swelling remained, pink and puckered, but all things considered, she'd escaped relatively unscathed.

A chorus of mating calls croaked, buzzed, and chirped from the shallow water, and June smiled, figuring love was in the air today. Which brought a question to her lips.

"Do you believe me when I say I love you?"

If she hadn't felt Luke's muscles stiffen, she would've repeated herself. But he heard. He understood.

After a long minute, he said, "I believe that you believe it." She turned his words over in her mind while he absently stroked her arm. "You love the man you think I am," he continued, "but not the real me. You don't know the real me. There's not much to love."

June's pulse quickened. She hated to hear him talk like that. It wasn't just the dismissal of her feelings, but Luke's genuine disdain for himself. It both angered and saddened her. "Let's pretend we never grew up together," she said, propping herself on one elbow. "That we met for the first time when I came back to town. This is what I'd see: a man who works hard to help his neighbors—not for money, or because the court ordered him to—but because it's the right thing to do. A man who takes care of his friends. He makes sure I get home okay after work. He's patient. And a generous lover. Really, really generous."

Luke smirked and tugged her on top of him. "You're confusing generosity with greed." His hands traveled down the length of her back and settled on her bottom. "I'd be inside you right now, if you weren't so sore."

"Don't change the subject." June kissed him softly. "I know the man I'm in love with. Better than he knows himself."

"You think so?" He rolled her back onto the blanket and leaned up, looking out over the murky water. His voice darkened. "Ever heard of an OTH?"

"No."

"Other Than Honorable. It's how I was discharged from the army."

June's mouth fell open, not from disapproval, but because she couldn't believe he was talking about it. Caressing his arm encouragingly, she asked, "What happened?"

"The short version? I beat the shit out of my commanding officer."

She couldn't stop her brows from ratcheting skyward. But she knew Luke. He must've had a good reason. "And the long version?"

He pulled in a deep breath and sighed loudly before glancing down at her. "You really wanna know?" When she nodded, he eased back onto the quilt. He took her hand and splayed her fingers, fidgeting with them as he spoke. "I told you a little about my ex-wife, Ada. How it was really bad between us?" June nodded, and he continued. "When I knew it wasn't gonna work, I asked for an annulment, but she wouldn't have it. Probably 'cause she hadn't gotten her green card yet. Anyway, she'd been sleeping around behind my back. I think she knew I'd divorce her, and she wanted to snag another soldier first—someone who'd bring her back to the states. An officer this time. Eventually, she hooked one. My boss."

"Oh, sugar!"

"Exactly." His lips twitched in a grin. "An asshole named Captain Pratt. I didn't know about it, but Trey did."

"Wait," June interrupted, "I thought officers couldn't do things like that. Commit adultery."

Laughing, he gave her a look that made her feel naïve, then kissed the back of her hand. "Technically, they can't. But it's hard to prove, and it happens all the time."

"Oh."

"Anyway, Trey thought I really loved Ada—he didn't

know any better—and he tried talking to Pratt, to get him to break it off with her."

"Did it work?"

"No. The guy just balked and denied everything. And you know Trey—he wouldn't let it go. He started snooping around, following them to see where they met, stuff like that. Finally, he came to me and spilled everything." Luke laughed without humor. "Poor bastard was sweating like a whore in church. He was afraid I'd shoot the messenger."

June understood. She'd been the messenger once and had lost a friend in the process.

"Anyway," Luke continued, "when I told him I wanted a quick divorce, he came up with what we *thought* was a brilliant idea to make Ada cooperate."

"Let me guess. To catch her in the act?"

"More or less." Frowning, he waved away a mosquito. "We followed her and Pratt to their favorite hangout, some dive bar off post, to take pictures with a disposable camera left over from my wedding." He shook his head cynically. "Seemed like a good idea at the time."

It seemed like a good idea to June too. "What went wrong?"

"I'd just snapped a few shots of them kissing when one of Pratt's buddies—another officer—noticed us and went ape-shit. He came storming over for my camera, and Trey stopped him. They started throwing down, and then Pratt charged me like a bull."

"Uh-oh." June saw where this was headed. "What's the penalty when someone gets busted for adultery?"

"Discharge—an OTH, like mine." Locks of ruddy,

brown hair blew across Luke's forehead with the breeze, and he pushed them back, face hardening as he replayed the events. "Pratt wanted my camera. Bad enough to fight for it. But I held him off and stuffed it in my back pocket. That's when he got Ada involved."

June didn't like the sound of that.

"I guess he'd agreed to marry her, and she didn't want her new meal ticket getting discharged. So she threatened to tell Command I'd cheated first. When I didn't take the bait, Pratt asked her, *What about all the times he hit you?*" Luke tightened his grip on her hand. "I swear to God, June, her face lit up like the goddamned sun. She started spewing lies about how I beat her, and Pratt kept egging her on. She even said I made her miscarry our baby—the one that never existed. Claimed she could get her doctor to swear to it, if she paid him enough."

He paused to take a deep breath. Though five years had passed, his jaw clenched in obvious frustration, not that she blamed him. June stroked his chest until his tense muscles relaxed beneath her touch. A few seconds later, he swallowed hard and continued. "Then Pratt said 'Keep the camera, you stupid hick. Nobody's gonna believe a wifebeater over me. You'll be in the brig by morning, and in a kraut prison till you're thirty.'" With his free hand, Luke scrubbed his face. "And then I completely lost it. I went off on him."

"Of course you did!" She would've snapped too.

"No, June." He shifted his gaze, locking his green eyes on hers. "I messed him up really bad. Broke his jaw, his nose, maybe even a few ribs. I don't remember."

"Good."

"*Good?* Jesus, I snapped and beat a man till my knuckles bled! That doesn't scare you?"

"No." Not only had Pratt slept with Luke's wife, he'd tried framing him for spousal abuse. Besides, she'd known Luke all her life, and though he'd gotten into a few tiffs in high school, he'd never hurt anyone.

"Well, it scares me. What if it happens again?"

June reached up and caressed his cheek. "*Has* it happened again?"

"No, but—"

"But nothing. That man attacked you, then pushed and pushed, until he got the reaction he wanted. Pratt got what he deserved."

Luke shook his head. "The army disagrees with you. The only thing that saved me from getting a dishonorable discharge was those damned pictures. They took the affair into account and lessened it to an OTH."

"What about Trey?"

"Same thing—OTH for striking a superior officer."

"And Pratt?"

Luke released her hand, turning his gaze to the clouds. "Last I heard, he lawyered up and got transferred stateside. I don't know if he married Ada, but I like to think so. A fitting punishment for both of them."

"What a mess."

"No shit." Luke plucked a tall blade of grass, then began snapping it to pieces. "My career? Gone, just like that. World War Three could break out, and they wouldn't call me back. And folks don't exactly go out of their way to hire you when you've got an OTH on your record."

That explained Morris Howard's second chance.

He'd helped Luke build a new career when no one else would have him. And then Luke had done the same for Trey and the steady rotation of troubled men who worked with Helping Hands.

"That doesn't seem fair." June swept bits of grass off the blanket. "You didn't do anything wrong."

"The hell I didn't." His voice went sharp, eyes narrowed. "Don't do that. Don't make excuses for me. I agreed to live by a code of honor, and I broke it. Nobody put a gun to my head. I made a stupid choice. I hurt someone, and I deserve the consequences."

June straddled Luke's lap, taking his chin so she had his full attention. "Doesn't change anything. That officer shouldn't have slept with your wife. And don't even get me started on the fake abuse charges."

"It doesn't excuse what I—"

"No. You made a mistake, and you've moved on with your life, as you should. You're a good man. I love you." She kissed him hard on the mouth, trying to force away the remnants of his self-hatred. When he shook his head to object, she pulled him closer. Eventually, he softened enough to return the kiss.

A buzzing noise sounded from Luke's pocket, the vibration tickling June's inner thigh. She scooted aside to let him answer the call, but she never stopped soothing him with gentle touches.

Luke checked the incoming number and tapped his phone's screen. "Let's hear it." He nodded in response to whatever was said on the other end. "Great, thanks." Then he disconnected, short and sweet.

"Good news?" she asked. They could use some.

"The best. That was my realtor. He thinks we'll have

multiple offers by tonight." The hope of a quick sale seemed to lift his mood, bringing out a tentative smile. "And he loved your ideas—the colors and furniture and girly stuff. I never thanked you for that."

It still wasn't a *thank you*, not really, but June grinned and rested her head on Luke's chest. Part of her wanted to continue their conversation, but she thought better of it. If, deep down, Luke didn't believe she loved him, repeating the words wouldn't make a difference. She wrapped an arm tightly around his waist and sighed.

That's when they heard the first of the distant sirens.

Chapter 21

LUKE YAWNED BEHIND HIS FIST AND SQUINTED UP AT the cloudless, blue sky. He directed his dubious gaze at the trees, whose leaves rustled lightly in the cool breeze. With no scent of rain weighting the air, he wondered if someone had fired off the weather sirens by accident.

"They still run drills the first Tuesday of the month?" June asked, obviously just as puzzled.

"Yeah." But this was the last week in September. Not a test. "Guess we should head back to Pru's and check the forecast." Late summer storms could creep up quicker than a duck on a beetle, and he had no intention of getting caught in the open.

With a groan, he rolled off the blanket and then reeled in their empty fishing lines. Thankfully, nothing took the bait. The last thing he wanted to do was untangle a crotchety snapping turtle or unhook a puny trout. He'd hoped to wrap June in his arms and enjoy a long nap, since neither of them had slept much last night. They still could, he guessed, just on Pru's sofa. Not quite the same, though.

June shook out the blanket and slung it over one shoulder, as Luke grabbed their untouched picnic basket. While they walked back to Pru's, Luke couldn't help tuning out June's soft prattle to consider what his agent had said. Multiple offers didn't necessarily mean a bidding war. If he'd listed the house when he'd originally intended—if Trey's injury hadn't set him so far back—he'd be in a better position to negotiate. But with his land coming up for auction in a week, Luke didn't have the luxury of holding out for the highest bidder. The buyer who offered immediate closing would win his home.

His heart accelerated, and despite the new chill in the air, he lifted a shoulder to wipe sweat from his temple. He'd really cut it close this time, but everything would work out all right. Worst-case scenario: he'd clear just enough to buy his land and then crash with Pru while taking on small projects to build up more capital. Start flipping hovels again, just like before. The idea of living with Pru, especially at his age, made his stomach feel heavy. He wanted stability and independence, not only for himself, but for June. It was hard feeling like he deserved her. Unnatural. But if he could get that land, build a fine home near the pond, show he had something real to offer—maybe then she'd get someone else to run Luquos and come back to Sultry Springs.

"Hey," June said, giving their linked fingers a tug. "Where'd you go?"

Luke gave an apologetic smile and brought her hand to his lips. "Nowhere special."

"Looks ominous." She raised her chin to the sky, which had transformed into a sickly shade of green in the brief time he'd zoned out. Heavy clouds began to race past while the wind whipped the ends of his hair into his eyes. He picked up the pace, and by the time they rushed through Pru's back door, the putrid sky opened up and pelted the earth with tiny hailstones.

June shook out her hair, and chunks of ice the size of frozen peas clinked to the linoleum floor. While she scooped up the mess and tossed them into the sink, Luke grabbed a peanut butter sandwich from the picnic basket and joined Pru in the living room.

"Had no idea this was comin'," Pru said, gesturing to the same faded oak console television where he and June had watched cartoons as kids. Weatherman "Pudgy Paul" Stockman warned in a chipper voice to expect a series of violent storms throughout the day and swept his hands over a local map splotched with greens and reds to indicate rainfall.

Luke plopped down on the sofa. "Guess fishing's out."

"We can lie around here just as well as the pond," June said. "Scoot down." He moved to one end, and she stretched out, resting her head in his lap. Sliding a gaze at his sandwich, she opened her mouth for a bite.

He broke off one corner and touched the bread to her lips before yanking it back again and popping it into his mouth. When she puffed out that pouty lower lip, he bent down to kiss it. Pru pretended not to see their playful exchange, but he noticed a smile dance across her cheeks, before she turned and left the room.

"Plus," June added, "it's been too long since we had a good storm."

That's right. He'd forgotten how much June loved thunderstorms. She used to sit on the front porch and watch them roll in, until the lightning came too close, and Pru would make her come inside. By that time, she'd be half soaked, with snarled, windblown hair, but always grinning. Like she'd harnessed a force of nature or something.

He tore his sandwich in two and handed June half while finishing the rest in one overstuffed bite. Then a mixture of drugging sensations—the steady, rhythmic pelting of ice against the roof, sunlight slipping behind dark clouds, June's soft curls tangled within his fingers—lulled him into a trancelike state, until his eyelids grew heavy as cinder blocks. He knew better than to take June upstairs to his bed, even for a chaste nap. Pru would beat him senseless with her heavy, hardback Bible. Instead, he lay down beside her on the narrow couch and pulled her tightly against his body. She burrowed her cheek into his chest, and he was out cold within minutes.

The next thing Luke knew, Pru's large bony hand was clamped around his shoulder. "Come on," she said, giving him a hard shake. "Time to move down to the cellar." In her other hand, Pru gripped an emergency radio with a built-in flashlight.

"Huh?" Still in a fog, he helped June sit up and then stumbled off the sofa. How long had they slept? The room was black as night, but it didn't seem like that much time had passed.

"Tornadoes?" June asked in a cracked whisper. Her eyes widened, reflecting the dim, flickering light from the television. June's love of thunder and lightning didn't extend to tornadoes, which had always transformed her from a brave, smiling girl to a quivering, weeping mess huddled in the corner.

"Yep," said Pru. She nodded toward a stack of neatly folded blankets on the recliner. "Grab those."

"Lucky!" June shouted, whipping her head from side to side. She didn't have to wait long. A soft mew sounded from the hall, and Lucky hopped in with that awkward three-legged gait. Luke grabbed him in a football hold, determined not to let the scraggly thing blow away once they stepped outside.

June scooped up the blankets and held them against

her chest, gripping them like a pillow and burying her face in the fabric folds. He wrapped one arm around her shoulders, leading her out the back door behind Pru.

The sudden change in pressure made Luke's ears pop, and he tucked the cat between his body and June's to protect it from hailstones and the hard, scraping wind. The sky's eerie glow barely illuminated the heavy aluminum doors in the ground that led down to the cellar. Bits of dried leaves and dust sandblasted Luke's neck as he ducked his head and pulled June forward, her muscles rigid beneath her cotton dress. He released her only long enough to heave one door open and usher her inside, followed by Pru. Then he stepped down and bolted the doors shut, hearing ice clunk and ping off the metal. Luke felt along the damp cement wall for the light switch and flipped it on, bathing the dank space in the flickering glimmer of a single fluorescent bulb.

Warped wooden steps creaked beneath their feet, replaced by the grit of dirt beneath their shoes, as they descended into an area no larger than a generous walk-in closet. The air was thick with mildew, and a sharp metallic scent emanated from a rusted shelf pressed against the far wall. Two tattered canvas cots lined the remaining walls, dusty, but certainly more welcoming than a seat on the bare earth. A lone cricket chirped, competing with the howling, whistling wind from above.

With a groan, Pru eased onto the far cot and began tuning the radio to the strongest station, and once Lucky's paws hit the ground, he gave a half-hearted hiss and joined her. "Too bad we're a bunk short," Pru said. "Hope you two don't mind sharin'." She did a better job of hiding her grin this time.

Luke uncurled June's fingers from the blankets and spread one onto the other cot, then sat down and pulled her onto his lap. Instantly, she wrapped her arms around his neck and pressed her lips to his shoulder.

As a kid, he'd never liked spending the night in the storm cellar—who would?—but June used to cry in great, hiccupping sobs that had made his lungs feel heavy. He'd always tried, without much success, to distract her with stories or jokes, but this time he held her tightly in his arms and rocked her from side to side.

"You're safe down here," he whispered. "Nothing can touch you." She nodded and loosened her grip a bit. "Anyway, it's just a precaution, right Pru?" He raised a brow at June's grandma, hoping she'd play along.

"That's right. Worst'a the storm's in the next county."

He wasn't sure which county Pru was referring to, and he was afraid to ask. Jesus, please not Hallover. Anywhere but there. He'd always teased June, saying her bad luck was more contagious than measles, but Luke didn't really believe in luck. He hated the idea that his failures were someone else's fault. He and June had a measure of control over their fates, just like everyone else.

But listening to the radio, Luke began to wonder.

"…in Hallover county, where reports indicate a touchdown with significant property damage…"

Maybe control was an illusion.

Something heavy clattered outside the cellar doors, and June jumped in his arms. She cleared her throat and said, "Probably nowhere near your house." Her trembling fingers stroked his hair as she tried to offer comfort. "It's a huge county. Could've touched down anywhere."

"…now four confirmed touchdowns in Hal—"

"Hey," June said, three decibels too loud. She took his cheek and steered his gaze away from the radio as Pru turned it down to a low murmur. "I just remembered something. A bad dream I had last night, something about snakes. It reminded me of a hypothetical question I read in a book once. If someone offered you a million dollars, would you agree to have horrible nightmares every single night for a year?"

"Kind of random, isn't it?" Luke wasn't fooled for one second by June's sudden interest in conversation starters. She was trying to distract him, just like he'd done for her all those years ago. Sweet, but ineffective. Nothing short of having her naked beneath him on that cot would push the thoughts of storm damage from his mind.

"I wouldn't do it," Pru said. "Only got so many nights left. Don't wanna waste 'em." She scratched Lucky behind the ears and cocked her head to the side, as if in thought. "But young'uns like you? Maybe the money'd be worth it."

"Yeah," June mused. "I don't know. A million dollars would give me a lot of security, but all those nightmares would drive me crazy after a few weeks. And losing sleep would affect my health. So I guess it comes down to which is more important—financial security or emotional security. I think emotional. So, no, I wouldn't do it either." She squeezed Luke's arm. "How about you?"

Heaving a sigh, he shook his head. "Doesn't matter anyway, 'cause it would never happen, but I guess I would. I can take a few bad dreams." The words stumbled from his lips, but he wasn't thinking about nightmares, or listening as June and Pru continued the debate. Only wondering how much damage his house could sustain and still be ready for closing within a week. He could handle a few missing shingles, replace some siding and a window or two. Beyond that, who could he call to help with repairs? Trey and Pauly, for sure. Maybe a few other guys from the crew. He couldn't pay them until after closing, but they'd probably be okay with that. Yes, it could still work out. But despite that thought, his heart still thumped against his ribs. If only he'd known about the land auction, before he'd tied all his money up in that damned house.

"What do you think?" June asked, tugging at his shirt sleeve. "About cutting off both thumbs to add ten years to your life?"

"Hmm?" Her shoulders sagged as she probably realized the distraction wasn't working. He remembered the feeling. None of his best jokes could ever keep her from crying until the threat of twisters was over. "Sorry, Junebug. Too much on my mind. Let's just lie down, okay?" He needed quiet, to think through all the possibilities and all his options. No matter what, he had to find a way to buy his land. Pru used to say there was a key to unlock every door. His mind reeled with the quickest ways to fix storm damage with no cash on hand, to find the key.

They nested together like spoons on the cot, but neither slept. June continued to flinch at every sound, while Luke drove himself half-mad envisioning a timber-littered hole in the ground where his house used to be. And wondering who would scoop up his land at auction. How many years would pass before it came back on the market, if ever?

Many hours later when the wind died down, he

gave up on sleep and unbolted the cellar doors. A fallen branch blocked the way, but he managed to dislodge it enough to wriggle out, pull the branch aside, and then let June and Pru out into the muggy, early morning haze.

Glancing around, Luke noticed some superficial damage to Pru's wood siding, one cracked windowpane, and a couple trees he'd have to cut down before the next storm, but nothing that required his immediate attention. He circled the house and did one more inspection—both inside and out—to be sure they'd be safe when he left.

"Wait," June said, grabbing his forearm. "I'm coming too."

Luke shook his head. "No telling what's going on over there. Could be live power lines down, the roads might be blocked. I might have to walk at some point."

"But—"

"Unh-uh. Stay here, and help Pru clean up the yard. I'll call when I know something."

Before she could object again, Luke planted a quick kiss on her forehead and hopped into the truck. He didn't know what he'd find in Hallover, and if he broke down, he didn't want June there to witness it. Or worse—to patronize him and stroke his face and say everything would be fine.

Though it went against his every instinct, he drove ten miles below the speed limit and kept his eyes trained on the road. *Everything's gonna be okay*, he promised himself. But repeating the words didn't ease his mind, so he cranked up the radio and let the thumping bass push out all conscious thought.

Chapter 22

IT TOOK A FEW MINUTES FOR JUNE TO IDENTIFY THE cause of her unease. It was too quiet. For the first time since her arrival at Gram's house, the whip-poor-wills, doves, and quail had fallen silent. Shielding her eyes, she gazed at the battered, half-stripped trees and wondered where all the birds had gone. Even the crickets and cicadas were mute. Maybe they'd burrowed underground or simply blown away. Who knew? But no wind blew now, that was certain, and it didn't help counter the sun's brutal rays. June heaved a sigh and raked another bag full of leaves and twigs before returning to the sanctuary of Gram's air-conditioned kitchen.

"Luke call yet?" she asked Gram, while blotting her face with a paper towel. Three agonizing hours had passed since he'd left, and she'd expected to hear something by now.

"No." Grammy offered a cool glass of iced tea. "But Burl did. Shooters lost power, so no need goin' to work tonight. Said to tell you good-bye and good luck in Austin."

"Oh." That's right. Her month of service was over in a few days, and she'd have to return to Luquos. The thought left her with a stirring of excitement in her breast, as well as anxious tingles prickling the surface of her skin. But she couldn't leave without knowing Luke would be okay. "Gram? What if Luke's house is too damaged to list? Is there another way for him to get the cash in time for the auction?"

"Sure. I could take out a second mortgage, but he'd never agree to it." Grammy shook her head and smoothed the front of her blue cotton dress. "Prideful man. He'll do it himself or not at all."

"Can he use the Hallover house as collateral for a loan?"

"No." Gram's expression hardened into a look June knew well. "That ex-wife 'a his ruined his credit before the divorce. Ran up all the cards before shackin' up with another man. That's why he uses cash from every sale to buy the next house."

"How much do you think it'll take to win the auction?" Maybe she could scrape together a couple thousand bucks, if she picked up a few bartending shifts.

"Hard to tell without knowin' who's biddin'." With a shrug, Gram glanced to the side like she was calculating numbers in her head. "I think it went for sixty last time, but it could go for less. Could go for a hundred. No way to tell."

Whoa, a hundred thousand dollars? June squeezed her eyes shut and said a quick prayer for Luke. Hopefully, his house was still in decent shape, and all this speculation was for nothing; otherwise, she'd be useless as boobs on a bull.

Deciding the break was over, June headed back outside to continue raking. She made a deal with herself—if she didn't hear from Luke in one hour, she'd go looking for him. Yeah, that sounded perfectly reasonable to her. Luke had said to stay put, but he'd also promised to call. She'd give him one hour to honor his side of the bargain before she tracked him down.

Fifteen minutes later, a humid breeze from her car's open windows tossed her curls into the air as the miles passed by. She twisted her stereo dial to find some local information about road closures, but the six stations her dilapidated radio picked up yielded nothing useful. The scene outside her window seemed promising though. Nothing worse than the damage at Gram's house—a few trees uprooted in the fields, and leaves carpeting the asphalt—so far, she'd only had to slow down once to steer around a branch protruding onto the road.

As June approached Hallover County, the knot in her chest began to loosen. Luke's phone battery had probably died—that's why he hadn't called. After all, there'd been no way to charge it last night in the cellar. She'd just relaxed into her seat and released a quiet sigh of relief when she saw it: the mahogany desk with beveled etching along the top. The one she'd selected from the furniture rental store because it complimented Luke's master bedroom perfectly. Now it lay in the middle of the road with its legs broken in half like matchsticks. A cold weight settled in June's belly as she slowed down and passed it on the grassy shoulder.

Before long, she spotted Luke's black truck parked alongside the road in front of a massive fallen oak that had blocked the way. She pulled up behind him and continued on foot.

―⁓―

From a battery-operated radio in the kitchen, The Police complained about getting wet beneath the world's umbrella. How fitting. Luke switched the radio off, clutched it in his palm, and then threw it out a broken window and into the sodden backyard. It landed with a dull thud beside a cluster of wilted golden flowers June had planted out front last week. He was wet, all right, just like everything else inside this goddamned house. Funny thing about a roof—it only worked as long as it was attached to the walls.

He pounded his fist against the granite countertop, then winced in pain, remembering too late that he'd put that same fist through the drywall a couple hours earlier. Cradling his hand against his chest, Luke scanned the kitchen again, taking in the splintered furniture, the soaked walls, and the warped wood floors. And that was just the surface damage. His place was in worse shape than the Jenkins home had been, and how long had the crew worked on that project? Six months, at least.

It was over. His dream of finally owning the Gallagher land, of building his home there, was over. But why? Why the hell couldn't he catch a break, just this once? Looking at the neighborhood, you'd think God Himself had reached down and flicked the roof off Luke's house before leaving everyone else to live in peace. It wasn't enough that he'd lost his mama, been played by his ex-wife, and then booted out of the army. Now he was pushing thirty with no money, no prospects, and he didn't have a place to sleep that night. He'd have to go crawling back to Pru. Again.

The light crunch of glass beneath shoe soles sounded from the foyer, and from the slow, tentative footsteps, he knew it was June. Damn it, why hadn't she stayed home? The worst part of all this shit was knowing he had nothing to offer anymore. He didn't want to face her. Not like this—a worthless, broken man inside his literally broken home.

"Hey," she whispered from behind.

Luke turned to the window. June's voice was thick with pity, and he didn't want to see it in her eyes. "You shouldn't have come."

"You didn't call."

"Look around. I was occupied." Which was a lie. He'd done nothing all day—there was nothing he *could* do.

He heard June step forward slowly. "The furniture's insured. Just so you know." When he didn't respond, she continued in a softer voice, "Decorations, too. I paid the extra nineteen ninety-nine. It's not something I'd normally do, but I just—"

"Good to know." Until then, he hadn't given a thought to all the staging crap she'd rented. At least he wasn't on the hook for thousands of dollars worth of furniture he hadn't wanted to begin with.

"How about the house?" she asked, placing one hand lightly on his shoulder. "Is it insured?"

Luke shrugged from beneath her touch and moved toward the back door, picking up chunks of drywall and wood off the floor as he went. Although he'd paid for the house in cash and insurance wasn't mandatory, he'd bought a cheap policy. But it was only worth the appraised value at the time of purchase—less than twenty-five percent of what the property had been worth when it went on the market a few days ago.

"Yeah." He tossed the debris out into the backyard. "But it won't pay much." If he really stretched his dollar, he'd have enough to buy supplies for a new roof, maybe new floors and drywall, but there'd be nothing left for labor, appliances, or landscaping. And there'd sure as hell be no compensation for the hundreds of hours he'd spent busting his back in this place.

Several minutes ticked by in silence before June cleared her throat and said, "I feel like this is my fault. If it weren't for Trey's accident, you'd've had this house finished and sold weeks ago." Even though Luke couldn't see her face, he knew she was chewing the inside of her cheek and staring down at her shoes, just like every time she thought she was in trouble.

Ever since they were kids, June had taken her licks and kept trailing after him—no amount of roughhousing or teasing could ever repel her. For whatever reason, she'd convinced herself that she loved him, and unless he forced her to let go, she never would.

"You're probably right," he said, closing his eyes and hating himself for what he was about to do.

"How can I help?"

"Help?" Luke whirled around and finally faced her. "Like you helped Karl break his nose?"

June's mouth formed a little pink O, and she shook her head, sending her brown curls in motion.

"No?" he said, raising his voice. "How about the way you helped Trey off the roof? Is that how you wanna help?"

"Don't." Her voice seemed so tiny in the open kitchen, but she squared her shoulders bravely and tugged at the hem of her white tank top. "Don't be like this—"

"Oh, I know! What about the time you helped yourself to an armload of snake venom?" Luke was shouting now, charging ahead until he could see the faint mark he'd left on June's shoulder when they'd made love. He quickly tore his gaze away and looked directly into her welling eyes. "In case you haven't noticed, your help is toxic, and your luck is deadly. Everything was fine until you came back to town." Then he pointed to the front door and said in the coldest voice he could muster, "Take your *help* back to Austin, and ruin someone else's life."

Her voice trembled, and one tear spilled onto her cheek, but she stood a little taller and rested her fingertips on his chest. "I told you I wasn't leaving, and I meant it. I love—"

"You never could take a hint." Luke wrapped his palm around her fingers. He probably held on a beat too long, but he managed to set them by June's side and let go. "You've followed me around since we were kids. It's time for you to stop acting so damn needy and leave me alone for once." Then he turned away before she had a chance to see the pain on his face. "Go on. And don't come back here again."

He sucked in a deep breath and held it while June made one of those awful choking noises that came from trying not to cry. He felt like the biggest shit on the planet, but she'd be better off without him. He knew this as certainly as he knew the sun would rise in the east the next morning. Finally, after the longest few seconds of his life, she left the kitchen, and the quick crunch, crunch, crunch of glass beneath her shoes echoed from the foyer.

Luke's rib cage seemed to constrict and crack, the jagged, calcified edges of bone virtually piercing his lungs. He ached to run after June and snatch her into his arms—he knew she'd forgive him—but that would only prolong the pain. It was time to focus on the future, lousy as it might be. At least he had nothing left to lose, so life couldn't possibly get any worse.

He got to work cleaning up the wreckage, confident that tomorrow would be a better day, if only by default.

Chapter 23

LUKE REACHED BEHIND HIS NECK AND TUGGED OFF HIS dampened T-shirt. Even though fall temperatures had finally kicked in, demolition work was brutal, and it always made him sweaty as hell. He stifled a yawn and tipped back a cold Mountain Dew while watching Trey use a rented forklift to haul another load of shingles onto the front lawn.

He owed his buddy a lot, and not just for his help with the house these last two weeks. Trey'd offered to let Luke crash on his sofa, which had saved him the humiliation of asking Pru if he could move back home. And when the Gallagher land had gone to auction the week before, Trey had done his damndest to keep Luke distracted—he'd even sprung for beer at Shooters that night. It didn't change the fact that a stranger now owned his land, but he appreciated the effort nonetheless.

"That's the last of it," Trey said, limping over on his new walking cast to join Luke on the front stoop. "I'll tarp it later." He eased down onto the bottom step and groaned in relief.

Luke yawned behind his fist and nodded. "Thanks."

"Am I keepin' you awake?"

"Haven't been sleeping. Just need this caffeine to kick in."

"I know my couch isn't too comfortable, but, hell, you've slept on worse. Remember that field exercise—"

"It's not that." It was the dream, the same one he'd had every night since June left town. Little details changed, but the basics stayed the same. She'd stand before him, smiling with outstretched arms, and whisper, *I love you, Luke. I love you so much.* But when he'd run to hold her, everything would change. Slowly, her face would transform from adoration to disgust, as if she'd seen a rotting carcass on the side of the road. Then she'd shake her head and hold one palm forward. *You hurt me, Luke. You're just like your worthless daddy. I could never love you. No one could ever love you.*

Then he'd wake up gasping like a drowning man and lie awake the rest of the night. "Hey," he asked Trey, "if someone offered you a million bucks to have nightmares every night for a year, would you do it?"

"I dunno." Trey shrugged. "Probably."

"Yeah, that's what I used to think." But not anymore. Seeing June again and again—coming so close to having her in his arms and then suffering that heartbreak and rejection every time—was mental torture. No amount of money was worth it. Thinking about her made his guts ache, and even though he tried to force her from his mind, she crept in whenever she damn well pleased. He wondered what she was doing at that very moment. Probably balancing the books for her new bar or something like that. Did she ever think about him?

"Why'd you ask? Having nightmares?" Trey snorted a laugh and elbowed him in the knee. "Maybe *you're* the one with the vadge, my friend. You wanna borrow my old teddy?"

"How 'bout I ram it up your—" Luke forgot all about his buddy's teasing when a caravan of nearly two dozen cars and trucks pulled into view. Each vehicle slowed to a stop on the road's shoulder. Then, like ants scurrying around a dead grasshopper, people exited their cars and swarmed his front lawn. "What's all this?"

"Hey," Trey said, holding one hand out in a defensive gesture, "it wasn't me. I told them you wouldn't like it. June arranged all this before she left."

"What the hell are you talkin' about?"

"She talked to the preacher at Miss Pru's church, then she tracked down every single family Helping Hands has ever worked with."

"And?" Luke stood, feeling little prickles at the base of his skull.

"And all these people are here to help. You know, to rebuild the house."

Holy sheep shit. He couldn't believe June had done this. She had to know it would drive him crazy to have a hundred strangers milling around his place—to be indebted to all those people when he could do the job himself. "Why would she do that?" he muttered to himself more than Trey.

"*Why?*" Trey shook his head and scoffed. "Because she loves you, numb-nuts."

———~~~———

"Slow down, Lucas." Pru's large hand reached out and snagged his belt loop. Luke stopped, but nodded toward the sixty-foot extension ladder propped against his brand-new roof. "I know," she said with a quick nod, "but take a minute to drink somethin'." Her blue eyes narrowed, and she thrust a water bottle at his chest. "That's an order."

"Yes, ma'am," he said with a fake salute and a smile in his voice. Chugging the icy water, he took a moment to observe Pru and her flock of church ladies as they prepared to feed the masses. They gossiped and chirped happily while arranging platters of ham sandwiches, potato chips, and chocolate chip cookies on the folding tables they'd assembled in the backyard.

He'd never thought it possible, but the crowd worked like a well-oiled machine. Trey had grouped everyone by ability, and then he'd assigned each group a task. From framing the roof and nailing on shingles to basic cleanup, everyone—no matter how skilled or raw—pitched in. It reminded Luke of an Amish barn-raising he'd seen once in a photo documentary. If things continued this well, the roof and drywall would be finished by the end of the day. Another group had promised to return tomorrow to help install the new wood floors, and yet another the following day to paint, stain the floors, and landscape with donated flowers and shrubs.

Luke realized it was possible to have the house ready to show within a week. It was still too late to buy his land, but the prospect of having all that money in the bank made his chest feel lighter. And since he was in no hurry this time, he could hold out for the highest offer. If the final bid was high enough, maybe he could track down the SOB who'd bought the Gallagher property.

"Hey, Luke." A round-bellied man pushed back his tattered Stetson, revealing a bush of wiry gray hair. "You probably don't remember me. Jim Robins. You replaced all my windows after a hail storm a few years back."

"Sure." Luke extended his hand. "Mill Creek Drive, right?" It had been one of Helping Hand's first projects.

"That's the one." Jim's face brightened, and he gave a vigorous handshake.

"Thanks for coming out."

"Nah, I'm the one who should be thanking you." The old timer pulled a white handkerchief from his shirt pocket and dabbed at his forehead. "Been pretty useless since my knee went out. Feels good to give something back, you know?"

It had been like this all day—Luke trying to show his gratitude, but receiving thanks instead, especially from the Helping Hands families. Even though it seemed backward, he kind of understood. Nobody liked being on the receiving end of charity—he sure didn't—and it must've been a relief to pay off that imaginary debt. Still, he made a point to stop and shake the hand of each volunteer before the day ended.

Eight hours later, Luke stood on the front stoop waving as they all drove away. Well, all but one. Old Judge Bea lingered inside the kitchen, pretending to inspect the repairs, but Luke could tell he wanted something. Bea wasn't the kind of man who lingered. If he wasn't on his way to supper, he had an agenda.

Luke picked up a few discarded water bottles and tossed then into the kitchen's recycling bin. "Hey, Judge. I'm about to head back to Trey's. Want me to walk you out?" Which was his most tactful way of saying, *Saddle up and ride out, old timer*.

Bea leaned against the island countertop and lowered his white caterpillar eyebrows. Clearing his throat, he pulled a folded sheet of paper from inside his jacket pocket. "Wanted to give ya this in private."

"What is it?" Luke wiped his palms on his jeans

and reached for the document. He opened it and stared blankly at a solid block of legal text. "Am I being sued?"

"No, it's a deed transfer. Came across my desk this morning."

"Deed?" What the hell was this? Luke didn't recall transferring ownership of any properties recently. The last house he'd flipped had closed more than six months ago. He brought the form to the window to read it by the fading sunlight. The property description listed his old address—the house where his mama had lived, and the surrounding acreage—with Mae-June Augustine as grantor. He shot Bea a questioning look.

"She didn't tell me anything," the judge insisted with a shrug, "but it's yours now. She beat all the other bids fair 'n' square and signed it over to you."

"This must be a mistake." Or a really cruel prank. Luke shook his head and tossed the document on the counter. "June didn't have any money. It was all tied up in that—"

Oh, shit. A bowling ball settled in Luke's stomach. He knew exactly where she'd found the cash, and the re-alization almost made his knees buckle. She'd somehow sold her bar—the one she'd worked ten years to open— and walked away from her dream. He couldn't believe she'd done it. "Why?" he whispered. Why would June give up everything for him, especially after the way he'd treated her?

The answer was finally clear, her sacrifice an unmis-takable message where words had failed. She loved him. She really loved him.

Chapter 24

"*ALEGRAS, BONITA*." ESTEBAN TUCKED A WAYWARD CURL back into June's twist and brushed his thumb over her cheek. "Smile. It hurts my heart to see you like this."

"Hurts your tips too," added Tony, the bar manager. He used to call her boss, but now, their roles were reversed. And he wouldn't let her forget it.

June flashed the brightest smile she could manage and shifted uncomfortably in her leather pumps. She'd gotten used to going barefoot or wearing sneakers back home, and now her old wardrobe felt unnatural. By the end of each shift, her feet throbbed in pain, but she was grateful for the work. It not only helped rebuild her anemic checking account, but provided a distraction from her thoughts too.

"I'm fine, Esteban." She squeezed his arm. "How's the temperature in the back tank? They get it fixed?" It wasn't her job to manage those details anymore, but she couldn't help asking. "I'd hate to lose any more jellies."

"All taken care of." He gave her a consoling pat on the shoulder before strolling toward the back office with Tony.

It turned out Esteban had grown to enjoy managing the day-to-day operations at Luquos while June was away, and when she'd asked him to buy her out, he'd happily agreed. It was what she'd wanted, but going from owner to bartender just plain sucked. Watching

Esteban receive all the praise and attention on opening night while she'd served drinks in the shadows had left June with a perpetual lump in her throat.

She sighed and rested her elbows on the bar's immaculate lacquered surface. Soft jazz played from speakers in the ceiling while the gentle glow from the aquarium wall provided the only light. Tranquil, for sure, but Luke was right. It was kind of boring. Without the rush of a noisy crowd, each shift dragged on like a three-legged turtle.

There'd be no escaping her thoughts on a slow night like this. She'd try to focus on creating a new drink recipe or perfecting an old one, but in the end, she'd probably end up replaying her one night with Luke, just like she always did. What they'd shared during those hours had transcended sex—they'd loved with everything, body, spirit, and beyond. Coming so close to reaching her goal—to reaching Luke's heart—seemed to make the disappointment of losing him even more devastating. Weeks had passed, and she still couldn't look at a hammer or screwdriver without breaking down in tears. And considering all the maintenance the back tank had needed, she'd cried a virtual tsunami watching the workers come and go.

A middle-aged man in a dark suit approached the bar, and June straightened to take his order. "Welcome to Luquos," she said with a forced smile. "What can I make for you tonight?"

"I'm looking for Mae-June July Augustine." He leaned in close, then shook his head and snickered. "What a fracked-up name, huh?"

The smile fell from June's lips. "That's me."

"Oh. Sorry. This is for you." He handed a large manila envelope across the bar. "You've been served. Have a nice evening." Then he turned on his heel and strode away, just like that.

June's heart leapt up and sprinted inside her chest. Sweet mother of Stevie Ray, she couldn't handle any more bad news. With trembling fingers, she tore open the envelope and pulled out two heavy sheets of paper bound with a small, red paper clip. She squinted in the dim light and scanned the first page.

Dear June,

Don't worry, you haven't been served. I just wanted to get your attention.

   Remember the letters Mrs. Moore made us write to ourselves in senior English? I decided to repeat that assignment, and I've written another letter to my future self. It's attached, and I'd like you to keep it and give it to me in ten years.

Thanks a bunch,
Luke

"What on earth?" June kicked off her shoes, code violations be damned, and pulled the second page free. She glanced around the bar, half expecting to see Luke wearing his old teasing grin. He wasn't there, of course, and she felt like an idiot for getting her hopes up. She backed away from the bar and closer to the aquarium's pink glow to read his letter.

Hey, you good-looking son of a biscuit-eater!
(You've cut back on the swears since becoming
a dad.)

I'll try to keep this short. The kids are prob-
ably getting into something while your back
is turned, and there's not much time to read.
You're happily married to your best friend
(Junebug, not Trey) and living with your three
sons in the house you built behind the pond.
June wants to try again for a girl, and you're
more than happy to keep practicing. She's the
most important person in your world, and if she
wants a dozen babies, that's fine by you.

You used to struggle with saying the L-word.
I hope by now you can tell June how much you
love her every day, but if not, I know you're
showing it. And that's what matters. If actions
speak louder than words, then you're practi-
cally shouting your love from the rooftop with
a bullhorn. You wake up each morning and kiss
the birthmark on the side of her neck, then bring
her coffee in bed. And speaking of bed, you're
always thinking of new ways to keep her swear-
ing like a truck driver. Sometimes life is chaotic,
but you're living the dream, buddy. And, though
you probably don't like thinking about it, you
almost ruined everything ten years ago.

No matter what June said back then, you
couldn't believe she loved you. You were so
convinced she was better off without you that
you pushed her away each time she got too
close. In fact, you pushed her right out of Sultry

*Springs. It wasn't until she gave up everything
for your happiness that it finally sank in to your
thick skull: she's loved you since you were kids.
And you've loved her half your life; you just
couldn't admit it.*

*So, here's what you did to get her back.
You paid some guy twenty bucks to give her a
letter—the very same letter you're holding in
your hands right now—and you waited for her
in the parking lot outside Luquos. Even if—*

June gasped and stopped reading. She brought a hand
to her heart, and the letter fluttered to the floor. Holy
sugar, Luke was outside right now, waiting for her. Legs
twitching to run, she inched away from the aquarium
wall and toward the front entrance, but stopped herself.
Should she make him wait a little longer, maybe until
closing? Would rushing out there make her look "so
damn needy" like he'd said weeks ago? Before June
could answer her own questions, she'd ducked beneath
the counter, sprinted across the lounge, and bolted out
the front door.

The asphalt felt cool and gritty beneath her feet, and
the night breeze lifted a strand of hair from her twist.
She pushed it behind her ear and scanned the parking lot.

There he was, sitting on his truck's tailgate with his
denim-clad legs dangling over the edge. When he noticed her, he hopped down and gave a timid, sideways
grin. The streetlight's glow highlighted the auburn hues
in his hair and cast shadows beneath his cheekbones. He
stroked the strong edge of his jaw, widening that grin
into a magnificent smile. God, he was breathtaking, just

like always. June forced herself to hold back and not rush headlong into his arms.

"Hey," he said softly, then nodded toward her bare feet. "No shoes? I guess you can take the girl out of the country, but you can't take the country out of the—"

"You think this makes up for everything?" June shifted her weight to one hip and folded her arms beneath her breasts. "That one letter fixes it all?"

He raked a hand through his hair and moved closer. "No, I don't think that."

"Sure sounds that way to me."

"I know I've been an ass—"

"You got that right."

"But I'd planned on making it up to you." Inching forward, as if approaching a wounded animal, he reached for her hand and took it in his warm grasp. "Every day for the rest of my life." Slowly, tentatively, he placed a kiss inside her palm before adding, "You've given me so much, but I have to ask for more."

"Like what?"

"Like forgiveness." He intertwined their fingers and lowered his head until they were eye-level. "I didn't mean anything I said that day at the house. I swear it on my life. I didn't mean one word. Can you forgive me?"

"Maybe." Of course she could forgive him. She already had. "What else do you want?"

"You. All in. I want to give you my name." He knelt at her feet, pressing his palm against her belly. "And my children. The land, the house—you can have it all—it doesn't mean shit if you're not there to share it with me. I'll bet we can even talk Burl into retiring early if you want to buy Shooters. We belong together, Junebug.

Tell me what I have to do to make that happen. I'll do anything you want." He knelt there in silence, lips pressed together and waiting for her response.

A warm flutter tickled the inside of her chest like parakeet wings. "You could start by asking."

"Will you marry me?"

"I need to hear you say it." June tugged on his hand, until he stood. Luke had never said he loved her, not out loud. After all these years, she deserved to hear the words. She closed the distance between them and took his cheek in her palm. "Tell me."

His green eyes warmed, and his face broke into a genuine, no-holds-barred Luke smile—the one that sucked the air from her lungs each and every time. "June Augustine," he whispered, "I'm so in love with you. I promise to love you every day until I die, and then some. Will you marry me?"

June nodded vigorously because words wouldn't pass through her thickened airway. Luke pulled a ring from his back pocket and slid it onto her finger, but all she saw through the tears was a vague, blurry glimmer. She didn't care if he'd given her a plastic twist tie. June's heart swelled beneath her ribs as if it couldn't hold any more joy.

Luke wrapped her in his strong embrace and brushed his lips tenderly against hers. "You know," he said, "I never thanked you. For getting all those folks to help rebuild the house and for buying my land. When the house sells, we can use the money to buy back your share in Luquos."

Laughter bubbled up from June's chest. Technically, it still wasn't a thank you, and technically, she didn't give half a damn. She shook her head. "No. I want to go home, to Sultry Springs."

"I think we should get your shoes first though." Luke scooped her into his arms and carried her toward the front door. "Oh, and Junebug?"

"Yeah?"

"Thank you."

Epilogue

PRUDENCE FOSTER SHIFTED ON HER WHITE FOLDING chair and gazed at Gallagher pond, where hundreds of drifting, floating candles flickered in the twilight like bobbing fireflies. A slow, clumsy bumblebee drew her attention to clusters of lilac and honeysuckle, which hung in great waterfalls from the wood trellis at the end of the aisle. Their sweet, floral scent mingled with distant burning leaves to create a perfume no man could catch in a bottle. As much as she'd wanted June and Lucas to take their vows in The Lord's house, she had to admit they'd done a right fair job transforming this overgrown lot.

Pastor McMahon caught her eye, smiling and tipping his bald head as he stepped beneath the wooden arch, and she returned the greeting with a nod. She loved seeing Brother Mac in his long, white, ceremonial robe, complete with a red cross affixed over his heart to remind everyone who they should thank for this happy occasion.

"Hi-ya, hon." Gerty Bicknocker nudged Pru's arm from the row behind and settled into a seat beside her date, an old widower she'd nabbed a few weeks ago. More hair sprouted in the man's ears than on his head, but at their age one couldn't be too picky. "Saw June back at the house," Gerty said with a slow, solemn shake of her head. "She looked so much like Becky it gave me chills."

Goose bumps rose to the surface of Pru's own skin, and she tugged a thick, wool sweater around her shoulders. "She's wearin' Becky's old dress. Said she didn't care if it was twenty years outta style; she wanted to feel her mama here today."

A lump rose in Pru's throat, and all the swallowing in the world wouldn't push it down. She felt her daughter's presence like a warm shawl, fresh from the dryer, an almost painful swelling in and around her rib cage, somehow crushing and caressing at the same time. Pru reached into her pocket and felt for Becky's hair ribbon. It always made her feel close to her baby girl, and though she didn't need it today, her fingers worked the frayed ends out of habit.

Becky'd had her faults, but she'd loved June something fierce. Yes, she was here all right, and June didn't need a dress to make that happen. Pru didn't trust herself to speak without breaking down, so she turned to watch the wedding party join Pastor Mac.

Trey limped into place, so handsome despite one gray trouser leg bunched above his plaster cast. It seemed that thing would never come off. He was such a sweet boy, much too good for the floozy cocktail waitress he was dating now. What he needed was a nice girl like June. Pru decided to get right to work on that, tilting her head and considering June's bridesmaid, a bartender from Austin whose name she couldn't recall. No, she wasn't right either. A pretty young lady, but she wouldn't quit making eyes at that Esteban character, June's former business partner. Pru had met him earlier that evening, and he reminded her of a lecherous old man the way his gaze followed every pair of breasts in the room. Anyone interested in a man like him probably wasn't a nice girl at all.

When Lucas stepped into view, Pru forgot all about matchmaking. Praise Jesus, he looked so striking in his creased, black suit that she brought a hand to her heart. He'd even gotten a haircut, shearing off the reddish tips that used to curl against his shirt collar. His freshly shaved face beamed with nervous pride, like a man on top of the world with nowhere to go but up. This was the man she'd prayed Lucas would become, the potential she'd seen in the angry and broken twelve-year-old boy.

She'd never told anyone, but Lucas and June had saved her life. When her beloved Jacob was called home after forty-seven years of marriage, she didn't know how to keep on living. And then, just when she'd thought God's test was behind her, she'd lost her only child, her sweet Becky.

Caring for little June had seemed too much to bear, but Pru couldn't send her off to live with those trash Augustines in East Texas, so she'd pushed aside her grief and focused on raising that grandbaby. And Lord have mercy, when Lucas came along, he was so wild she didn't have two minutes to think about her loss. Those kids tried her patience—heck, they tried, convicted, and hanged her patience—pushing her sanity to the limit, but they filled her once empty home with the sounds of family again: laughter, tears, clattering plastic toys, cartoons, bare feet slapping against the hardwood floor.

Now, all these years later, Pru finally understood God's plan. Those children had needed her—and each other—and Becky's loss was a part of that. It didn't take away the pain, but it softened the edges a good bit.

"Would everyone please rise?" When Pastor Mac lifted his leather Bible, chitchat turned to light shushing, and then half of Sultry County stood from their plastic seats and turned to behold June, the most beautiful bride ever to walk God's earth.

June really did favor her mama, light brown ringlets spilling free and brushing her shoulders, her only veil a circlet of daisies. Even from the front row, Pru noticed a deep pink blush dust the apples of June's cheeks. She'd never looked happier, and Pru offered yet another silent prayer of thanks for this bounty of joy. The dress really *was* twenty years out of fashion: a white, knee-length, baby doll sheath so typical of the age of free love Becky had idolized, but somehow it worked, blending with the natural elements around her. Linking her arm through Judge Bea's, June leaned in to whisper something in his ear, and they both laughed before gliding forward. Though every person in attendance watched June, she only had eyes for Lucas, the man she'd loved since the days of mud pies and hopscotch.

Instead of an organ, June and Bea marched slowly to the music of buzzing cicadas, dried leaves tossing in the breeze, and crickets' love calls punctuated by the occasional croak of a bullfrog. When they reached the end of the aisle, Bea lifted June's hand to his lips before placing it in Lucas's eager grasp. With a wide grin stretching his thin mouth, Bea backed away and took the seat beside Pru. His usual white, bushy hair was slicked into submission with pomade, and she noticed its biting scent when his sleeve brushed hers.

"We done good, didn't we?" he whispered while the pastor began his sermon. "I told you it'd work out in the end." After a light chuckle, he added, "Mae-June and Lucas together for life. God bless Texas—we're gonna need divine protection!"

"Ten years ago, I'd've never dreamed it."

Pru patted her old friend on the knee and remembered the day June had dropped out of college, particularly the fight that'd followed. They'd both said hurtful things, and June had sworn never to return home. Once Pru's anger had simmered down, the new silence in her house had worn on her nerves like an ulcer, and she'd wondered how she'd manage without those kids around to drive her crazy. She'd written to Lucas and apologized, but making things right with June hadn't been as simple. A true friend, Bea had offered a shoulder to cry on and a way to get June back in Sultry Springs. *It might take years*, he'd said, *but this bench warrant'll get her home again, and then I'll manage to keep her here awhile. Just be patient, and put it in The Lord's hands, Prudence.*

She'd never expected nine years to pass before her granddaughter returned, but thank God for every long minute. Had June come back any sooner, Lucas wouldn't have been ready to give his heart—it was still too hardened. Providence had ensured everything happened just as it should.

Pru dipped her head in prayer along with the congregation. After "amen," she leaned forward to hear the vows.

"I, Lucas Jonathan Gallagher, take you, Mae-June July Augustine, to be my wife..." With a smile bright enough to blind the archangels of heaven, Lucas took June's face in his hands and kissed her before saying another word.

"Hey now, Luke," Pastor Mac chided while laughter broke out among the guests. "You're jumpin' the gun."

A few seconds passed before Lucas released his bride and resumed the vows. When June's turn came, her voice trembled with unshed tears.

"...to love and honor you all the days of my life," she said, her voice cracking on the last word. "And after that too. Because one lifetime's not enough."

Lucas gathered June into his arms and held her close, only releasing her long enough to exchange rings—six inches of space between them seemed too much to bear. It brought moisture to Pru's eyes, and she used her sweater's sleeve to dab at her cheeks.

After the closing prayer, Pastor Mac invited Lucas to officially kiss the bride. With a whoop of pure joy, Lucas wrapped both arms around June's waist and lifted her off the ground while they kissed for what seemed like an hour.

"Okay, buddy." Trey tugged on Lucas's sleeve. "Save somethin' for later. She's not goin' anywhere."

"No," Pru whispered to herself. "She's not goin' anywhere." After the honeymoon, her family would return home, filling her walls once again with love and laughter, until Lucas built a house of their own on the land right here behind the pond, where they'd just promised to share one life. She'd been blessed beyond her greatest dreams. What more could she want? Well, maybe some great-grandchildren to keep her young, but that could wait. After all, you couldn't rush providence, and Pru was mighty good at waiting.

Acknowledgments

Sultry with a Twist would probably be sitting on my hard drive if it weren't for the support of several dedicated guides who helped me navigate the winding road to publication.

First, to my amazing agent, Nicole Resciniti, thank you for falling in love with my characters and for taking a chance on their creator—a slightly neurotic newbie with no pub credits. I'm still in awe of the way you "finessed" me into bringing this book from category-length to single title. You're a genius—literally!—and I'm so grateful to have found you.

A huge thanks to my editor, Leah Hultenschmidt, for giving June and Luke a loving home, and for making their story shine. Additional thanks to assistant editor Aubrey Poole and publicist Danielle Jackson. Big, squishy hugs to my critique partners, Carey Corp, who promised to never let me fail, and Lorie Langdon, who talked me down from the ledge by continually reminding me, "These are *good* problems to have." Girls, I'm not sure I would've even made it to the query stage without your encouragement. More hugs to my sisters at the Ohio Valley Romance Writers of America for their advice and cheerleading along the way. As Linda Keller said, "You'll come for the writing, but you'll stay for the writers."

I'm grateful to my online buds at The Nest—the NBC

Writers—for helping me with everything from plot brainstorming to query critiques. Our weekly check-ins and your pompom-waving motivated me more than you know. You ladies rock. Another thank you to my awesome "agency sisters." I'm so glad we found each other.

Much appreciation to my friends—you continue to amaze me with the depth of your support, especially you, Heather. Sometimes I think you're happier for me than I am, and I love you for it. Donna, I can't thank you enough for all that you've done. Next time we get together, drinks are on me!

Last, but obviously not least, much love to my family, who make all things possible. Mom and Dad, thank you for fostering the lifelong love of reading that led me to this career. I won the cosmic lottery when I landed with the two of you. Also, I hope you skipped the dirty parts when you read my book, but if you didn't, then lie to me and say you did. To my siblings, thanks for the laughs. In fact, it was a slap-happy writing session with my sister, Jamie, that prompted me to name my heroine Mae-June July Augustine and give her an incontinent, three-legged cat.

Hugs and kisses to my kids, who are *not* allowed to read this book until I'm dead. Thank you for putting up with the never-ending supply of Little Caesar's pizza that sustained us when Mommy was busy writing. And to my husband Steve, all my love and gratitude for being a true hero: kind, honest, selfless, and supportive. Luke Gallagher has nothing on you, babe.

About the Author

Macy Beckett is an unrepentant escapist who left teaching to write hot and humorous romances. No offense to her former students, but her new career is way more fun! She lives just outside Cincinnati in the appropriately named town of Loveland, Ohio, with her husband and three children. *Sultry with a Twist* is her debut romance.

For sneak peeks and giveaways, please visit her on the web at www.macybeckett.com, and don't forget to say hello on Facebook, Goodreads, and Twitter.

Available in March, Trey's story: *A Shot of Sultry*

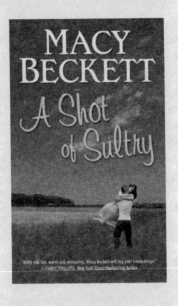

Golden boy Trey Lewis, with his blond hair and Technicolor-blue eyes, is a leading man if Bobbi ever saw one. He's strong and confident and—much to her delight—usually shirtless. He thinks keeping his best friend's baby sister out of trouble will be easy. But he has no idea of the trouble in store for *him*…